THUNDER HORIZON

THUNDER HORIZON

BOOK TWO OF THE DARK SUN DAWN TRILOGY

Stephen Zimmer

SEVENTH STAR PRESS

Cover art: Bonnie Wasson
Cover art in this book copyright © 2017 Bonnie Wasson & Seventh Star
Press, LLC.

Editor: Scott M. Sandridge
Published by Seventh Star Press, LLC.

ISBN Number: 978-1-941706-57-2

Seventh Star Press
www.seventhstarpress.com
info@seventhstarpress.com

Publisher's Note:
Thunder Horizon is a work of fiction. All names, characters, and places
are the product of the author's imagination, used in fictitious manner.
Any resemblances to actual persons, places, locales, events, etc. are purely
coincidental.

Printed in the United States of America

First Edition

ACKNOWLEDGEMENTS

I would like to thank my beloved Holly Phillipe, for being a bedrock of support and encouraging me to get back to a strong writing rhythm once again. It has not been easy, but I hope this book shows it has been worth it. I am blessed to have Holly in my life.

I would like to thank Bonnie Wasson for the wonderful artwork gracing the cover of *Thunder Horizon*. I am honored to have Bonnie as a cover artist. She definitely works magic with her artistic talents and it is always a thrill to see her visual portrayal of Rayden Valkyrie.

I would like to thank my editor, Scott M. Sandridge, for all of his enthusiasm and work on this book and the trilogy. It gives me great confidence to know Scott is watching my back on this journey, and wants to see the Rayden Valkyrie novels be the best they can possibly be.

I would like to thank my dear friends Eric and Kylie Jude, for putting up with my crazy journey and always being there on the rough days to help me get up, dust myself off again, and keep moving forward. I drink a bourbon toast to both of them!

I would like to thank Christina Butcher, for never wavering in her confidence in my path. A truly amazing friend.

I would like to thank Frank Hall for helping me on many fronts, and keeping the maelstrom from becoming overwhelming. I am very blessed to have him as a true friend on my journey.

As always, I want to thank my mother, who is never gone from my heart or my world. I miss her dearly. Her encouragement of my writing path resonates in my life each and every day.

Last, but certainly not least, I want to thank my loyal readers, who are the ones that make all the sweat, blood, and tears involved in writing novels worthwhile. I put my all into every book, as that is the least I can do to honor those who take the time to adventure in my worlds. Onward and Upward!

DEDICATION

To the One Who carries us through the storms.

To my mother and father, for giving me a home in the truest sense.

To my sister, who reminds me that family is forevor.

To my beloved Holly, for giving me a true home once more.

CHAPTER 1

Rage flowing through iron guzzled the blood of doomed men. Frenzied cries abounded, cloaking the sprawling meadow teeming with battle-maddened warriors.

Cleaving through the roiling masses, flowing golden hair whipped about, accenting flashing blades leaving mounting dead in their wake. One a sword blade, and the other an axe, the weapons conveyed the ferocity of their blue-eyed, lethal wielder.

With the northern maelstrom at the height of its fury, Rayden Valkyrie thundered into the enemy ranks. Balance, speed, and synchronicity of motion overwhelmed one warrior after another.

Whether skilled with sword, spear, or axe, none of the warriors in her path proved to be a significant obstacle. With swiftness and accuracy, her weapons found their way past shields and blades alike, and deflected the few strikes sent her way.

Blood served as her war paint, spattered across her face such that her icy gaze shone all the brighter. Terror gleamed in the eyes of more than one warrior having the misfortune to stand in her path.

Instinct, judgment and training honed over many long years filled with strife and war propelled her toward the fortuitous chance she recognized, only a few strides ahead. One more

1

enemy warrior hewn down with a single stroke of her sword cleared the way.

Stepping over the body of her latest fallen adversary, Rayden closed the distance, knowing the momentum of an entire battle stood before her.

Greeting Rayden's advance, a long blade slashed toward her. Sweeping her own sword up to intercept the sharp, rushing iron, Rayden weathered the tremendous power behind the attack, absorbing the blow through solid form and balance in her block and stance.

With a shift of body and footing that took place the moment the clang of the blades rang into the air, Rayden transposed from the defensive into the offensive, initiating an attack with the axe gripped firm in her left hand. Putting all her strength into the assault, she loosed a war cry that carried the force of her fury and will within its rising tenor; reaching a crescendo culminating with the finish of the axe's arcing path.

Iron tore into exposed flesh and burrowed deep.

A lightning bolt searing through the midst of blood-drenched carnage, Rayden levied a decisive blow.

A mountain of a warrior collapsed heavily to the ground, his eyes carrying a stunned look before glassing over, and his storied long sword, Death's Fang, tumbling from a lifeless hand. Nagradak, the renowned chieftain of the Runi, and the most feared among their warriors, had fallen.

Deadly purpose reflecting within an icy gaze, Rayden did not pause a moment to savor her momentous victory, though many enemy faces in the vicinity, witnessing the slaying, displayed looks of shock and dismay. Striding onward, she cast her gaze about with weapons at the ready, prepared for any new threats or opponents to engage within the swirling chaos of battle. Those around the fallen enemy chieftain melted away from her approach, a nascent panic taking root and sprouting fast within their eyes.

All around her, emboldened warriors of the Gessa tribe pressed the attack with vigor. A surging wave empowered by her slaying of the Runi chieftain Nagradak, the Gessa hacked, slashed and stabbed, filling the air with the roar of their cries.

The body of the chieftain now lying well behind her, the head twisted in a grotesque manner from the axe strike landed at the end of her soaring war cry, Rayden kept moving forward. A brushfire through the enemy masses, panic and fear radiated from the killing blow and spread across the open ground in moments. Splintering apart, and losing their focus in the throes of disintegrating resolve and rising terror, many Runi proved easier fodder for the invigorated Gessa.

Yet not all among the enemy horde sought to flee. Several remained who were still possessed of courageous heart; resolute in facing death with weapons in hand. These warriors stood their ground, all across the battlefield, including a few bracing at Rayden's approach.

Fighters skilled and strong, those before Rayden each met an honorable demise at the end of her blades, while droves of their lesser comrades found themselves cut down from behind trying to run away.

The metallic clash of sword blades rang out, a powerful blow aimed toward Rayden's head blocked firm in its path. Already in motion before the swords embraced, her axe completed a short, rapid arc, cleaving deep into the brawny warrior's side.

The thick-bearded fighter's eyes widened in a look of agony and shock, freezing him in place for an instant, and leaving him vulnerable. Rayden pivoted, bringing her sword about in a vicious slash, finishing the kill.

All falling in swift fashion to her blades, three more stout warriors engaged her in combat by the time she reached the far edge of the battlefield. Around her, the broken remnant of the

Runi host fled in haphazard desperation through the trees; their hopes of taking Gessa lands left shattered upon the blood-soaked ground behind them.

Rayden came to a halt at the edge of the trees. Staring into the dense shadows beneath the boughs of the old forest, she found that despite her disgust with cowards she still held a little pity for the enemy survivors.

Scattered and having cast aside all caution, the Runi warriors would find no succor or refuge in the woods. Deep within the shadows of the forest, the nightmare that had driven the Runi to strike at the Gessa awaited the tattered remnants from the battle.

There would be no respite. The enigmatic menace roving the shadows would slake its thirst for human blood in abundance when night fell.

"They will not return. You know they go to their doom," a booming voice called to Rayden from behind. "A fitting end for such craven fools."

Rayden gazed into the shadows a moment longer, before turning to face the towering, broad-shouldered warrior striding toward her. His braided beard streaked with silver, and crow's feet radiating from the corners of his slate-gray eyes, Eigon no longer held the glow of youth.

Despite the advances of age, great power still flowed through his muscle-thickened limbs, and an abundance of martial experience more than countered any slight loss in quickness. To their mortal peril, more than one brash, fast young Runi warrior had learned a final, unforgiving lesson about the value of experience that day.

Eigon trudged up to her side, still clutching his gore-coated sword blade in his right hand. Blood yet dripped from the end of the honed metal. Two warriors coming together with the hellfire of battle still flowing within their veins, his iron-hard gaze met her own.

Rayden nodded. "The night will bring them terror and death, but that is not what bothers me. Their lands touch your own, Eigon ... and there is no wall between. What lurks in those shadows makes no distinction between Gessa and Runi. It only sees humans ... and it sees humans as prey."

Eigon looked off into the woods for a few moments. A grim countenance accompanied the unwavering stare he cast back to her. "No, it matters not what tribe its victims are from. It hunts human flesh. It will not be long before what drove the Runi into us is here among our people, on our lands. And it is not just my lands, Rayden. They are your lands as well."

Rayden said nothing to dispute the old chieftain, though in her heart the lands of the Gessa she could never view as her own. A powerful, large tribe of the north, the Gessa had made her welcome as a child, and given her refuge and a place among them.

Now, many years later, she had returned to aid them in a dark hour. Nevertheless, the lands she recognized in her heart as her own, the lands of her mother and father, were little more than a distant memory.

Her thoughts drifted for a moment, taking her far from the battlefield and forest. Flickers of recollections crossed her mind.

She could see the kind eyes and face of her father, a bear of a man imbued with a rare sort of wisdom and intelligence. She could still remember the feel of his massive arms embracing her; precious moments when all the fears and worries of a little girl fled away.

Beaming like the sun of a midsummer's day, her mother's smile yet shined from within Rayden's mind's eye; an expression that had always reminded a little girl that she was loved and belonged. Though much smaller in stature than her father, her mother carried strength of heart to rival the man she loved and had devoted herself to.

A distant, wondrous time, in a place where the sun caressed the ocean's surface and graced it with a jeweled sheen, where vigorous mountains soared high, to where a small, golden-haired child believed they kissed a cerulean sky, dwelled as a precious treasure within the vault of her memory. In one cruel, brutal day, all had been cast into shadow and cold, throwing Rayden at a young age upon a perilous journey without any true destination; at least not a destination she could fathom.

That journey, without any clear notion of a destination, yet continued. At present it had led her to the edge of a forest, at the end of a blood-drenched battle.

Sweeping away the sharp-edged, heavy feelings, and batting away the dark thoughts mocking the impossibility of her heart's desperate hopes, Rayden forced the trace of a grin to her lips. Her gaze softened with the genuine gratitude and affection she held toward the old Gessa chieftain.

His face had been young, and his body showed few scars, when he had first embraced a golden-haired, blue-eyed child; a child emaciated, hollow-eyed, and with a tear-stained face swathed in blood and grime.

"You have long given me a place among you," Rayden said. "You have honored me greatly, and counted me as one of your own people. It is something I will never take lightly."

"The blood is not so different as you may think," huffed Eigon, a smirk showing through his dense beard. "The tribes of the north are connected to each other. Even the far north, from where you hail.

"Perhaps one day it will no longer be like this, where blood must flow between the tribes. Perhaps one day we can see that we can still follow our tribal ways ... and share common cause."

Rayden sensed the lament beneath his words and knew the spilling of Runi blood gave him no joy. Before he said anything more, she sought to lift his spirits.

"What would you do without the challenge of battle, Eigon? I cannot see you passing your days tilling dirt and watching over fields," Rayden jested, a smile coming to her lips at the thought of the great warrior laboring in fields of crops.

Looking bemused at her remark, Eigon shook his head. "No, I was not born to plow soil. These hands were made to wield a sword and to hunt. No different than you, though your hands found their way to wielding both sword and axe, together."

Rayden caught the deep respect woven into the chieftain's words. He had never cajoled her to seek a husband, or take any other path than the one she had chosen to walk upon. Eigon had always advocated and encouraged the freedom of her will, and for that alone he would always have her undying loyalty.

Hearing a growing murmur from behind them, Rayden glanced back, peering beyond the chieftain to the ground held by the Gessa warriors. Her grin spread further. "It would seem our conversation is brought to an early end. I believe you are being sought out, by quite a few others."

Eigon smiled. "That is one thing I've learned about being a chieftain. You are always sought out. By those wanting something from you, or those wanting to drive an axe into your skull. Sometimes I am not sure which of those things is worse."

The two shared a moment of laughter, though Rayden's expression took on a serious hue when the levity ebbed.

"Sometimes you are sought for reasons of gratitude, in being the rare kind of chieftain that you are," Rayden said, thinking of what Eigon meant to her, and nodding her head toward the mass of warriors coming up behind him.

The throng of warriors spread out, forming around the sides of Rayden and Eigon, though none took so much as a step beneath the trees. More than a few cast wary glances into the forest.

Before long, several hundred Gessa warriors had gathered

at the cusp of the tree line. One man stood forth at the head of the multitude around Eigon and Rayden.

"Eigon! Chieftain of the Gessa! This battle is ours!" roared the young, blond-haired warrior, a mountain of a man himself.

The warriors around him lent their voices to a thundering ovation honoring their storied, beloved chieftain. There would be time enough for mourning later. The moment at hand demanded the celebration of a hard-fought victory.

Though lauding the older chieftain, the young warrior stood tall and proud at the head of the other Gessa, and there had been no hesitation in his stepping forward to speak on behalf of the gathering. Rayden did not miss the spark of ambition shining within the younger warrior's eyes.

The presence of ambition never bothered her, as ambition itself could be as much a force for bettering oneself as it could be a source of corruption. She had always found Alcedan much to her liking, and hoped that he did not pursue a path of folly with his ambitions. Rather, she wanted to see him prove himself worthy of leadership in the fires of battle and other trials; to where he ascended one day by acclimation rather than blood, when Eigon's time upon the world came to an end.

For her part, Rayden believed the powerful warrior had the strength to channel his ambition into a positive force, but that assessment would not keep him shielded from her scrutiny.

"Alcedan, your blade, and that of many other brave Gessa, won this day, as sure as mine did," boomed Eigon in response, his tone of magnanimity ringing genuine to Rayden's ears.

His acclamation of Alcedan came as no surprise. She had never found Eigon to be a self-absorbed leader, such as the ones she often encountered in the warmer climes farther south. True confidence radiated from the older man, in a way that did not hesitate to recognize the achievements of others around him.

"But it is our chieftain who stands upon the edge of the

battlefield, where our foe has been driven into the shadows," Alcedan replied. "You have set the example for us to follow. As you always have. Above all of us, this victory is yours." Rayden caught a deferential edge to Alcedan's voice. The tone gave her encouragement that the young man might have the priceless and uncommon gift of wisdom, to a degree that would help him govern any ambitions he harbored.

"And let us not forget Rayden Valkyrie, who was first among all of us to the edge of this battlefield," Eigon said, raising his blood-stained sword into the air. "It was Rayden's axe that felled Nagradak and the Runi's resolve to continue fighting. Nagradak was one of the greatest and most fearsome warriors to ever take a field of battle. None withstood that blade of his, Death's Bite, until Rayden."

Brandishing weapons at the chieftain's gesture, the warriors raised their voices once more, this time in sonorous acclaim to Rayden. A raucous cheer filled the air and swelled in vigor.

Rayden accepted the outburst of praise in silence. She nodded to the other warriors, seeing the affection held for her reflected on many faces, veteran and younger alike.

While appreciating their outpouring of commendation, she took her own satisfaction in seeing the faces of many warriors she had trained in combat. Perhaps something she had taught them, or in the discipline she instilled in all who she trained, had made the difference between them standing before her now, full of life, or lying cold and dead upon the field of battle. Of all rewards, seeing the light of life within the eyes of the survivors that she had trained stood far above any spoils of war or cheering throng.

When the accolades finally ebbed, Eigon's face took on a more somber look. Eyes drawn toward the chieftain, the quiet grew thick about him. He waited a few moments before he addressed the assemblage.

"We have won a great victory, and there is much to celebrate, but many have fallen this day," he said in a solemn tone. "We must remove their bodies from the ground where they fell, and honor every one of them. We will give the bodies of our foes to the fire as well, for many of them showed a true warrior's heart this day."

The chieftain's words shadowed Rayden's own heart. The most difficult part of a battle about to commence, the aftermath would reveal the identities of many she knew who had fallen that day. Likely, one or more she counted as a friend.

A battle was never free of a heavy price, only the foolish or those who intended to take no risk themselves rushed into a war. Many of the youngest Gessa warriors, experiencing their first major bloodshed, would be taking a hard, life-changing lesson from the crimson-draped field that day.

"Let us begin the task, so that no scavenger can gorge itself upon the flesh of brave warriors," Eigon said. "Let us give their bodies to the fires, now that their spirits are with the gods."

At Eigon's dismissal, Alcedan and the other warriors turned and began heading away from the forest. They did not have to walk far to come across fallen warriors, with numerous Runi dead littering the ground approaching the trees.

"Come, Eigon, let us turn our thoughts to honoring courageous warriors," Rayden said in a low voice, when the throng around them had fully dispersed.

Warriors all across the battlefield were now dragging the slain toward a central area, with weapons and other items being collected in another place. A weighty pall hung over the gloomy scene, any words spoken among the laboring Gessa warriors delivered in whispers or low voices.

Eigon did not answer her at first. He gazed in silence for many long moments upon the dour undertaking.

The years looked to carry a little more weight on the chieftain's face when he finally looked back to her. "Yes, let us honor them, but you and I both know there will be no rest with what is coming. We must prepare ourselves. Will there be any time to gather our breath?"

Rayden nodded, a grave look on her face. "A shadow spreads over us, and we can only march forward to meet each day as it arrives. Though it gives me no joy to say so, what dwells in that forest has plenty of Runi to feast upon tonight. It is likely we will get a short reprieve."

"A grim thought, but no less true," Eigon replied. His next few words took on an edge of bitterness. "If only those fools had come to entreat with me, instead of rushing into this reckless attack. I do not know what madness consumed Nagradak. He should have known I would have given the Runi refuge, and we could have faced this new enemy together, shoulder to shoulder, shield to shield.

"And now? What of their elders? Their women and children? They are gathered somewhere, out there among those trees ... They will soon learn of what happened today, and how many husbands, sons, and fathers fell upon this field. They will swiftly lose all hope."

He grew quiet for a moment and Rayden knew the old chieftain did not speak the words lightly. At the core of his spirit, he mourned the unnecessary loss of life.

Eigon then continued. "I share your thoughts on this. We will get a reprieve tonight ... and maybe for some days to follow. Let us gather our breath. Come, the fires will burn bright this night, taking up the bodies of many good, brave warriors, from both tribes. Their spirits already journey in the light of a different realm."

He took a step away from the forest's edge. She made no reply and strided along with him.

Side by side, each silent and reflective within the spheres of their own thoughts, Rayden and Eigon made their way across a quiet, open field, one no longer engulfed in the horrors of battle.

***

The shouts and laughter of warriors sounded in the distance, where larger fires blazed, hosts of flames kindled far from the battlefield. The great pyre to which the bodies of the fallen Gessa and Runi warriors had been given had long since ebbed to stillness, leaving behind mounds of ash.

Hearts now turned toward thoughts of victory, comrades, and the relief of survival, replacing the somber, mournful atmosphere governing the moments when the smoke from the pyre reached toward the heavens during twilight's approach. Even so, more than a few emotion-laden moments were taken to speak the praises of the fallen Gessa, whose ashes now drifted across the battlefied in the embrace of the chilly night winds.

Set farther away from where copious amounts of meat roasted and drink flowed in abundance, two friends sat together in quiet, under moon and starlight.

"I did not doubt you would return to stand with us, Rayden Valkyrie." Her face illuminated by the crackling flames of the small fire before them, the auburn-haired, broad-shouldered beauty smiled, as she turned her face toward Rayden. "And I know that your blades did much to win this day and defend our people. All speak of how you slew Nagradak. No warrior had ever prevailed against that one. It is said you crushed the Runi's will to fight in that moment. Many Gessa lives were spared when the Runi splintered. No woman among the Gessa has ever done what you have, Rayden. You are like no other."

"Have I not taught you to swing a blade, Erethea? You could have fought at my side, and so could many more of the women among the Gessa," Rayden replied. "You underestimate your own skill."

The smile on Erethea's face faded. "I cannot risk my

sons losing both their mother and father in a single day. If the settlement is overrun, then it will be seen what I can do with a blade. Until then, Jarut will carry the spirit of our family into battle."

"I understand," Rayden said, holding her expression steady, despite the sharp inner pangs that Erethea's words evoked. She understood all too well the agony of losing both a mother and father in a single day. In that light, Rayden could never find fault with Erethea's decision. "But I also know that you are more than capable as a warrior. As are many of the women here."

"It is not an easy manner of living, unlike those places you tell us about far to the south," Erethea said. She looked back to the fire, the flames dancing within her blue-green eyes, growing quiet for a few moments. "Dwellings of stone, behind great walls. Carts filled with clothing, food, and more, streaming into those places you call cities. Here, there are no walls. There is no abundance of carts at hand with the things we need. We must make, hunt, and grow everything we can. We are the stronger for it, but strength does not make it easy."

"Everyone is needed here," Rayden answered, nodding her agreement, thinking of the great merchants of the south, living softer lives of comfort and luxury made possible by the sweat and hard labor of many. "And raising two strong, healthy sons, as you have, is as important and difficult a task as any."

Erethea kept staring into the fire. She asked in a low voice, "How long will you remain among us?"

Rayden could see the plea in her friend's eye and knew Erethea wished her to stay.

"I will not leave the Gessa while this danger from the shadows threatens," Rayden declared, eyes bright in the glow of the flames.

Her thoughts dwelled upon the people living under the shadow of grave threats; both the Gessa and also those such as the Tega, who lived under the growing shadow of the Teveren Empire.

Many faces paraded through her mind.

The first was that of young Hamilcar, the boy she had saved from the fires of an altar in the city of Kartajen. When summoned by the Gessa, she had chosen to leave him with the freed slaves who had been given refuge on the lands of the Tega.

To bring him along would have been more than reckless, but a part of her still felt deep pangs at their separation. The bond grown through the struggles they had faced together had taken a familial nature.

She had guided and protected the young boy, and in her own way nurtured him. Having been given over to the priests of a dark god for sacrifice by his own mother and father, the boy carried the kinds of invisible wounds that were not likely to ever heal in full. How the boy learned to live with those wounds would determine whether he grew stronger, and became an even greater kind of man than he might have become before, or succumbed to darker, colder paths.

Rayden yearned to know how the boy fared. Her heart rested a little in the knowledge that she had entrusted his care to a good, honorable man, Annocrates.

One of the freed slaves, Annocrates may not have been the strongest warrior, but he was among the strongest when it came to matters of trust and character. He was the kind of man that Hamilcar needed in his world; a true father-figure, where the boy's own father had proven abhorrent and unworthy of the title.

Rayden missed Doros, wishing that she could have accompanied the woman on her quest to discover the fate of her family. Had it not been for the urgent situation facing the Gessa, Rayden could see herself going on the journey with Doros to search out her brother, sister, mother, and father. She hoped with all her heart that Doros one day reunited with all four of them, and that they would never be scattered apart again.

She thought of Ammanus, whom she had been separated from during the events in Kartajen involving Hamilcar and the harrowing escape from the city. Though crass and given to prurient interests, Ammanus possessed a good heart and his company often lifted her spirits.

Rayden wondered where his path had taken him. Whether he had remained across the sea or taken passage to Teveren lands she did not know. She only knew he had the wit and resourcefulness to find his way through all manner of situations, and had little doubt that wherever Ammanus had gone he was enjoying ample food, drink, and the company of women.

"What are you thinking of, Rayden?" Erethea asked, interrupting her ruminations.

Rayden looked away from the dancing tongues of fire. "Shadows ... and those living under them."

"Probably all over this world," Erethea responded. "Seems like shadows are spreading everywhere in this time."

Rayden nodded, with a grim expression, thinking of how those growing shadows had driven the Runi into a disastrous battle. "Indeed they are."

Erethea smiled. "For my part, I am glad you are here with us, to help us face the ones we live under."

"And it brings joy to my heart to see you again," Rayden stated, her face softening. A smile bloomed on her lips. "It has been a long while since we sat together like this. I have missed such nights."

"Far too long," Erethea said, and Rayden could hear the regret in the woman's voice. "I am never alone with my sons and Jarut, but I do not have any friend such as you. One I can confide in ... one who holds my trust. One whose counsel I treasure."

"I feel the same as you, Erethea. Friends such as you are rare in this world," Rayden said. "The more lands I visit, the more that becomes clearer to me."

"You have crossed a great many lands," Erethea said. "I can't even imagine it."

"A great many," Rayden agreed, feeling a tinge of weariness at the words.

"You have seen and experienced much more than any of us," Erethea said.

"Not always for the better," Rayden responded. "It is a cruel world we live in. A world unforgiving and callous. It is a world full of predators, power-hungry conquerors, slavers, thieves, and the wicked. Wherever I have gone, it has not taken long before I find myself in conflict with such filth."

Rayden's gaze hardened and her tone grew firm. "Believe me, as long as I can breathe I will go against such adversaries, with everything I have left within me."

Erethea shifted over and set her hand lightly upon Rayden's shoulder. She smiled and spoke in a soft voice, "It is also a world which has honor and compassion. A world with courage and love in it.

"It is a world with friendships and family ... and family is not always of blood, Rayden. Family is something much more. In a world where we do not choose the family we share blood with, do not underestimate what it means to be chosen as family."

The words caught Rayden off guard. Looking to Erethea, she could see the deeper meaning echoed in the other woman's eyes. Rayden knew that Erethea looked upon her as both friend and family, in the most genuine sense.

"You will always have a place under my roof, should you ever need one," Erethea said. "No matter where your travels may take you, I want you to know that."

Rayden made no reply. She took Erethea into an embrace, hugging her friend tight before the firelight betrayed the glisten manifesting on the surface of her eyes.

CHAPTER 2

Moonlight kissed jagged rises looming above the Gessa settlement. Rayden stared in silence toward the shadowy mountains, brisk winds whipping about her face. The icy tendrils brought with them an invigorating sensation that carried throughout her body.

Around her, the spirited conversations of other warriors could be heard. The hunting party preparing to set out, it would not be much longer before she would be trekking through a pine-scented wilderness.

The thought proved highly welcome and brought heightened anticipation with it. Rayden much preferred the untamed environs and the unfettered freedom the wilderness offered over settlement life, even if life in the former had rougher edges and held far more peril than the latter.

Many days had passed since the battle with the Runi, and she had found herself growing restless. Training at arms had taken up a portion of each day, but many long periods of idleness remained to be endured.

She filled those periods as best she could, from giving young warriors tutelage in weapons to lending a hand in various tasks. Whether cutting wood or going to accompany a nervous swine herder agitated by the swelling fears of dangers in the forest,

Rayden did her utmost to contribute to the needs of the Gessa.

Unease hovered over all in the settlement, and it thickened by the day. Every man and woman of the Gessa knew time grew short.

The menace lurking in the shadows of the Runi lands would not spare the Gessa. Sooner or later it would make an incursion into their lands and be among them, killing at will. Answers had to be sought.

The Gessa still had to carry on with their daily lives, and hunting remained a needed task. Ample game could be had in mountainous lands opposite from where the things stalking the territory of the Runi dwelled.

With no reports of anything amiss in that area, Alcedan and several others from Eigon's core retinue of warriors had decided upon a hunting expedition. When asked to join them, Rayden did not hesitate. A hunting foray into the mountainous terrain she knew well had offered a chance to offset her increasing restlessness enduring the routine of settlement life.

Rayden heard a brusque laugh behind her. Turning, she saw Alcedan looking her way. A grin spread upon his face, he rested his left hand on his hips, his right gripping a long spear and pair of javelins.

"Something amuse you?" she asked in an even tone.

"You seem fascinated with the mountains," Alcedan replied. "We will not be going that far tonight. And we will not be climbing to their summits."

"No, and it would not be wise to brave the snows on those heights," Rayden said, thinking of the icy, treacherous realm crowning the upper reaches of the great rises. She doubted Alcedan had much experience in such a harsh environment.

"No, it would not. I have only been that far up the slopes a couple of times," he said. "I do not feel right in leading anyone up there, when I would not have confidence myself."

Rayden nodded, pleased with his response. Alcedan's candor and honesty both surprised and impressed her. His words served as more testament to her hopes of the spirited young warrior having the gift of wisdom.

A tall, dark-haired warrior walked up and smacked his hand down upon Alcedan's shoulder, in the casual manner of a comrade. Jarut's voice carried an air of eagerness imbued with impatience. "About ready to head out? The night is not getting any younger or warmer!"

"It appears that way," Alcedan replied with a grin, giving the other man a vigorous slap on the back.

"Let's not waste another moment of starlight and clear skies," Jarut replied. "It is an advantageous night to begin a hunt."

Jarut remained the boisterous fellow Rayden had known before, but she sensed a more mature version of the man who stood before her now. From everything Erethea had told Rayden, Jarut had grown into a dedicated father and husband in the time Rayden had been away from the Gessa on her journeys. Knowing Erethea, Rayden doubted Jarut would have survived long otherwise, but it was good to hear nonetheless.

"It is a high honor to have you going with us tonight, Rayden Valkyrie," Jarut said to her, his tone sincere.

"A good hunt in the night benefits mind, body, and spirit," Rayden said. A touch of a grin played about her lips. "It is much better than standing around here and watching plants grow or chopping wood."

"We know she can fight, and she has wisdom too! I agree with her!" Jarut said, slapping Alcedan on the back again. He hefted up the spear gripped in his other hand. He stated with an air of growing restlessness. "We should not wait any longer! The night grows older!"

Rayden chuckled, though she could not disagree with his desire to set forth. Every fiber of her being strained to enter the wilderness.

Alcedan looked about, and a moment later called for the hunting party to head out. Rayden counted ten warriors in all when they started forward through the trees, including herself.

She held onto a javelin for the hunt, though she carried both axe and sword at her side. The last couple of days she had included some additional time for practicing spear-throwing in her training. Rayden had tightened up her form and accuracy, giving her full confidence of her readiness should she gain an opportunity to bring down some quarry.

Abundant moonlight aided their trek. Branches creaking and leaves whispering proved the hunting party's only significant accompaniment for quite some time, the peaks of the mountains drawing ever closer.

No conversation took place among the warriors. Rayden strode near to Alcedan at the forefront of the loose column, with a few men sent farther ahead to scout. All kept their wits and senses attuned to their surroundings, ready for the slightest sound or disturbance.

While the hunting party had the reassurance that the ground they roved lay on the other side of the Gessa lands from where the Runi border was located, Rayden could not avoid thinking about the lethal menace now facing the tribe. She wondered how much longer it would be until the forest she walked through held the same threat that plagued the Runi. In her eyes, it stood merely a matter of time.

The moon rose a little higher, and they soon came upon one of the men who had gone forward to scout, a lithe warrior named Mardan. Kneeling down, he gave close scrutiny to a series of impressions in the ground. He did not turn his head at the approach of the others.

"These are not too old, we are close to it," Mardan said in a low, tense voice. He looked up, and Rayden saw grave concern etched in his face. "We should go no farther. We risk too much."

"Snow Lions?" Jarut whispered, taking a knee by Mardan and eyeing the impressions. Mardan nodded back to him. Jarut continued, "But why? This far from the heights? What are they doing so far down the slopes? They never come this low."

"How close is it?" asked Alcedan. A gust of icy air blew over them.

"Very close," Mardan answered, his eyes displaying anxiety.

"It is good we are downwind," Jarut said, another current of air passing over the group. "They will not have our scent."

"Beollus and Iannos are farther ahead," Mardan said, and the implication in his words hung thick in the air between the rest of the hunting party's members. "They must have overlooked these tracks. We cannot call out to—"

A roar erupting out of the darkness cut Mardan's words off. The pitiful nature of the scream that followed told Rayden all that needed to be said.

In an instant, the hunters had become the hunted.

A young warrior ran through the trees to Rayden's left, heading in their direction. Behind him, the light of the moon glinted off a dense coat of white fur, covering a large, muscular form bounding fast after the man.

She knew the creature at once. A Snow Lion closed in upon Beollus and swiftly drew closer to the group.

"Break apart, and try to surround it!" Rayden called to the others.

Clustered they risked losing several of their number in a whirlwind of claw and fang. If they could harry it from many angles, they stood a chance of confusing the beast and creating openings to strike.

The other warriors adhered to her command, scattering apart before the onrushing beast.

Setting her feet, and changing her grip on the spear she

carried, Rayden stood her ground and did not take to the shadows herself. The pursued warrior had only one sliver of a chance to survive, and that fraying thread lay entirely in Rayden's hands.

Raising her weapon up, she reared back.

The distance between the running warrior and the beast evaporated. In another moment or two, Beollus would find himself engulfed from behind and ripped apart by the claws of the Snow Lion.

Rayden hurled the spear, sending the missile through the air with great velocity. A piercing, bestial cry split the night.

The Snow Lion skidded to a halt and thrashed about, the spear embedded deep in its flesh just behind its shoulders. Rayden knew precious few moments remained until the creature lashed out in agonized fury.

"Get far behind me, now! This is my fight!" Rayden shouted to the young warrior, who continued past her with a terror-stricken countenance. Her eyes remained fixed on the Snow Lion, her hands instinctively taking up both sword and axe.

The beast gathered itself and squared toward Rayden. Letting loose a guttural roar that shook the air, the Snow Lion exposed a huge set of fangs. Its eyes glowed bright, reflecting the moonlight and lending the beast a surreal, otherworldly countenance.

Enraged in its pain, and denied its initial quarry, the beast crouched lower, tensing. Its gaze locked on Rayden, the creature sprang toward her in an explosion of movement.

Extremely broad paws, well-suited for prowling the snow drifts of the cold realms it inhabited, propelled the beast across the ground.

With a quick upward motion and flick of her arm and wrist, Rayden hurled her axe toward the charging Snow Lion. The axe spun tight, and the blade drove into the beast, landing more truly than had the spear, cleaving deep into the creature's skull at its left eye.

The Snow Lion emitted a higher-pitched cry. Rayden dived to the right, just before the beast rushed through the space where she had been standing.

She landed hard on the rough ground. Incurring cuts and scrapes from the debris on the forest floor was nothing compared to what the claws of the Snow Lion would have done to her flesh.

The creature twisted and whipped about in throes of great pain, one eye blinded from the axe blade. The beast batted the axe free from its eye, yowling in a new burst of anguish.

Rayden gained her feet and moved in, slashing hard with her sword blade.

The Snow Lion swiped its right paw at her approach, a strike coming within an arm's length of mauling her. Rayden countered, delivering a vicious slash that almost severed the limb, crippling the beast.

No longer able to support any weight upon its right front leg, the creature struggled to remain upright. Growling, the beast bared its fangs toward Rayden, the gleam of its lone remaining eye reflecting pain, confusion, and even a little fear.

Rayden did not hesitate, hacking at its other forelimb, wounding the creature again and rendering it more vulnerable. Blood spattered all over its white fur as she chose her spots and delivered several more heavy blows, strikes that finally left the beast inert, and seemingly lifeless, under the night sky.

Not about to take any chances, she delivered one more strike with her blade, chopping deep into its neck with full force. Pulling the sword back and breathing heavily, she reached down and yanked her still-embedded javelin free.

Backing away from the creature's body, she did not let her wariness down for even a moment, just in case a flicker of life remained within the massive beast. She had witnessed more than one death spasm before, and even devoid of life the creature could mortally wound a human with ease.

With great care, she retrieved her axe from where it had fallen. Returning it to the loop in the wide belt at her waist, she kept both sword and javelin in hand.

She remained in place, listening for any indications of other Snow Lions or her companions. The moonlight filtered through the trees, casting shadows that danced when an icy breeze whispered through the branches.

Looking around, she sought out the young warrior who she had saved, but could find him nowhere in sight. At some point during the struggle, he had fled deeper into the woods.

Before anger at Beollus' absence took root, she reminded herself that she had told him to get far behind her, and that she claimed the fight against the lion as her own. Nevertheless, she found herself disappointed in the young man.

"Rayden," Jarut said in a low voice, stepping into sight from the trees to her left.

She had already squared towards him, weapons in hand, at the sound of his approaching footsteps. Seeing the tall warrior emerging from cover, she lowered her weapons, but not her vigilance. There was no telling how many Snow Lions could be in the vicinity.

Pounding footsteps carried through the trees as others drew near. Jarut gazed upon the dead form lying near to Rayden.

He looked back to her with an expression of amazement. "You slew the beast, by yourself."

"And there may be more of them, do not let your guard down," Rayden admonished him in a terse voice.

Others from the hunting party began returning.

"It is not likely there are more," Alcedan's voice interrupted from the shadows, as the brawny warrior emerged into sight and walked up to them. "A male Snow Lion does not hunt alone. Had they been moving together, the females would have been with him. I believe this was a lone creature."

Alcedan's judgment made sense. Had there been a full pride, Rayden and the other warriors would have found themselves beset by many female Snow Lions. Had an entire pride attacked, Rayden doubted any of them could have survived the night.

Yet one thought lingered, as she recalled the lions of her travels far to the south. Another possibility remained; a troubling one.

"It still may not be alone," Rayden said.

"It is just a lone male, without a pride," Alcedan reiterated, with a dismissive air.

"Why do you say it may not be alone?" Jarut said, looking concerned.

Before she could answer, Rayden heard the shuffling of massive paws on forest debris, preceding a booming roar that shook the night. A great shadow burst from the trees, engulfing one of the hunters.

She whirled toward the movement. A fearful, grating scream turned into a gurgling croak beneath the reverberating growls of the raging beast.

"Stand together!" Rayden called to the others. "It is among us! We must fight!"

Jarut, Alcedan and a warrior named Temmas remained with Rayden, spears at the ready. Nearby, the others grouped together.

The Snow Lion turned to face Rayden and the three with her. The fur about its jaws coated in gore, the creature snarled and exposed an array of fangs glistening with a crimson hue.

With a thick, flowing mane framing its angry visage, another male Snow Lion stood before them, one every bit as large and powerful in form as the first. The presence of a second male Snow Lion did not suprise her in the least.

On her journeys far to the south, Rayden had witnessed pairs of male lions roving the wilderness together; both as hunters without a pride of their own, and as co-regents of one.

She doubted the beast before her ruled a pride. Brothers hunting together, the two Snow Lions prowling the lower forest terrain in the shadow of the mountains had not yet taken command of a pride, or the area would have been swarming with females.

With a cry, and without warning, Temmas lunged forth and stabbed at the lion. The beast swatted the head of the spear away with ease, and sprang with claws outstretched at the exposed, defenseless warrior.

Rayden pivoted and thrust with her spear. The iron tip reached the lion and tunneled deep behind its shoulder a moment after its claws shredded the front of Temmas' body from his chest to stomach.

Alcedan and Jarut followed an instant later, plunging their spears deep into the body of the lion. The creature grunted and fell heavily to its side, wheezing with three spear blades embedded far into its flesh.

"Stay back," Rayden cautioned the others, eyeing the labored breath of the beast as life seeped from its body. Keeping her gaze fixed on the beast, she took up her axe again, holding both of her weapons at the ready.

The Snow Lion's side heaved one more time and became still. The forest took to silence once more.

Still keeping their spear tips leveled toward the beast, the other group of hunters made their way over. Faces tense and eyes wide, they glanced between their companions and the prone beast.

"Two male lions?" Jarut queried, with an air of confusion. "How can this be?"

"I have seen it before," Rayden said. "A sliver of fortune is with us, as I have seen two males command a pride in the lands far to the south. If these lions had such, we would be overwhelmed."

"It took several of us to kill it, and we lost Odaces and Temmas," Alcedan stated with a tone of bitterness, his face shadowing at the pronouncement.

"We need to find the one of us who is missing," Rayden said, taking quick assessment of their numbers.

" We ... we lost Iannos," ventured a nervous-sounding voice.

Rayden glanced over toward Beollus, the young man whose life she had saved by her intervention. His face still held a look of terror, but she knew his fear now derived from a reason other than Snow Lions.

"Iannos too?" Alcedan whispered, eyes downcast. "Not Iannos..."

"The beast took us unawares, like a shadow rising to life, we never saw it coming," the young warrior added. "It leaped upon Iannos, and he was dead before I knew what was happening. I ran back."

"You fought with Rayden then?" Alcedan asked the young warrior. "When you saw she stood her ground? You turned and fought with her?"

"I do not think he did. His face betrays him. Rayden brought this monster down herself," Jarut interjected, casting the young man a sharp glance. "I think Beollus ran past her, and continued running."

"You ran? And left Rayden behind?" Alcedan asked, his eyes remaining fixed to the ground. The distaste thick in his tone, he repeated," Beollus ... you ran? What of when the beast attacked Iannos? You ran then too. Did Iannos stand a chance if you had not?"

"Iannos was dead. The beast was upon us," Beollus replied, a pleading edge to his voice. "There was nothing I could have done."

"You did not have to run again," Alcedan said.

"He made no sound ... nor struggled ... when I realized what was happening," Beollus stammmered. "He was dead ... I swear."

Rayden saw that Beollus had misunderstood Alcedan. She could see the ire swirling within the tall warrior's gaze as he stared at the ground.

"I'm not talking about when the beast attacked," Alcedan said, his jaw growing taut.

Alcedan slowly brought his eyes up. Death brimmed in the gaze he cast Beollus. He gripped the hilt of the sword he carried.

Rayden knew his intent at once. She stated, firm, "Hold, Alcedan."

"This is not your concern, Rayden Valkyrie," Alcedan said. "No warrior of the Gessa runs when another is being attacked."

"If they were unawares when the Snow Lion attacked, it is all but certain Iannos died in an instant, I believe that," Rayden said, knowing she tread on fragile ground. "And when he reached me, I told him to get far behind me. I told him it was my fight. He could only have gotten in my way. He listened as you all listened to me, when I recognized the beast and told you to scatter apart."

She hoped she did not have to raise her weapons against Alcedan, but she would not allow the young warrior to be slain in her presence.

Alcedan turned towards Beollus. "It would have been better for you to die fighting the beast than abandon Rayden, no matter what she told you. You saw her taking a stand. You should have remained with her."

He took a slow step toward the young man.

Though Beollus looked terrified, he stood his ground. "I am sorry, Alcedan. This was a monster I had never seen before. I could not stand against that beast alone when it killed Iannos. In my fear I did as I thought Rayden told me, when she called to me."

Alcedan took another step forward, the grip firm on his sword. Threat coiled in the cold night air.

Rayden stepped forward, getting between the two men. She fixed a hard gaze upon Alcedan.

"Had Iannos even a slight chance, it would have been a disgrace for Beollus to run," Rayden stated, in a slow, measured tone, her gaze unwavering as it held that of Alcedan. "There is no saving a man or woman when a Snow Lion springs upon them out of the night. Beollus could not have reached Iannos in time to save him.

"And had I not told him to get far behind me and claimed the fight to myself, you would be justified in your rage, Alcedan. Spare him now, and let him be measured when everything stands more clear."

Alcedan glared toward Beollus, and then turned his heated gaze back toward her. She could see the agitation escalating in the tall man. "Do not interfere in the ways of the Gessa, Rayden. Our blood is not that of cowards. He saw you taking a stand against the same threat facing him, and he continued to run."

Rayden girded herself for combat. She admired Alcedan's courage. He knew her to be the better fighter, but would not back away from the confrontation because of it.

"I do not seek to interfere in the ways of the Gessa," Rayden replied. "I have seen men taken unawares by lions much less formidable than this one. Truly, Beollus stood no chance of saving Iannos ... and I will tell you one last time ... I told him to get far behind me, and he did. I commanded him, as I did the rest of you."

The tension in the air coiled even tighter. Every instinct warning her, Rayden could sense an impending attack. Her focus settled and her breaths came steady.

"Would you kill us all here, Rayden? Where these lions did not?" Alcedan asked her, his eyes harboring an iron glint.

"Alcedan, I would die for you, or any of the warriors here ... Jarut ... Beollus ... Gerran ... Ussala ... Mardan ... any of you, if that is what it took to save you," Rayden said. "I chose to stand ground against the lion to see that Beollus lived.

"I ask you to trust my judgment, and spare the life I risked my own for. Would you dismiss my judgment and seek to kill me? Would you punish a young warrior for following a command?"

A flicker of surprise crossed Alcedan's face. The questions struck him hard, but she could see that he remained angered that Beollus had completely abandoned Rayden to her fate against the lion.

He stared into Rayden's face for many moments. She kept herself poised for the first instance of movement, indicating the beginning of an attack, sword and axe at the ready.

Finally, the hard edges in his face eased, like a storm receding, and he nodded to her. "You have done so much for the Gessa, Rayden. You are a part of us too. I trust your judgment. I always have. I will not take this matter any farther."

Relief flooded Rayden, even as her estimation of the warrior grew. He had just proven himself a man who could reign in his emotions and exercise better judgment when the moment called for it.

Beollus may well have continued running whether Rayden had told him too or not. He remained unmeasured, and the day might come when she would not step between him and one like Alcedan. But this was not that time, and the young warrior had only done as she had commanded him.

The surviving members of the hunting party tarried long enough to skin the pelts of the Snow Lions, in addition to cutting a few choice portions of meat for a later meal. A heavy, brooding atmosphere filled the night, weighing down hearts and minds.

Gathering wood, the hunters set about a grim task that had to be completed before they moved onward. The mangled bodies of the three slain warriors could not be taken back to the settlement. Nor could any member of the hunting party abandon the fallen where they lay.

Before helping to carry Iannos's body, Rayden satisfied any lingering doubts about Beollus's claim. Iannos's throat had been torn wide open, the ground beneath him soaked in blood. No warrior could survive such a wound.

Flames consuming their forms, Odaces, Temmas, and Iannos were given final respects, and spared the indignity of scavengers. Their weapons were taken up and distributed among the survivors to carry for the time being.

Assembled around the makeshift pyre, the rest of the party shared no words as the fire burned. Each dwelled quietly within the sanctuary of their own thoughts and memories.

Rayden stared deep into the fire, the blazing tempest transforming the flesh of warriors into ash and smoke. To her eyes, the rising tendrils drifting high into the night sky hinted toward something else; a transition of worlds, of the kind spoken of by shamans, priests, and seers.

The deeper longing that always tugged from within her began welling up. Dreams of another reality began forming out of the mists of her mind.

Visions that each brought the sharp sting of sorrow in their wake, figures long-missed from across the years began emerging from those inner depths of memory. With the passing of time, their numbers continued to grow, adding to the heaviness of heart manifesting in such moments like she endured at the present.

Rayden wondered, if she lived long enough, whether the day would come when she could no longer bear the remembrance of cherished individuals who had been lost to her from violence, disease, or the ravages of time. Summoning her willpower, she forced her mournful thoughts away, before she found herself consumed with melancholic feelings.

Walking away from the crackling, hissing fire, she gazed into the trees, and took in a long, slow breath. The chill of the night seeped into her lungs, a cleansing feeling that buoyed her encumbered spirit.

She heard footsteps coming up from behind her. She glanced to her right, though she knew the step of Alcedan well enough. The tall warrior nodded to her, a somber expression outlined in the moonlight.

"The night weighs heavy indeed," Alcedan stated, in a low voice.

"Death is the risk each one of us takes, every single day ... and I'm not speaking of just warriors," Rayden replied with a solemn air. She looked to Alcedan. "Who knows what tomorrow will bring? Who can even promise we will survive the rest of this night? Nothing is certain. We can only choose to live strong in the time we have at hand."

"And I am with you in that choice," Alcedan replied.

The hint of a smile flickered upon Rayden's lips. "You are one who lives strong, and may it be so always. The storms coming upon these lands will need to be faced by those such as us."

"That is why I wish to speak with you, now," Alcedan said.

When he grew silent, she asked, "Yes? What worry plagues you?"

"The question raised by Jarut ... Snow Lions, this far down the slopes of the mountains," Alcedan stated, letting the implications hover in the air between them.

"Far from where they have always roamed," Rayden said. "White coats of fur do not blend well among these trees. The Snow Lions are ill-suited for the lower ground. No, they have traveled far from their dominion and shed their advantages. No light reason caused that."

"And that is what troubles me," Alcedan said.

"You are wondering what could have driven them so far away from the snow-filled heights they call home," Rayden said, bringing her gaze to meet that of the other warrior. "My thoughts dwell upon that also. It is a grave concern, and I have no immediate answer."

"What possibly could drive two male Snow Lions out of the mountains?" Alcedan asked. For an instant, a glimmer of fear passed across his eyes. "There is no stronger predator in those heights."

To Rayden, the presence of fear in the warrior's eyes reflected no weakness in him. Only the most foolhardy abandoned such a quality. A healthy part of a warrior's essence, fear instilled forethought and discipline when facing a dangerous threat.

"Whatever the cause may be, it is something we are in no condition to face this night," Rayden answered in a firm tone.

"Yet we must learn what it is," Alcedan said. "The Gessa live beneath the very slopes these Snow Lions abandoned."

"When dawn's light falls upon the mountains, we will seek answers," Rayden said, nodding.

A foreboding notion came to mind. She thought of the Runi tribe. Akin to the Snow Lions, they had abandoned their lands.

On gut instinct, she suspected the cause of both exoduses to be the same. The answer to the Snow Lions' presence on the low ground would likely bring them the answer to the enigma plaguing the Runi lands.

"What are you thinking? I see that something bothers you greatly about all of this," Alcedan observed, staring at her face.

"It may be nothing," Rayden answered. "Or it may be that the same terror drives both man and beast from their longtime dominions."

"If that is so, then whatever plagued the Runi, is surrounding our lands," Alcedan said. "That would be ill-fortune to us all."

"It is a possibility we cannot cast aside," Rayden said. She then cautioned the warrior. "Yet we must not be rash, until more is known."

"We cannot walk away and leave this mystery in the shadow

of the mountains," Alcedan said. "We must continue the hunt, even if its purpose has changed. But if we discover the causes behind the Snow Lions and Runi are the same, and find what drove the entire Runi tribe to war against us, how can the few with us here hope to face it? How will we survive to warn the others? We have already lost three of our number this night."

"If it is the same menace behind all of it, then we must find a way, or none may survive," Rayden said. "For now, let us all try to get a little rest. I will take up the first watch of the night."

Turning, she lay a hand upon his shoulder and then continued back toward the others. With myriad thoughts swirling in her mind, having the first watch would not be a burden. Rest would not find her easily in what remained of the night.

***

Around midday, the sun's rays sifting through the towering pines revealed a stark vision of slaughter. Limbs, heads, and other bodily pieces riddled a blood-soaked stretch of ground.

A terrible stench permeated the air, a nauseating aroma born of death and rot.

All of the warriors clutched their weapons, taking each step in careful silence while eyeing the carnage. A brief examination of the mutilated carcasses testified that the carnage had occurred not long ago.

Rayden could not believe what she saw, strewn among the trees. The remains of several female Snow Lions, eviscerated and torn to pieces, had been left to the denizens of the forest.

A broader search of the area, revealing the absence of young cubs or an adult male, told her the group of female Snow Lions most likely had been on the hunt.

Whatever killed the beasts had done so with a savage ferocity. The tell-tale marks of lengthy talons and huge bite wounds on the lion corpses told of another kind of animal; though other kinds of wounds she came across left Rayden deeply perplexed.

More than one wound she examined looked to be the result of a weapon. A few appeared to have been inflicted by spear, while others looked to have been caused by a blunt type of implement, such as a war club.

Stomaching the horrid smell, almost unbearable at close proximity, she kept to her inspection, intent on finding the answer for certain. At last, she came across a sight that confirmed her troubling inclinations.

Just past the bashed-in skull of a Snow Lion, an unmistakable weapon lay upon the ground. Though crude, nothing more than some rough leather strips lashing a stone head to a stout wooden shaft, the weapon belonged to no wild beast.

A sentient mind had fashioned and wielded the object.

The presence of a weapon only deepened the mystery. There were no human tracks to be found, and most of the bloodshed had been caused using talon or fang.

"Come here, quickly," Mardan exclaimed, from several paces to Rayden's left, in a hushed voice carrying a thick sense of nervousness. "I found something all of you will want to have a look at."

Rayden and the others hastened toward Mardan at once, gathering around the spot on the ground that he gestured at. Her eyes took in the sight he had called them over to witness.

The clear outlines of a couple large footprints lay exposed to her eyes. Elongated, the impressions in the ground held evidence of claws.

Apprehension gripped her. Unfamiliar in shape, the tracks spoke of no creature she had ever encountered in the northern lands.

Gauging by the footprint of an average human, whatever made the tracks had to be very large in size. It also walked upon two legs.

She had no doubts of it possessing tremendous physical power, enough to rip the mountains' fiercest predator into pieces. The testament to its strength resounded from all the gore and parts of Snow Lion corpses scattered all around Rayden and the other warriors.

In light of the fact that the killings had not taken place all that long ago, Rayden knew the unknown creature could well be close in the vicinity. Perhaps it watched them now, veiled in the shadows.

"Keep your wits about you, and have your weapons at hand," Rayden told the others while looking around the area, scrutinizing every last bit of shadow and foliage.

The others needed little prodding, most looking edgy and casting their gazes about in a state of wariness.

Several more pairs of the unusual footprints came to light as the warriors scoured the area. The additional tracks revealed more foreboding discoveries; more than one attacker had been involved in the slaughter.

Judging from the impressions, Rayden determined that no more than four of the mysterious creatures had been involved in slaying eight Snow Lions.

"A beast that carries weapons," Alcedan remarked in a voice barely above a whisper, kneeling down at Rayden's side while she examined some ground. "What manner of creature is this?"

Rayden thought of the race of beings with dog-like heads who dwelled in lands far to the east and carried weapons, but knew those creatures did not possess the kind of claws or jaw strength that could inflict the vicious wounds she had come across on the Snow Lion carcasses. She thought of monstrous entities in more than one of the lands she had traveled that could change shapes, many able to take human guises, but those did not wield weapons when taking the form of beasts.

The tracks in the ground also had no resemblance to those

of the wolf-men living in lands to the north of the tribes.

Whatever had created the tracks represented something entirely new to her experience. The specter loomed of a creature able to combine the savage ferocity of a large, bestial predator with the weapon-wielding ability of a human.

The weapon they discovered, and the types of wounds that appeared to be inflicted by weapons, hinted at cruder skills and techniques than those possessed by a tribal warrior. It remained the only consolation to be found within the miasma of carnage.

Rayden held little doubt that the new revelations shared a connection with the dire plight of the Runi. She did not want to begin thinking of the possible numbers of the creatures that roamed the woodlands, knowing there had been enough to drive an entire tribe from their lands.

When nothing more could be found, the group decided to continue onward. Moving away from the blood-drenched scene, the warriors walked in silence for quite some time, careful to keep every step light upon the forest floor.

All listened and watched for any hint of the creatures that had killed the Snow Lions, but the woodlands remained draped in a pensive silence. No bird or beast disturbed the stillness.

Rayden knew the creatures that made their home in the woodlands were well-aware of the lethal threat stalking the shadows. The pervading silence served as a stark warning to the warriors; the slayers of the Snow Lions were yet near.

With the shadows growing longer and the day waning, the group finally drew to a halt, needing to take a brief respite.

"Still, a mystery looms. What of Weimassa?" Jarut asked the others, when they were all gathered together. "I have been thinking of this as we walked. She is not far from here. She dwells somewhere in the shadow of Axe Mountain, which we can see through the trees now. Unless we find something soon, it seems the only other way."

"The mountain witch? Have you lost your mind?" Gerran retorted. The stocky, dark-haired warrior's voice ran thick with incredulity. "She's no priestess of our gods."

"If anyone knows of what killed those lions, she will," Jarut countered, holding the other's gaze.

"And wield her dark arts upon all of us," Gerran riposted, his voice rising a little more. "I am not about to face the powers of a mountain witch. Not on her own terrain."

"Sorcery is nothing I wish to chance," added Mardan.

Rayden understood their reticence, having experienced far enough of witches and sorcerers throughout her years. Despite the things on her behalf that Dreaghen had done, even he gave her pause. Such individuals wielded powers and arts that transgressed the natural laws governing the world, and that alone made her wary of all practitioners of sorcery.

"She is likely to want these mountains rid of whatever the creatures are ... as much as we are," Jarut replied, his voice also growing in volume, along with the glare in his eyes. "Weimassa and the Gessa have a common threat."

"Jarut makes a point," Ussala said, rubbing his knees where he had taken a seat at the base of a tree.

"And would you be reckless and bring sorcery upon us too?" Gerran said, casting a hard glance at Ussala and looking more agitated.

"Hold your tongues!" Alcedan interjected in a stern, lower tone, glowering at the two warriors. "A danger we do not understand roams these woods. You have seen what it can do. Do you wish to draw those things to us now? When we know so little?"

Ussala and Gerran looked to him, and shook their heads.

"It is still a way we may learn what these things are, without needing to find them," Jarut said, after several moments passed, his voice returned to a quieter level.

"More than one man has gone to her, and never come back," Gerran said, lowering his voice as well. "That is well-known. The priestesses have warned us. The witch is said to lure men to their doom. Great beauty masking a demon's heart and hungers."

Rayden thought of encounters in her past involving such seductive predators, who lured a singular, vulnerable kind of victim. The recollections gave her an idea.

"No man has returned ... but what about a woman?" Rayden asked, looking to the faces of the others. "One who has faced many who wielded the powers of sorcery and magic."

She looked to the faces of the men around her, letting the idea take root in the minds of the proud warriors. Searching out a mountain witch stood a course of action teeming with perils in itself, but Jarut had touched upon a possible truth.

The things stalking the mountains and forests could be just as much of a threat to the witch as they were to the Gessa. A lone witch, even a powerful one, would be sorely beset with a menace that had driven the Runi from their lands and into reckless battle.

Over the course of her journeys, Rayden had witnessed more than one instance of longtime enemies coming together to face a common foe. The possibility loomed that the witch would welcome the chance of gaining new allies, at least while under the same shadow of threat.

A part of her wished she could summon Dreaghen and seek his counsel, but the enigmatic sorcerer appeared only when he desired. If anyone could cast light upon the mind of a mountain witch in circumstances like those facing the warriors, Dreaghen could.

The others looked to each other, but not one of them offered a response. Worry creased the face of Gerran, while furrows of deep concern spanned Alcedan's. Rayden could sense that none of them held much appetite for her to take such a risk upon herself.

"A woman seeking the witch out may stay her hand just long enough to speak of the danger stalking these woods," Rayden said. "It is a risk, of that there is no question, but we are left with few choices."

"What if she is the cause of it?" Gerran asked. "Is that not possible too? A witch can summon things of the darkness."

"Think upon what has happened, Gerran. The witch had no interest in pushing the Runi to war against us." Rayden said. She paused, eyeing the young warrior. Feeling more strongly than ever that whatever had befallen the Snow Lions had a connection to the terror spurring the Runi into fleeing their lands, she continued. "My instincts tell me that this threat is as much of a danger to her as it is to us. I do not believe she would seek to kill me outright."

"If you are not right about this, you may forfeit your life," Gerran said. "Do not be a fool. Not even you can overcome dark sorcery."

"Do not judge so swiftly!" Rayden snapped, irritated with the young warrior's assumptions. "I have been pitted against sorcery more times than I care to count."

Gerran's eyes widened at her sharp response. His next words carried a deferential air. "I meant no offense, Rayden Valkyrie. I speak only out of concern. You are valuable to all of us."

Rayden nodded to him, and said in a more level tone of voice, "The witch may exercise dark arts, but she is still a creature of flesh. Honed iron has power no flesh is immune from. My blades have sent more than one witch or sorcerer into the arms of death."

Rayden looked over to Jarut. She could tell at once that he chafed at the idea of her shouldering the risk by herself. His eyes reflected his stony visage, but he held his tongue.

Rayden deemed it a wise decision on the part of the warrior. Whether Erethea's husband or not, he, like Gerran, tread on thinning ground with her.

"It is a great risk for one warrior to take, when many would share it together," Alcedan stated.

Rayden thought of the mutilated bodies of the Snow Lions. "Walking through these woods right now is a great risk. Not even a hunting group of Snow Lions can tread it safely. The witch is not far from here. I wish to chance it. Better for one to take a risk than all ... often, one may succeed where larger numbers will fail. A solitary woman approaching the witch will raise far less alarm than a group of warriors."

Alcedan held her eyes for a few moments, and finally nodded. "We would not try and stop you."

"Nor could you stop me," Rayden replied, correcting him, her eyes glinting like ice-blue blades. "Await me here. I will return. It is my intention to return with the answers we seek. Take this spear into your keeping. I will keep my sword and axe in hand at all times."

She extended the javelin she carried toward Alcedan.

"Then may Otan watch over you," Alcedan replied, taking the spear from her.

Taking up her sword and axe, she gave Alcedan a nod. Turning, she headed into the woods with soundless steps, bearing north and setting her eyes on a mountain summit that had the general shape of an axe blade.

***

Rayden moved through the trees with extreme caution, stopping every now and then to listen in silence. Winds passing through the boughs of the trees met her periodic assessments, but nothing else of significance disturbed the air.

She could feel the brooding tension saturating the atmosphere, prodding her every instinct. Both axe and sword remained firm in hand, for a moment unprepared could make the difference between living and dying.

A threat bringing blood and death in its wake, something deeply amiss and undoubtedly unnatural pervaded the woods. Answers had to be unearthed.

Angling for the north, Rayden used the majestic summit of Axe Mountain as her guide. She knew the peaks towering about her with great familiarity, having trekked among the lofty giants for many years while growing up.

Axe Mountain had always been a favorite of hers in its resemblence to one of the two main weapons she carried with her. Now, it served as her beacon.

If the tales spoke true, she would find herself at the witch's homestead at the cusp of nightfall. No matter how much she would have preferred it to be the outset of day, Rayden knew it would not take long to determine whether the witch stood on the ground of alliance or hostility.

A cascade of thoughts ran through her mind, but foremost among them loomed the issue of how the witch warded her grounds. A being living alone in the depths of the wilderness, and especially a figure practicing magical arts, would not be likely to leave their dwelling unguarded.

Rayden could draw upon her own wealth of experiences, but she knew she had not faced every kind of magical art in the world. She had to bear in mind the things she had heard spoken of, in addition to the times she had been faced with the things of witchcraft and sorcery.

Stories abounded among the Gessa and other lands regarding the powers of witches. Whether whispered by mothers to children, or told around the fires of warriors, over copious amounts of ale, the tales of witches carried an abundance of truths woven throughout them.

None of the tales boded well for Rayden's purposes. From summoning demonic entities out of abyssal depths to possessing the ability to shift their forms, witches were known to employ an array of powers that would prove daunting to even the best of warriors.

The slower pace onerous, Rayden could only set her mind to endure, unable to afford taking any risks. Seeking out a witch steeped in dark arts, and moving through woods containing an unknown, lethal menace, left no room for errors.

With light fading and shadows growing, Rayden came upon the dwelling of the witch at last. Within a small, cleared space stood a circular hut covered in animal skins.

A fire pit had been carved out of the ground a short distance beyond the entrance to the hut. A small timber enclosure stood to the right, now devoid of any livestock; or whatever a witch chose to harbor.

Rayden stood still at the edge of the clearing, every sense heightened. Her hands clasped both sword and axe with tighter grips.

She did not want to present an aggressive posture, but she could chance nothing when she had no inkling about what guarded the witch's domain. Her gaze remained poised for any flicker of movement, the perception of which could give her the sliver of warning needed to defend herself from attack.

A light trickle of laughter flowed through the trees, like an approaching breeze, raising the hackles on Rayden's neck. She could not locate the source, but the sound heralded a being confident and well-aware of Rayden's presence.

Movement on the other side of the clearing to the left of the hut drew Rayden's eyes. She steadied herself, balanced in stance and weapons at her sides, while taking in a sight both fascinating and unsettling.

Drifting across the clearing, just above the ground, a transparent figure in the shape of a woman approached Rayden. Her long hair flowed behind her, billowing, though no wind coursed through the air to buoy it.

Eyes pits of black, the specter otherwise would have appeared most comely. The stunning vision of beauty, if in a state of flesh and blood, would captivate a young, lusty warrior like Gerran with ease.

Rayden could only hope that her instincts proved correct, if the ghostly apparition before her turned out to be a representation of the witch. If taking an incorporeal form, the witch held an appearance that had nothing to do with intent of seduction. If the figure represented some manner of guardian apart from the witch herself, Rayden had to discern the situation at hand quickly.

"I have come to warn, or beseech, but I did not come with a desire to harm," Rayden said aloud, the specter drawing ever closer. Though unnerved at the presence of a spirit-creature, she remained set in place. "I ask only to speak with you, before you decide if what I say is a warning or not."

"To warn? Or beseech? You do not know why you have come?" a breathy voice answered, a cold, mirthless smile forming upon the apparition's lips. "Harm? You could not inflict harm upon me, no matter what you desired."

"I came to warn the one who dwells here, if she does not know what stalks these woods. And I have come to beseech her, if she knows what blight lurks in the shadows," Rayden responded in an even tone, watching for any sudden movements if the apparition proved to be a distraction for something else. "I know not if you are a guardian or the one who dwells here, known as Weimassa among the Gessa. I ask only for a moment of time with the one who lives here, before you seek to cause me harm."

The spectral being broke into raucous laughter, a hollow, joyous sound, one that curdled Rayden's blood. The figure's voice carried a maniacal edge, a distinct element the blond warrior had heard more than once before, coming from those clenched in the throes of madness.

"You are far, far too late to warn," the ghostly figure replied, solemn and fixing her black eyes upon Rayden. "And far too late to beseech. Go ahead ... look for yourself ... in the trees beyond the hut. No harm shall come to you ... at least on my part."

The translucent being shifted course, drawing farther to the side and opening up a channel for Rayden. Choosing to accept the invitation, she started forward and walked across the clearing, heading in the direction indicated by the specter.

Rayden glanced a few times in the direction of the specter. The entity kept its place, hovering above the ground and watching her with a leering smile.

Stepping forward, Rayden reached the trees. Eyes widening, she looked upon a gruesome sight.

What remained of a woman's body had been scattered all about the trees, much like the bodies of the Snow Lions. Chunks of flesh, lengths of innards, and torn limbs littered the ground.

Rayden's breath caught in her throat when her gaze set upon a severed head, glassy eyes staring back at her.

It took little discernment to see that the head had been bitten off, though that realization did not cause the shock enveloping Rayden. The face looking back at her mirrored that of the apparition watching from a short distance behind her.

Rayden whirled about, looking at the ghost still hovering in place. She knew the truth of it.

"That was ... your body," Rayden uttered, reeling inside. "You ... are Weimassa."

"You should have brought your warning much earlier," the apparition said, with a lilt in her voice that Rayden took to be a trace of regret. "And maybe I would still be in flesh."

"What ... did this?" Rayden asked, still trying to regain her equilibrium following the startling revelation. "When?"

"It does not matter whether you know or not, as it is too late for you as well," the apparition said, turning her head, as if listening to some sound Rayden could not hear. "But you will know in a moment what did this. You will have the answers you came for."

The crazed laughter sounded from the apparition once more. Rayden's eyes widened further, the voice becoming more distant as the witch's spirit faded away before her eyes.

A low, rumbling growl surged from the other side of the clearing, a short distance beyond the spot where the witch had been. Rayden locked her eyes in the direction of the disturbance.

A dark form, huge and towering, separated from the trees. Shaggy, coarse fur covered its entire body.

At a loss for answers, Rayden had not seen or encountered anything like the creature she saw looming in the open ground.

The beast's large head resembled that of the hyenas she had encountered in the desert lands far to the south. Broad, powerful jaws set into a shorter muzzle contained a fearsome set of teeth. Upright, and oriented toward her, a pair of circular ears crowned its head.

Thick of neck, the creature had a brawny upper torso with powerful-looking arms ending in sets of curving, sharp claws. By contrast, the beast's legs extended long and lean in proportion, hinting at an extended stride and speed.

Not one of the wolf-men inhabiting the far northern reaches, the creature bore no resemblance to anything Rayden had encountered within the tribal lands.

Something new and dangerous faced her; a creature that could tear Snow Lions apart, limb from limb.

Within the grasp of its right fist, the monster clutched a wooden haft with a stone lashed to the end by hide strips. Images of the dead Snow Lions and a broken weapon flashed through Rayden's mind.

The answer to the mystery stood incarnate before her. Taking a couple of long strides toward Rayden, the creature's lips parted in a vicious snarl, saliva dripping from its jaws.

"Come, devil, if you would like to know death," Rayden said to the beast, squaring towards the creature with her weapons in hand.

The thing emitted a higher pitched, chortling sound, catching Rayden off guard. Unless she misread the response, the creature had understood her meaning, and mocked her with some kind of laughter.

In a way, she hoped that to be so, as it would indicate the presence of arrogance in the beast. Rayden had exploited the overconfidence of many opponents across the years. Hubris had a tried and true way of exposing weaknesses that a focused warrior could exploit.

Her suspicions became confirmed a moment later, when the beast flung the crude weapon it carried aside. Looking back to her, it spread its arms wide, extending its talons with a swelling growl coursing past its dagger-like teeth.

The beast lunged forward and rushed her, a murderous look blazing within its golden eyes. The creature's speed astonished her, but Rayden still managed to execute a dexterous move, just as the creature reached her.

With great swiftness, she pivoted to the left and dived low. The creature barreled into empty space where it had expected to take her to the ground. Committed to its strike, the beast lost its balance and stumbled down.

Rolling over and getting to her feet, Rayden charged the beast. The creature reacted, whipping about into a crouching position, but not before her axe lodged deep into the space between its neck and right shoulder.

Jumping backward, Rayden slashed desperately at the beast with her sword, striking at the nearest part of its body she could reach. The creature swiped at her with tremendous speed, ripping through air, the talons passing uncomfortably close to her body.

The end of her sword sliced through fur and flesh on the lower part of its leg, eliciting a high-pitched yelp from the stricken beast.

Gnashing its teeth and reaching up, the thing tore the axe embedded in its back free, sending a spray of blood outward. It tossed the axe far into the trees, loosing a terrible, undulating cry of pain.

Eyes burning with fury, the beast started for Rayden again. The creature yelped once more, putting weight on its injured leg.

The leg still functioned, but the wound slowed the beast enough for Rayden to take some initiative.

Down to one weapon, she raced toward the witch's hut and kept her body low. With the creature's sight of her blocked, Rayden quickly searched out impressions in the hides that she could grasp, hoping the timber frame underlying the animal skins proved strong enough.

Pressing hands and feet inward, Rayden climbed up toward the center of the hut. She listened to the sounds of the beast approaching, hearing its staggered, heavy gait. Reaching close to the smoke-hole crowning the top, she looked around.

Rayden watched the beast tromp around the base of the hut, its head swerving to and fro, searching for her. Favoring its right leg, a grating, sustained growl issued from the depths of its throat.

A brutal end awaited her, if the creature could match its intent. She knew it would not leave, and sooner or later it would look upward.

Only death could end the confrontation.

At the moment, she had gained a little advantage with the beast having lost track of her whereabouts. The slightest leverage could not be discarded against a foe that could kill Snow Lions.

When the beast stepped into the ground just beneath her, Rayden sprang from the roof of the hut, her leap one of the most calculated gambles she had ever taken.

The creature turned its head upward, just as Rayden plummeted down toward it, both hands gripping her sword overhead.

Putting everything she had into the blow, Rayden chopped downward. Sharp-honed iron blasted through skin and bone, burying deep into the monster's skull.

Letting go of the sword, Rayden hit the ground hard. Regaining her balance, she scrambled back in haste from the stunned creature, keeping free of the range of its talons.

The beast remained upright for a moment longer, swaying in place with the sword protruding from its head. Its eyes held no focus, and only a breathy gurgle emitted from its throat.

Then, the best fell heavily to the ground, collapsing forward.

Rayden stayed back. She did not approach the beast until she had found and retrieved her axe from where the thing had hurled it.

Returning to the body, she did not bother to check the creature for signs of life. Instead, she hacked its head clean from its shoulders, leaving no chance that the beast held a flicker of life within it.

Only then did she take up her sword, pinning the beast's head underfoot and yanking the blade free from where it had lodged in its skull. In a burst of anger, she kicked the head away, sending it tumbling across the forest floor.

Shadows and the coming of night engulfing the area, Rayden weighed whether to go or wait until sunrise to begin the trek back to the others. A ripple of thunder, and a brisk gust of icy wind, decided the matter for her.

The scent of rain carried in the air. The thought of hiking through dark woods caught within a storm's grip held no appeal for her. She chose to wait out the night.

Rain began falling in a steady torrent shortly after nightfall, prompting her to seek shelter inside the witch's hut. In the darkness of the interior, little could be made out of the former occupant's possessions.

Rayden found a few hides that she made use of for warmth, as it did not take long before a biting chill permeated the forest air. Wrapped snug, she settled herself in and began a vigil, unable to discount the possibility of things natural or supernatural making an appearance.

Listening to the periodic booms of thunder, the lashing wind, and the incessant beating of raindrops on the hides covering the timber-frame, Rayden had only her thoughts to keep her company throughout the duration of the night. Unable to sleep, she remained alert, a part of her expecting the witch's apparition to return.

To her relief, nothing disturbed the night, beyond the sounds of the storm outside. Whistling blasts of wind and pattering rain proved much more preferable to snarling beasts or the sepulchral voices of disembodied spirits.

Grateful for the shelter, Rayden kept her fatigue at bay. Listening for any hint of something other than a storm, she had her weapons close at hand.

When morning's light broke across the woodlands, Rayden got out from under the hides and emerged from the hut. She found everything where it had been the night before.

A bright sun beamed down upon a dampened forest, rays of gold slicing through the boughs of the trees, the musty scent of which surrounded her. A chill yet lingered, but already had begun dissipating within the sun's warming embrace.

While repulsive, the head of the beast that had attacked her would be needed, or at least serve as an object of considerable use. Walking over, she secured her axe at her waist. Reaching down, she grabbed the head up by the back, finding the object to have a significant degree of weight.

Carrying the head in one hand and her sword in the other, Rayden paused a moment before leaving the grounds. Looking back, she eyed where the pieces of the witch's corpse marked her brutal fate.

Rayden turned back, and strode toward the witch's dwelling. Leaning over, she set the monster's head down by the hut's entrance.

Rummaging inside the dwelling, Rayden found a small digging tool. She took a few moments to churn up the rain softened ground near to the fire pit.

Grabbing up most of the remains of the witch in a few trips, Rayden piled them into a haphazard mass within the fire pit. She proceeded to cover everything with the loose soil and debris she had prepared beforehand. Finishing the makeshift grave, she stacked the rocks ringing the fire pit all over the covering of dirt she had fashioned.

"You lived as you wished," Rayden spoke into the air. "Your choices are yours alone, however you now answer for them. I pay you for my night's shelter with this burial."

Turning, Rayden strode away from the grave. She diverted her course long enough to retrieve the head of the beast, before continuing toward the trees on the southern edge of the clearing.

Out of the corner of her eyes, a flicker of movement preceded the voice that followed in the wake of her steps.

"Thaaankk youuuu," sounded the airy voice, just above a whisper.

The voice held no trace of madness or sliver of mockery. The tone sounded gentle in Rayden's ears, perhaps even a little joyous.

Rayden looked to the right, and beheld the apparition, hovering in the air once more. This time, eyes harmonizing with the rest of a human appearance replaced the dark pits that had been there before.

The apparition's form looked a little brighter, and less translucent. A smile graced a countenance relaxed and peaceful.

As Rayden watched, the apparition disappeared, vanishing in what resembled a radiant burst of sunlight.

Continuing through the trees, Rayden held no regrets about bringing peace to the witch's spirit, even if the woman had her own atrocities to answer for. Torn into pieces by a predatory monster, the woman had met with a grisly fate.

Rayden pondered what kind of realm awaited the witch's spirit. She thought about the apparition, wondering if the things she had done, in slaying the monster and burying the witch's remains, had somehow spared the spirit from lingering about her former dwelling.

Death held such a great mystery about it. Rayden had witnessed far too much to discount the possibilities of worlds beyond, but neither could she say anything for certain about the nature of those realms.

Rayden could only wish that those she cared for, who had left her world, found their way to safe harbors. Whether she would ever find her way to such a place of refuge, and reunite with those who had died, she could not say.

Yet if a witch said to have engaged in dark arts could find redemption, Rayden could take a little encouragement as she continued walking her own path.

Though the urge to hurry back to the others flowed through her limbs, Rayden held her pace back. Repeating the caution she had exercised when seeking out the witch's abode, she took her steps in disciplined wariness.

She hoped to avoid encounters with beasts like the one she had slain. Rayden knew more of the monstrosities roamed the woodlands, and did not relish the thought of encountering them in numbers.

Seeing her carrying the severed head of one of their brethren would only serve to empower a tremendous rage in creatures already possessed of fearsome natural attributes. Rayden hoped to avoid such an inferno.

Fortune graced her return trek. Though a heavy silence continued to reign, no more of the beasts emerged from the shadows to confront her.

A feeling of gladness filled Rayden's heart when her eyes finally took in the sight of the other warriors. All were present, indicating that nothing had happened to them while she sought out the mountain witch.

An air of excitement and curiosity surrounded her return. Alcedan and the others stared in wonder at the head grasped in her left hand.

She raised it upward, so the others could gain a clearer look at its features.

"This is what we are facing," she announced. "This is what killed the Snow Lions ... and the witch."

"I have never seen the like," Alcedan exclaimed, his gaze fixed upon the head.

"Nor have I," Rayden said. "But now I understand why the Runi would embrace battle, over living with these roving the shadows among them."

She proceeded to describe the creature, emphasizing that it stood well over a head above the tallest man among the Runi or Gessa. Traces of anxiety manifested in the others' looks when she described the power, agility, and speed exhibited by the creature.

All gave Rayden their rapt attention as she told them of what had happened at the witch's dwelling; from the appearance of the apparition, to the discovery of the witches' remains, to the emergence of the beast and ensuing battle. She left out the burial of the witch, preferring to keep that part a private matter.

"We must return, and warn the others at once," Alcedan said when she had concluded her account, though the words were unnecessary.

Everyone, Rayden included, stood eager to depart the forested region hugging the base of the mountains. They now held the answers to a mystery that threatened the survival of their people.

Heading back, it proved difficult to rein their pace in, but they had to maintain caution while treading dangerous ground. Rayden and the others had to make certain the findings were conveyed to Eigon and the Gessa without a moment's delay.

After midday, the sounds of birds returned to the air, and they came upon a small cluster of deer. Watching the creatures bound away into the forest depths, Rayden welcomed what their presence signified.

The group now traveled through safer terrain. Accordingly, they quickened their stride, though not to the point of becoming negligent.

CHAPTER 3

A commotion broke out upon their return to Eigon's settlement. Shouts filled the air, bringing many from their huts. Children, women, and men alike ceased whatever they had been doing and swarmed the incoming warriors.

Talking excitedly amongst each other, they gawked at the head Rayden had returned with. All had expected to see quarry from the hunt like wild boar or deer, not the head of a monstrosity; of a kind that none of them had ever seen before.

At once, Rayden noticed that something of great importance had transpired since their departure. Armed warriors stood everywhere about the settlement, and several kept their positions despite the excitement over the hunting party's return.

The watchful state of the tribe troubled her deeply, as she and the others made their way towards Eigon's long house, located near the center of the sprawling mass of huts.

As the returning warriors approached the prominent structure, the grizzled chieftain stood awaiting them with a grim expression, flanked by several of the tribe's best warriors. Like the other warriors in evidence around the settlement, the men had weapons at hand.

Terian, the most respected priestess among the Gessa, stood with them as well. Long grey locks framing a narrow face creased with lines of age, the priestess had a look of deep concern. Her pale blue eyes fixed upon the head in Rayden's left hand.

Alcedan and Rayden slowed down, coming to a halt side by side at the forefront of their group.

Rayden's face remained unchanged, but the sight of three particular Gessa warriors standing off to the right caught her by surprise. Tall of stature, and strong of build, the trio looked weary and forlorn.

A shimmer of fear crossed all their faces as they gazed upon the object Rayden carried.

Setting his eyes upon the beast's head, and the Snow Lion pelts carried by the warriors with Rayden and Alcedan, a look of puzzlement and wonder filled the face of Eigon. He said, "Much has happened since last we met, both here and on your foray."

"What of the watch I see around the settlement?" Alcedan asked, looking uncomfortable with the presence of so many armed Gessa warriors. "Does a threat loom?"

"A threat surrounds us," Eigon answered.

"But the Runi have been driven off," Rayden said. "Should not warriors be standing near that boundary and not here?"

"We have others among us now," Eigon said, nodding to the warrior at his right. He said to the man, "Bring them here."

The warrior hurried off, returning soon with two others in his company. Looking upon them, and seeing the way they wore their hair, Rayden knew the pair at once to be Runi.

"What are they doing here?" Alcedan asked, with an air of agitation, casting the two men a hardened stare.

"Sometimes being a human is a greater bond than the tribe one is a part of," Eigon replied. "This is such a time."

"We understand what drove the Runi to the madness of seeking battle," Rayden said to Eigon. She lifted up the beast's head for emphasis, glancing toward the two Runi warriors. "This is what plagued them, yes?"

The terror in the faces of the Runi warriors answered her question strongly enough, but Eigon turned towards the men and asked them, "Is this the kind of beast you described to me?"

"It is," the closest man to Eigon acknowledged, with a nod.

"And they are many?" Eigon asked him.

The man nodded again, eyes fixed toward the head in Rayden's hand. He raised his eyes to her, looking her direct in the eyes.

"You killed it?" he asked.

"Yes, and it was no easy task," Rayden answered. "If there had been two, I would have stood little chance of surviving."

Her words evoked a look of amazement on the man's face.

"Grim tidings indeed," Eigon said, watching the man's reaction. He then eyed the Snow Lion Pelts. "You journeyed up the heights of the mountain?"

"The beasts drove the Snow Lions out of the mountains, and slew many of them on the lower ground," Alcedan said.

"What of the others?" Eigon asked, looking over the members of the small band of warriors. "More set out with you."

"Fallen ... an attack by the Snow Lions, whose skins you now see," Alcedan replied in a low voice.

"Dark days have descended upon us," Eigon said. He looked back to the Runi warriors and fell silent for several moments. Finally, he nodded to them. "I would have no honor to refuse you in such a time. Tell Carras to bring your people here. Bloodshed between us is folly, when we are all prey to a common hunter."

"Carras bids us to tell you that he will render you an oath, that the spilling of blood between us is forbidden, for as long as we are given refuge on your lands," the warrior stated, looking visibly relieved at Eigon's declaration.

"An oath to be enforced without mercy, should it be transgressed," Eigon replied in an even tone, his face etched into a somber expression.

The Runi warrior nodded. "We can expect no less ... and we can ask no more."

"Go then, take my reply to Carras and gather your people together," Eigon stated. "Return and you will be guided to land where you may find refuge among us ... until this danger is overcome."

In a respectful fashion, the two Runi warriors begged leave and departed at once, wasting no time in setting out for their lands. Rayden doubted all the Gessa would approve of the chieftain's decision to harbor the remnants of the Runi people, but she would have decided no differently.

Not all times were the same. An existential threat to humans overshadowed tribal differences and called for all the tribes to stand together.

When the Runi men had departed, Alcedan asked, "Carras?"

"The new chieftain, of what remains of the Runi," Eigon said. "I do not know him, but it would appear he possesses more wisdom than Nagradak did."

"I hope it is no trick," Alcedan said.

"I have read the signs, and the messengers speak truthfully," Terian said. "Carras is to be trusted."

"And if not, there's not enough of them left to be of any great threat to us," Eigon said, glancing at the priestess. "But you've never guided me wrong all these years. The favor of the gods rests with you. Seek their aid for our people. We are in a desperate time."

"I will go make sacrifice," Terian said, nodding to Eigon, before walking off.

"It would seem we have much more to talk about," Eigon said, returning his attention to Rayden and the others. "And there are families to give dark tidings to, of those who fell on your hunt. Do not delay in this."

Alcedan nodded. "I shall go and speak with the families

of those warriors, and tell them of what has happened. Rayden fought the beast whose head she now carries, and can tell you what she has learned."

Rayden did not envy the man of his decision. She had brought word of slain warriors to their families before, each instance a heavy burden leaving her with haunting memories.

Eyes filling with raw shock, to wailing, crying streams of tears, and even collapsing to the ground, the reactions of those learning of the deaths of loved ones stood an agony to witness. Rarely did Rayden feel as helpless as she did in the aftermath of delivering dark tidings to the family of one who had fallen.

Alcedan strode off to attend to the grim task. He took the other men away with him, leaving Rayden behind with Eigon.

"We are now surrounded?" Rayden asked, a few moments later.

"It would seem so," Eigon said. "Several of the Gessa have been killed, in places all around the edges of our lands. Most to the north, which looks to be where these creatures have begun making deeper incursions. It will not be long before they move farther inward, into every part of Gessa lands."

"Did they surround the Runi, at first?" Rayden asked.

"Yes, from what I learned from their messengers," Eigon said. "The deaths started on their borders, all around them, and then nowhere remained safe."

"They are not wild beasts, and something guides them by enough intelligence to know the lands of different tribes," Rayden said. "They are wielded with a purpose."

"If they are in great number, how can they be opposed?" Eigon said. "You said that fighting two may well have led to your demise."

"It would be best to bring the Gessa together, shoulder to shoulder," Rayden said. "Draw out the enemy and face them in strength, or be hunted one by one."

"Or set forth, toward the south," Eigon said. "Not as the Runi did to us, but seeking refuge."

"If other chieftains have the wisdom that you do," Rayden said, doubtful of the prospect. "What if they deny you?"

"I will have to get them to see that the threat against the Runi, and now the Gessa, is a threat against all the tribal people," Eigon said.

"The threat is in the south too," Rayden said, thinking upon the Teveren Empire and the gruesome sights along the Boreus Way.

Leagues of roadway lined with the crucifixions of slaves testified clear enough to the nature of the Imperator's spirit.

"The threat is to the north of us, and to the south of us, and likely pressing in at all moments," Eigon said. "Like the closing of jaws."

"Of a greater monstrosity ... the kind of wickedness that no amount of death can ever sate the hunger of," Rayden commented.

"Terian had a vision, of a great serpent coiling around a young boy and girl of our tribe," Eigon said. "I did not know what to make of it, but what you say brings me more understanding."

Rayden nodded. "It is like a great serpent, wrapping itself around the Gessa, the Runi, and all others."

"What is your counsel?" Eigon asked her.

"Bring the people together, for now. Scattered apart they are more vulnerable," Rayden said. "Send messengers forth. Take the head of the beast to show them. Have one of the Runi go in the company of your messengers, to speak as a witness of what happened to them. The head, the voice of a witness, and two tribes standing together may encourage wisdom in those who otherwise would seek folly."

"I still regret that the Runi did not come to us first, in the way that they have now," Eigon said. "I would rather have Nagradak and many other great warriors with us than the remnants, filled with so many who fled the battle. I fear we will need all the strength we can find to just survive what is coming."

"Face them in strength, not apart," Rayden said. "They may even be drawn out of the shadows and into the open that way."

"It would be better to face them on a field of battle than be hunted down in shadows," Eigon said, the fatalism clear in his voice.

"Let not despair get its hold upon you. Know that I will seek more answers, and more help for the Gessa," Rayden said, seeing the deep fatigue on the chieftain's face.

"Where can you go? What can be done at this troubling time?" Eigon asked. "We do not have long."

"I do not know, but Dreaghen may have some thoughts on the matter," Rayden said. "Whatever he may give me, know that I will pursue it."

"The ways of sorcerers are not ones I understand, but if there is something else we can seek help from, may the gods favor us," Eigon said. "I trust your judgment."

Rayden set down the head of the beast. "I will leave this in your keeping now. Time is short, and I will set out at once. I give you my word I shall do all I can to find a way to bring more help to the Gessa."

"I can think of no greater champion for our people," Eigon said.

Rayden bowed her head to the chieftain, honored by his words. "I will return, as soon as I can."

She turned away from the chieftain and made her way from the long hall, continuing out of the settlement and heading north, back into the depths of the forest. Though none interrupted her, seeing the resolute look on her face, many of the men and women of the tribe watched Rayden depart with a blend of curious and anxious looks.

CHAPTER 4

Thoughts swirled within a current of dissonance, clouding Rayden's mind. Staring into the moonless, overcast night, she had no desire to venture out on her own, so soon after returning with the hunting party, but nothing more could be gained awaiting the inevitable onslaught by the beasts.

The Gessa were being surrounded. The words of Eigon and Rayden's own experience with the hunting party clarified the truth of it. Driven by a diabolical intent, blood and terror would soon begin flowing among the Gessa.

Dreaghen had to be called forth. Perhaps the only one with an answer, or strong insights, the sorcerer could not fail to share what he knew with Rayden. The alternative would be to cast aside everything that he had labored to guide her through.

Not all that long ago he brought wolves to her, to guide her through the mountains and to the Kartajen encampment, where she met the general Mago. The general had then come to the aid of the slave rebellion against the Teveren Empire. His intervention gained the former slaves victory in battle, allowing them to survive and seek refuge in Tega lands.

Rayden needed the sorcerer even more now. The threat facing her represented something even more existential, not just to her, but to all of the people who had adopted her as one of their own.

"Dreaghen, I need your counsel now," Rayden whispered into the night air, wishing the words could fly to the ears of the sorcerer. "Appear to me."

Rayden kept a steady pace through the shadows, her steps quiet. Working her way deeper into the forest, she watched out for any sign of movement. Over a league passed without incident.

Skirting the edge of a lake, she espied a few deer on the opposite side. A part of her wished she could divert her course, and dampen the light hunger pangs within, but she had to keep pressing onward.

She knew that she put herself into increasing danger with every step, walking alone in the night, and heading north into areas known to hold the presence of the beasts. The display of recklessness her precise intention, she intended to provoke the sorcerer, one who she knew kept appraised of her whereabouts.

Whether in the form of an apparition or a dream, Dreaghen had a penchant for manifesting when she had genuine need of him, and she knew the road traveled two ways. The sorcerer had need of her, and she doubted he would allow her to jeopardize his own intentions for her path.

Rayden continued around the lake, reaching the far end. Before she stepped back into the trees, Rayden whirled about at a swell of light close behind her. She took up a fighting stance and raised her weapons.

An apparition hovered just above the ground, carrying enough distinctive features for her to identify the entity a few strides from where she stood. The soft blue glow emanating from the incorporeal form reflected off the shimmering lake surface.

Were it not for the circumstances, Rayden would have found the sight more beautiful. At the moment, agitation filled her spirit.

"Sorcerer, one day you will stand before me in flesh, and

it will take restraint for me not to pummel you," Rayden said. "You have an irritating way of making your appearances ... and you were about to let me walk straight into a horde of unnatural beasts."

"I did not think you so reckless." A hint of bemusement echoed in Dreaghen's tone. "I suspected your stroll through the woods toward the north to have more to do with calling upon me. And cannot a sorcerer choose the manner in which they appear?"

"At least you understood my need," Rayden said. "I counted on that. You've not led me astray. I didn't think you'd let me go astray now."

"Have I led you astray? Ever?" Dreaghen asked, sounding a little taken aback.

"Not yet," Rayden replied. "And pray for your own sake that you never do. Do not think you are invincible behind your sorcery. Many others who wield your arts have made that mistake ... and paid a bitter price for it."

"For just once I wish you would act like you are simply glad to see me," Dreaghen said, with a low chuckle. "Will I ever get a warm welcome from you?"

"Maybe, if you would make your appearances a little more anticipated, and less like an ambush," Rayden said. "And a part of me is glad to see you. I didn't want to hike through the woods for the entire night. I'd rather not fight any more of the beast men."

"What need brings you to summon me this time," Dreaghen asked. "Your whisper did indeed reach me."

"Good to know you bothered to listen," Rayden said.

"The wisest spend more of their time listening than speaking," Dreaghen said. "And the most intelligent discover how much less they know, the more they learn."

"I listen, and I have always been open to learning," Rayden said.

"Which is why I find you to be a warrior both wise and intelligent," Dreaghen said. "Two things I value in you, even more than your fighting ability. Now tell me why you have called for me."

"I am far from the Teverens and their Imperator, and now I see the Gessa and the other tribes in a fight for their existence against whatever sent these beasts to plague them," Rayden said. "I already sense an unnatural force behind them. There is a greater hand in all of this."

"The beasts ... another root of the tree we have spoken of," Dreaghen replied, nodding.

"If the tribes of the north all fall to this darkness, how can the Teveren Imperator ever be challenged?" Rayden said. "There are no other powers who can contend with the Imperator, other than the Kartajenians ... or the empires to the farther east, bordering the Teverens."

"The tribes will be needed in the struggle to come, for time is ever growing shorter," Dreaghn said. "Barriers weaken, and the Teveren Imperator will soon hold a power both vast and most horrific."

Rayden sensed the shift in the sorcerer's tone. Grave concern, and even fear, flowed in the words of the magic wielder.

"What power?" Rayden pressed.

"Severance of the barriers between worlds," Dreaghen answered.

"Does not the Imperator already hold that power? Does not that power reside among those who wield the dark arts?" Rayden asked. "They can conjure vile spirits, and I've seen men and women alike who are held captive by the wicked spirits holding dominion over them from within."

"Conjuring ... possession ... those wielding the dark arts have held such powers for ages," Dreaghen responded. "No, this something new. It will be something much more powerful, though what it is, I do not yet know.

"The Imperator and the sorcerers in league with him have not revealed it yet. I fear that when it is revealed, it will be too late. They are gathering a dark strength like no other I have witnessed. Everything ... the children taken for ritual ... the crucified slaves ... the wars ... those who die for the amusement of a blood-thirsting rabble ... all of it adds to their growing strength. Everything they do flows into their power ... building it ... growing it."

"Then the beasts have to be overcome, so that we can turn our attention to whatever the Teveren Imperator is preparing," Rayden said. "But these beasts may be far too formidable for even several tribes united to resist. I faced just one of them in combat. An army of them is something I do not wish to think about."

"Several tribes gathered could not stop them, if the beasts come in greater number," Dreaghen said with an air of certainty.

"What are they? Do you know anything of these beasts?" Rayden asked. "They are an inhuman race of creatures, in the way that the wolf-men to the north are ... but from where do they come?"

"They are not of a kind like the Varganir to the north of the triballands," Dreaghen said. "The air of dark magic surrounds them. It is undeniable. They are something unnatural and corrupted. They are not beasts of this world. I call them the Arguntier." The sorcerer's response gave Rayden pause and perplexed her. She had viewed them in an unnatural light, but only in terms of origin.

The beast she had encountered stood as physical, and in the flesh, as any other creature of the world, no matter how much ferocity and strength it held. The creature had displayed no hint of sorcerous or otherworldly abilities. It breathed, bled, and died, like any other living being.

"Then what are they?" Rayden asked.

"The nature of these beasts have given me some thoughts as to what the Teveren Imperator, and the dark witches and sorcerers gathered with him, are preparing," Dreaghen answered her, looking grim.

"No riddles or mysteries, sorcerer, speak plainly," Rayden stated, before Dreaghen could continue.

"I can only hazard a guess, based upon what I have learned, and what I know," Dreaghen said.

Rayden nodded. "Then what is it that you see?"

"You spoke of possession, and you have seen men and women in thrall to demons," Dreaghen said. "You witnessed one not long ago."

Rayden thought back to the crazed figure she had encountered along the grisly road known as the Boreus Way, lined with the crucifixions of slaves who had been part of the rebellion against the Teverens. Recalling the stench of death, she could see the madness filling the man's gaze as he scuttled among the suspended, rotting corpses.

She could also recall the wicked presence she felt about the man, and still hear in her mind the bestial, growling sounds coming from him, noises that in no way sounded human in origin. Rayden also remembered how he had scurried away when she had neared the two priests of the strange Creator religion.

Rayden nodded to the sorcerer. "I have witnessed possession many times, as you have said. The memory of my most recent encounter is still far too fresh in my mind. I would like to forget it."

"Possession is when a thing of the dark abyss takes dominion over a human," Dreaghen said. "What you face now is a form of possession, if I am seeing it clearly. Though very different than those others you have encountered."

"A form of possession? The creature I faced was in no way human. Those things may carry weapons, but the form and gaze of a beast is undeniable in them," Rayden said, thinking of the monstrosity she had fought at the hut of the mountain witch.

"Do animals have spirits?" Dreaghen asked her.

"I have no doubt of it," Rayden said, thinking of the spark of light she had seen in the eyes of many animals she had encountered across the years.

Growing up she had developed bonds with more than one special animal, each of which had distinct personalities and ways in which they conveyed meanings. Rayden had mourned the passing of more than one such animal, and felt the sting of loss not unlike that which accompanied the death of a person. In her eyes, only a creature with a spirit could be capable of becoming part of her, in such a way.

"Let me ask you this, then," Dreaghen said. "If a person can become possessed by a wicked spirit, and if an animal has a spirit ... then could not an animal become possessed by a wicked spirit?"

Rayden saw no fault in the sorcerer's logic, and she saw where his thoughts headed, but one undeniable reality vexed her. The thing she had encountered held a bestial countenance, but it walked upon two legs and carried weapons. It stood something much more than a feral creature.

"You have encountered those who can shift their form, yes?" Dreaghen asked.

"More times than I ever cared to experience," Rayden said, thinking of the variety of horrors she had witnessed across the span of her journeys. "I've seen some take the forms of wolves, snakes, huge bats, bears, boars, sea beasts ... and even lions."

"And many of those took on a shape combining the features of both human and animal?" Dreaghen asked.

"Yes, many times," Rayden said.

"Then what of an animal that could shift form and take on a few human-like features?" Dreaghen asked. "Like walking upright on two legs, when its natural form involved four legs."

"So you believe these are wild animals that can shift their forms?" Rayden said, not liking the thought at all.

"More than that," Dreaghen replied. "Wild animals that are governed by a dark spirit in possession of them, one that has shifted their form to its needs."

Dreaghen's notion sounded even worse. Bestial ferocity ruled with a merciless, ruthless intelligence presented a unique kind of threat.

"But if these beasts were once just wild animals, then they have come far," Rayden said. "The head of the one I felled was that of a hyena, an animal that does not dwell in the north."

"You know of the games in the Imperial City, yes? The blood games where man is pitted against beast, man against man, and beast against beast?" Dreaghen said. "Blood games on a great scale, often involving hundreds of creatures?"

"I have heard it spoken of, but have not witnessed them. Nor do I wish to see such a vile thing with my own eyes," Rayden said with a terse edge.

"The Teverens capture and bring great numbers of beasts to the Imperial City from afar," Dreaghen said. "I do not believe all of them become fodder for those blood games. I believe a great many become what the northern tribes are facing now."

Rayden recoiled at the idea put forth by Dreaghen. If the sorcerer was correct, it meant that the Teveren sorcerers had a means of channeling possessing spirits, of a wicked nature, into animals on a mass scale.

Further, it meant that collusion existed between the possessing spirits and those who exercised the power to channel them into the wild animals. The plague of beasts afflicting tribal lands and the growing shadow of the Teveren Empire carried out the same overall aims, leading toward something unprecedented.

The power to achieve all of what Dreaghen implied would

be far above the ability of any lone sorcerer. It all suggested a unison of effort far-reaching, of the darkest intent; an alliance involving a great number of others steeped in wicked powers.

"What other evils can they let loose, if they hold such great power?" Rayden asked, dismayed at the sorcerer's conclusions.

"A mystery for which I am yet seeking answers," Dreaghen said. "We can only confront what we are aware of, for now."

"Then I will set my mind to confronting the beasts," Rayden answered. "Tell me of something I can do, to bring help to the tribes."

"You are aware of another race that dwells on the border of tribal lands," Dreaghen said. "You just spoke of them."

"The wolf-men? To the north?" Rayden asked. "The Varganir?"

"The Varganir," the sorcerer confirmed.

Unease filled Rayden. A longstanding truce stood between the tribes and the Varganir, but the tales of older days involving encounters with the wolf-men were filled with blood and death.

Said to be the children of the god Weirgan, the Varganir were neither wolves nor men. No power of shifting forms resided within them.

In some ways, they reflected human kind. They walked upon two legs, spoke their own language, and many accounts existed of Varganir that could speak the words of the tribes. They had their own laws and rituals.

The similarities with humans did not go much farther. The Varganir had never displayed interest in the affairs of the tribes that bordered them. Rather, from what the tales indicated, the Varganir held an unceasing animosity toward the humans of all tribes and lands.

The hostility did not extend to the other race of creatures the Varganir's forms reflected. Able to communicate with wolves, the Varganir were said to maintain a close relation to the four-legged denizens of the forest.

Wolf packs and Varganir were said to often hunt together, and more than one tribal story spoke of the two besetting humans who had violated the truce and entered their territory. The tales served as a stark warning.

Rayden suspected a reason greater than matters of territory at the root of the enmity, but the cause remained absent from the tales shared among the tribal people.

"The witch whose spirit you encountered was no friend of the tribes, but the beasts were a greater adversary," Dreaghen said. "The Varganir are not beasts. They are natural in origin. They hold the gift of reason, but they have their own ways ... and they hold little regard for humans, who they view as weak and fearful ... and full of deceit."

"Many humans are," Rayden said. "And I hold little regard for the deceitful ones myself."

"They would view you no differently," Dreaghen said. "To them, all humans appear the same. They may even attack you outright. But they are the only others you could reach out to before the Arguntier flood Gessa lands with the blood of men, women, and children."

"You are counseling me to seek out the Varganir?" Rayden asked, a little incredulous at the suggestion.

"A desperate time and a desperate chance," Dreaghen said. "I do not know how the Varganir will receive you, but it will not be a friendly welcome."

"Makes me wonder what really happened, long ago," Rayden said.

"I do not have that knowledge," Dreaghen said. "But my instinct tells me it is something far more than border disputes."

Rayden took a deep breath. "I will seek them out. It is a desperate chance, but one that must be pursued."

"Only one such as you stands any chance," Dreaghen said,

with no trace of jest.

"Would they receive a sorcerer any better?" Rayden asked, smirking. "Perhaps you should make the entreaty."

"They would receive me even worse than you," Dreaghen said. "And know that I would make the entreaty, if I could do so."

Rayden found the last part of his response strange. Something deeper lay within the sorcerer's words, but she did not have long to think upon the matter before he continued speaking.

"It is likely that if they do not attack you, they will seek to measure you," Dreaghen said. "Let them test you. It means they are giving you a chance to prove you are something more than what they see humans as."

"I will do what I can to gain their trust," she reassured Dreaghen.

"Of all humans I have known, you are among the very few I would say are capable of doing so," Dreaghen said.

"Before I find out if I can gain their trust, I will have the lands of at least two tribes to cross before I reach the borders of the Varganir," Rayden said. "It will take some time, as I wish to avoid those of other tribes, who will not take well to a stranger crossing their lands."

"Look to the skies by day," Dreaghen said. "In this, I can be of help to you."

"I am grateful, for it is a treacherous path I am walking now," Rayden said. "I am not a powerful sorcerer, or a god, and you have called me to go against both ... and likely many of the first and more than one of the second."

"It would seem I have called you to undertake an impossible fight," Dreaghen said. "Just know that you are not the only one. Others taken up this struggle, using the gifts they have."

"Whether impossible or not, this fight must be embraced," Rayden said. "Failing to resist the Imperator only guarantees the victory of a darkness that would swallow all of us."

"I would like to ask you one question, Rayden," Dreaghen said. "It is a question I have often pondered, in the time before I sought you out, and even more so now."

"If I can answer it, I will, I am not given to riddles, sorcerer," Rayden replied.

"What greater journey are you on?" he asked. "I heard your tales from many lands you have traveled through, but in none of them could I sense your destination."

"If I could tell you, I would," Rayden answered, with a bittersweet edge. "I do not know. It may be near, or it may be too far for me to ever reach. I know only two things ... I will continue walking my path, and I will recognize my destination when I find it."

"Sometimes, you find when you are not seeking, and when you are seeking, you will not find," Dreaghen said. "Even so, I wish I knew the destination you seek ... as I would like to be able to give you any help I can on that journey."

She caught the regret in his voice. For a moment, despite the form he had taken by the lakeside, she did not see him as a sorcerer. He was just a man, with all the limitations, flaws and uncertainty of any other.

Giving him a warm smile in response, she replied, "I know you would, and I like this part of you, sorcerer. If you stood before me now, I would embrace you as a friend."

"And not pummel me?" he replied, grinning. "As you have threatened to do more than once."

Rayden laughed, thinking of all the frustrations caused by Dreaghen's enigmatic ways, the unsettling disturbances of her dreams, and the often unpleasant, sudden manner of his manifestations. "Not this night, but there's always tomorrow."

"Then I regret that I cannot stand before you now," he said. "But tomorrow, look to the skies, and I will help guide you through the lands of the other tribes."

"Then I will go seek the Varganir, and discover if I measure up to their test," Rayden said.

"I bid you well, and you carry my confidence, as always," Dreaghen said, the glow about him ebbing as his form faded from sight.

Rayden looked across the still lake a few moments longer, watching a breeze ripple the surface, before resuming her journey into the north.

***

After taking cover for some rest late in the night, Rayden set out at the cusp of dawn. Keeping to a brisk gait, with the sun crossing the cloud-scattered skies, she headed straight north.

With her mind set upon a great tract of territory that no tribe occupied, Rayden girded herself for a journey that would take at least a couple of days, at the pace she maintained.

Overhead, a large raven shadowed her movements. Gliding the air currents, it watched over her with diligence. Its sharp cries alerted her to any human or other presence ahead in the territory of the Arnan she crossed through.

She knew the creature to be a gift of Dreaghen, if not Dreaghen himself. Having seen the bird circling far above her at dawn's light, she had no doubt of it being the promised help from the sorcerer.

Its aid from the sky allowed her to maintain a quick pace, and skirt around any delays that would result from encounters with tribal warriors, wild beasts, or perhaps even the Arguntier. A few warnings from the raven prompted her to shift directions for a time, but she did not have to deviate far from her course before continuing northward.

Not wishing to arrive in the lands of the Varganir in a weakened state, knowing any test they gave would demand much of her, Rayden paused in her travel a few times to gain some sustenance through forage or hunt. Mushrooms and nuts gleaned from the forest, and a few eels caught in a stream using a makeshift trap, served as the core of her meals.

Though she would have much preferred the succulent meat of a roasted boar, and some cups brimming with ale, Rayden consumed more than enough to keep her strength up and hunger at bay.

When evening drew near, she pressed forward through the twilight until she could no longer follow the raven-guide. Only then did she come to a halt and fashion a little shelter from a mix of collected branches and undergrowth.

The nights passed without disruption. A few noises out of the darkness caught her attention, but they held no threat within them, being the sounds of animals going about their nocturnal routines.

No rain fell, the only condensation deriving from the mists of the pre-dawn. Time passed swiftly enough, and Rayden found herself enjoying the solitude, even if she had to maintain a high level of caution.

When night fell after the third day of the journey, Rayden pushed as far as she could, continuing a little after nightfall before allowing her body some needed rest. She had covered several more leagues that day alone, trekking through mountainous terrain. Striding up inclines with the air growing thinner, fatigue had finally begun to accumulate.

Deep into Cirna lands, she knew it would not be much farther to the edge of the Varganir territory. Her mind began to occupy itself with thoughts of how the mysterious race would greet her.

Sleeping lightly after concealing herself in some undergrowth, Rayden started out again before sunrise, picking up the raven's flight when dawn broke across the skies. Her breathing came a little easier, adjusting to the higher altitudes.

About midday, the raven called to her several times, in a manner different from the times it had warned her of something in her path ahead. After circling a few moments, it flapped away, and did not return.

Rayden knew the meaning of the raven's departure. She now walked in the lands of the Varganir.

The tranquility of the forest and the rays of light scattered about by the trees eased her spirits a little as she continued forward. Mountain air, crisp and fresh to her lungs, entered with each breath. The pleasant atmosphere helped to keep her disposition centered.

Rayden did not know what to expect, or how the Varganir would make their presence known. She could halt, and wait for them to come to her, or she could keep moving through their territory.

She opted for the latter choice, hoping to come upon them first, so she could determine her approach, as opposed to being ambushed. The early part of their first interaction would likely have a great impact on her chances to get a reasonable hearing from the creatures.

Though fraught with risk, if the creatures proved hostile, she kept her sword in its sheath and her axe in the loop at her belt. Empty-handed, she would not be suspected of being on some manner of hunt or bearing an aggressive intent.

The day passed without any encounters, or even signs of the Varganir. Growing a little frustrated, Rayden watched the shadows thicken and the sun's light recede, until night shrouded the forest.

Not long after nightfall, telltale howls sounded in the distance. Other howls responded, coming from another direction and sounding a little closer. Soon after those, another cluster of howls cleaved the night, coming from even closer.

Deeper and more resonant than that of any common wolf,

the series of calls let Rayden know that her presence had been noted; by the ones whose territory she trod upon.

She knew that she did not have much longer to wait for the Varganir to make their appearance, but decided to keep moving, still hoping to approach them first. Her heart began beating a little faster. She eyed the shadows with increasing vigilance, knowing the Varganir drew nearer with every moment.

Coming across an open stretch of ground, she hesitated, her instincts prodding her. No more howls had sounded, but the hairs on her skin tingled with the sense that she was not alone.

Stepping into the moonlit clearing and taking a deep breath, Rayden looked into the dense shadows ringing the space. The heavy silence gripping the night told her that the Varganir were now with her.

Looking as if they took shape from the darkness they strode out from, towering, broad forms encircled Rayden. Descending from elongated limbs and extended muzzles, a shaggy mass of fur covered the lupine beings. Many pairs of inhuman, golden eyes gazed upon her.

Rayden had encountered humans capable of taking the shape of wolves, whether from dark magic or some other art. She could not allow those experiences to shape the current moment, as she took in her first impressions of the Varganir.

The creatures before her had no human origin. Simply another race that shared the same world as Rayden, the Varganir were creatures of nature.

With bodies structured for power and speed, the Varganir presented a threat at any time. She stood at their mercy. Surrounded, she could not escape, and had to let fate take its course.

Seeing the Varganir looming around her, Rayden found it fortunate that the creatures did not exist in great numbers, or harbor the appetite for conquest that afflicted so many of Rayden's kind. It proved even more fortuitous that the Varganir were said to not have much of a taste for human flesh; though more than a few men and women had disappeared after entering the lands the creatures inhabited.

Rayden circled about with slow, purposeful steps, keeping a strong, confident posture, and looking up into each of the creatures' eyes. Her blood ran faster in her veins, but she exhibited no outward signs of fear.

The breaths of the tall beasts puffed outward in ghostly wisps within the embrace of the cold mountain air. The silvery, lunar light glinted off eyes and lengthy fangs alike.

Rayden broke the weighty impasse, speaking in a calm voice. "My name is Rayden and I have come to seek your help against something that will have the blood of my kind and yours."

At first, no response came from the creatures. The creatures continued their slow encroachment until Rayden found herself left with no more than a stride or two in any direction. She could read nothing from their gazes in response to her words.

She could only try again. "I am not here as a trespasser. I came here to find you. We both have an enemy, an enemy from the darkness. I have come to ask that we face that enemy together."

At last, one of their number stepped forward, emerging from the shadows toward the rear of the gathering and coming to stand before Rayden. A giant of their kind, the creature stood a full head taller than any of the other Varganir, and had a noticeably brawnier form.

To Rayden's eyes, the massive creature carried the air of Eigon about it. At once, she recognized the respectful, deferential postures from the other beasts, who had cleared a path for the prominent figure.

She held little doubt that she stood in the presence of their chieftain, or king. Rayden could only hope that the creature had at least a fraction of the wisdom and patience of Eigon.

"Enemy ... from darkness," the creature addressed Rayden in the tribal tongue. "Enemy ... in the lands. Enemy that hunts humans."

Though the words sounded stilted and guttural to her ears, they came as a relief. She could communicate, and being able to speak with one of them, especially a leader, gave her a sliver of a chance.

Rayden nodded. "Yes, the enemy that hunts humans. An enemy to your kind and mine. An enemy to Varganir and humans."

"Enemy to Rayden ... and Manak," the creature replied, pointing toward her and then placing its large right hand against its chest.

Rayden understood the gesture. With her right hand, she indicated herself and then the creature, saying, "Yes, enemy to me ... Rayden ... and to you ... Manak."

The creature turned to the others of its kind, and spoke in a language that Rayden did not understand. When no response came from the others, she guessed that Manak had translated their exchange. After addressing the surrounding Varganir, the wolf-man turned back to face her again.

"Enemy hunts Varganir kind, not human only," Manak told her. "Enemy hunts wolves ... and all things. It kills ... not for hunt ... it kills to kill."

"Varganir kind, and human kind, must fight together against enemy," Rayden responded, focusing on simplifying her words, and hoping most were understood by the creature before her. "Varganir kind and human kind must protect our lands."

Manak pointed toward her, extending a long, sharp claw in her direction. "You and human kind." It pointed toward itself. "Me and Varganir kind". It clasped its elongated hands together. "Fight enemy from darkness. This you ask?"

Rayden nodded. "Yes, that is what I ask. Or enemy from darkness will hunt Varganir kind here ... and human kind in our lands."

Manak addressed the other Varganir once more. This time, a few of the creatures spoke in reply. Though Rayden could not decipher their words, she could feel the rising tension in the air.

Manak replied to them with a growling undertone. One of the larger Varganir close by snarled in response, a clear display of anger.

Baring its lengthy fangs, Manak whirled toward the other. Straightening up to a full height, it tromped up to stand before the malcontent, and loosed a roar that shattered the relative stillness.

The ears of the other Varganir flattened to the sides. Though its lips remained pulled back and it continued to bare its fangs, it took a step backward.

Manak looked around at the other Varganir, as if to see whether any of them wished to issue a challenge.

The leader of the Varganir turned back to Rayden, and strode up to her. It fixed its golden gaze upon her.

"Human must ... " Manak began. It paused for a moment, and Rayden sensed the creature was searching for the right words to use. She waited patiently, not about to cause offense with interruption. Finally, it proceeded. "Human must show ... Varganir strength."

"You wish to test me, to see if I am worthy of the Varganir," Rayden replied, nodding, and recalling the words of Dreaghen. She then added, in a somber tone. "The Varganir see humans as weak ... so I must show that I am not weak. The Varganir do not trust humans ... so I must gain your trust."

"Yes," Manak said.

"What do you wish me to do? What test will show my strength, and gain your trust?" Rayden asked the creature.

"Slay troll ... troll that can kill Varganir," Manak stated.

"Only human who strong can slay troll."

Troll-kind a dangerous adversary, Rayden had faced them and similar creatures before. She had come to the brink of her own demise more than once in such encounters.

The brutish creatures were to be avoided, not sought out and confronted, but there were no other options. The Varganir leader's chosen test would be filled with peril, but it stood the only path to earning the respect and trust of the wolfish beings.

"I accept this test," Rayden said, lowering her head toward the Varganir leader in deference, and hoping the gesture would be interpreted in the right manner. "I will prove my strength to the Varganir. I will show that Varganir kind and human kind can stand together."

"Slay troll," Manak replied. "Then we judge what you ask."

***

Rayden worked her way up the mountain slopes, stopping now and then to examine the foliage and ground. It did not take long before she came across the first tracks.

Larger than those of a bear, and elongated in shape, the impressions included claw marks. Judging from the footprints, the troll that made them was not the largest of its reclusive kind, and far from one of the gigantic types she knew existed in the remote areas of the world. But neither was it the smallest.

Rayden estimated the troll to be taller and of larger girth than the Varganir leader. She had expected that, at the very least, not doubting it would be a creature of considerable size to be a danger to Varganir.

Nocturnal hunters, all varieties of trolls were formidable creatures as individuals. Making matters worse, some of the troll-kind lived in small packs or clans.

For the most part, trolls kept away from human settlements and dwelled in the deeper reaches of the wilderness. Yet they were known well-enough by the tribal people, and violent encounters took place on occasion between hunters and trolls.

Even the smallest of trolls could prove deadly, and unlike the Varganir troll-kind were well-known to harbor a taste for human flesh. Tribal lore spoke of many instances where children had fallen prey to the creatures, and any evidence of a troll near a settlement brought a swift response on the part of the warriors. The Gessa had slain more than one on their lands, though the last sighting of a troll had been several years before Rayden had come to live among them as a child.

Rayden halted in place, listening to a distinct, high-pitched chittering on the night winds. Another followed, coming from a different direction.

Unmistakable troll calls, the noises told her more than one of the creatures roamed the area she had entered.

To her best estimation, they sounded a fair distance away. Staying in place, she listened carefully. Not long after, the high-pitched vocalizations broke out again, this time sounding much nearer.

The trolls were heading in her direction.

Rayden took to the trees, working her way up the branches of a large pine until she found a solid, concealed perch far above the ground. Judging she had climbed far enough, a distance of over four times her own height separated her from the forest floor.

Adjusting her position, she settled against the trunk and waited. Another series of troll calls confirmed that the creatures drew closer. It would not be long before the beasts came into sight, if they kept to their course.

A large shadow cast by the moonlight accompanied a series of heavy breaths, a few paces to the right of Rayden's position. The creature that cast the shadow moved into her line of sight a few moments later.

Well over twice her height, the creature below had an elongated head, adorned with a pair of short, upright, oval-shaped ears. A set of broad, deepset eyes flanked the end of a short, tapering snout.

The troll's thick neck melded with a sweeping torso covered in dark, coarse fur. A short, narrow tail with a dark tuft at the end flicked back and forth, from atop its wide bottom.

Long of arm and leg, the troll's appendages appeared disproportionate when compared to the rest of its body. As the tracks had indicated, the creature had substantial claws at the ends of its extremities. Black and curving, they looked more than capable of rending flesh with ease.

The creature stopped, crouched, and sniffed at the air. A low, grating sound came from the depths of its throat.

Nostrils widening and chest expanding, the troll drew in a few slow, purposeful whiffs of the air. Moving independently of each other, and orienting to the front and sides, its ears rotated about, the troll listening to the night with great attentiveness.

Ears continuing to sweep back and forth, and body rigid, the troll remained still and vigilant. Looking from side to side, the creature appeared to become agitated. Its lips pulled back, exposing a glistening array of misshapen, jagged teeth.

A breeze passed over Rayden, flowing in a direction that would not betray her location to the troll. She could not take full relief from the icy current, though, as it could announce her presence to any trolls behind her.

A troll call sounded from nearby, and the creature beneath Rayden responded in kind. Becoming silent and still again, the troll remained in place, waiting.

Not long after the exchange, a second troll strode into view, trudging through the trees on the far side of the first.

A little shorter than its companion, the newcomer exhibited a series of prominent scars running down the right side of its face, and its left ear had been severed near the top. The creature had a grizzled, aged appearance, and it moved with a slight limp to its right leg.

The two creatures spoke to each other in low tones, their language sounding grating and guttural in Rayden's ears. With a look of wariness about them, the trolls kept taking in scents of the air while casting their gazes in all directions.

Reflective, like those of many nocturnal creatures, their eyes gleamed when they caught the moonlight. The creatures would have scant difficulty seeing Rayden. One look into the boughs would reveal her to them, but other than taking an occasional glance toward the sky, the trolls paid little heed to the heights of the trees where Rayden had positioned herself.

Despite the precarious risk, she did not second guess her choice to take to the trees. Though disadvantageous if revealed, her spot afforded her a solid vantage from which to observe the trolls.

The older troll with the discernable limp represented less of a danger than the larger, younger one. On the ground, she could evade the older one if need be, but the younger troll could outrun her with ease.

Both possessed tremendous advantages in size and strength, the latter proven many times in tribal lore to be bone-crushing against a human. Rayden's sword and axe could pierce their thick hides, but she would have to land blows at full force to do any kind of significant damage.

She hoped the trolls separated. Nothing could be attempted before then. She knew it would be reckless to engage two of the monstrous brutes at once.

Dawn's first rays would move them away, if they did not leave the area much sooner. The sun caused no harm to trolls, but the creatures loathed daylight and struggled in brighter luminance.

With the moon's location, Rayden estimated the night to have a little time yet remaining. She resigned herself to waiting for an opportunity to emerge. She could not become lax in her vigil, knowing that if a chance to strike at a troll presented itself she would not have long to act upon it.

The two trolls kept their positions for a short while, continuing to take in scents from the breezes. Fortune remained with Rayden in that the air currents did not change direction.

She could see signs of growing restlessness in the creatures. When they spoke to each other, the trolls sounded more irritable, and Rayden gained the sense that the older troll harbored a high level of frustration with the younger one.

A little more time passed, and the contentiousness between the pair increased. At one point, Rayden thought the younger one was about to assault the older. Baring its teeth and snarling, the troll shifted its feet, squaring toward the other.

The older troll showed no signs of backing down from the other's flare up. Glaring at the younger, it stayed its ground, feet set firm and posture strong.

After a sharp, angry-sounding exhange, the older troll abruptly turned away, and strode back in the direction it had come from. The remaining troll remained in place for a moment, glowering in the direction of the older one before starting forward itself, continuing in the direction it had been traveling in.

Rayden knew she had to move, or daylight would come and she would have the unwelcome choice of seeking out a troll lair or waiting for the next nightfall. The idea of going after a troll in the pitch dark of its subterranean abode would be the height of foolishness, and time stood precious with grave peril looming imminent over Gessa lands.

Now that the trolls had separated, and she could isolate one of them, she much preferred to bring her hunt to an end before dawn's light broke the horizon.

With nimble, quiet movements, Rayden climbed downward, lowering herself back to the ground. The wind direction favorable for pursuing the younger troll, she set out after the creature with a long stride and soft step.

The creature's hulking, shadowy form and heavy steps proved easy enough to follow. Drawing closer, and maintaining great caution, Rayden eyed the troll's form. Paying close attention to the manner of its gait, a thought took root.

Whenever it took a step forward, the backside of its other leg lay highly exposed, the substantial length of it adding to the prospect Rayden identified. A strike at the backside of the creature's trailing leg, low around its ankle, could cripple the beast in one blow.

If she managed to render the troll lame from the outset, the odds of prevailing would become much more favorable. The creature would be unable to rush her, and use its bulk to overpower her. It could no longer chase her if other trolls manifested and the need to flee arose.

Intending her axe for the strike, Rayden increased her pace and closed the gap between her and the troll. She watched for any sign that the beast sensed her, but it continued trudging onward and showed no hint of detecting her pursuit.

Matching her step to that of the creature, and springing forward to mitigate the troll's lengthy stride, she moved within striking distance. The musky scent of the creature filled her nostrils.

Whether sensing her or reacting to something else, the troll came to an abrupt stop, mid-stride, presenting Rayden with a prime opening. She reacted at once.

Hacking down with her axe, Rayden dealt a severe blow to the troll's right ankle. The blade cleaved deep, and Rayden tore it free. The creature flailed and bellowed in the aftermath of the strike, stumbling when it tried to bring its leg forward and stand upon it.

Barely managing to keep its footing, the creature remained upright. Favoring its wounded leg, the troll rotated in a clumsy fashion toward Rayden.

Glaring down at her, the troll bared its teeth and loosed a grating snarl, spittle flying from its mouth.

Staying at the perimeter of the creature's swiping range, Rayden began moving in a circle around the troll, forcing it to keep shifting to its right. Awkward of movement and in great pain, the creature struggled to turn and remain oriented toward her.

Slashing whenever she gained a propitious angle, she used her sword to open up several more wounds on the towering beast. Crying out and gnashing its teeth, the troll's claws raked empty air whenever it tried to lash out at her.

Bleeding profusely from the lower part of its right side, back, and arm, the troll began to slow. Patient and methodical, Rayden allowed the wounds to take their course, inflicting a couple more in the process.

Sensing the advancing weakness in the beast, Rayden calculated the time had come to finish the kill. Planting her feet, she halted abruptly. After a moment's pause, she thrust off her left foot and sprang to her right.

Her sudden shift caught the troll by surprise. Having turned about in a circle many times, at great effort, the troll became disoriented when it tried to react to her change in direction. Lurching to the left, it staggered for a couple of steps, before twisting, tripping, and falling over. Face down, the troll hit the ground hard.

Rayden did not waste an instant. She bounded in, landing her axe on the base of its neck before driving the tip of her sword through the back of the troll's skull. The creature's body went rigid, and then fell slack, a gurgling wheeze exiting its throat before falling into silence.

Rayden pulled her sword free and used her axe to behead the creature. Proof of her success would have to be taken back to the Varganir, and none of them could question a troll head.

The night fell into a calm silence, and no sounds of troll calls broke the stillness. The quiet did not mean that no other trolls had responded to the sounds of fighting.

Adept at stalking quarry, the creatures could also position themselves well for an ambush. Rayden could not let her awareness slack, for even a moment.

After taking a little time to catch her breath, she slipped her axe back into the loop at her belt and lifted the head up. The crest of short hairs running down the middle of its head afforded her a solid grip.

The head held considerable weight, but not enough to make walking with it too cumbersome. Starting forward, Rayden set out for the land of the Varganir.

***

Moonlight revealed a scene of carnage. Sprawled on the ground, the body of a large troll lay at an awkward angle. The torn left ear on its head identified the creature to Rayden at once.

The troll had been ripped into, mauled and gored with savagery. Disemboweled, its guts had been scattered all over the ground surrounding it. A terrible stench permeated the air; the pungency of an outright slaughter.

Indulging their appetites, the perpetrators of the brutal slaying remained present.

Jaws coated with blood, two Arguntier lifted their heads up from the carcass they had been feeding upon, fixing their light-reflective eyes upon Rayden. One had a head like that of a hyena, while the other's was more dog-like in nature, broad and shorter of muzzle.

Dark eyes narrowing, both of the creatures snarled, baring their lengthy fangs. Towering above Rayden, the beast men rose up from where they crouched at the side of the troll corpse.

Rayden flung the troll head she carried at the one to the left, the nearer of the two, and took up her axe at once. Batting the head aside, the Arguntier growled at Rayden, while its comrade sprang over the troll corpse, launching itself toward her.

Rayden dodged aside and slashed, but the creature proved too quick, and her sword passed through air. The other Arguntier made a gutteral roar and lunged at her, swiping its claws at her midsection.

Rayden jerked back just in time to avoid being gutted, though the tips of the beast man's claws tore through the cloth of her tunic. Hacking downward with her axe, she elicited a howl of agony as her blade bit deep into the creature's arm.

Maneuvering to keep both of her adversaries in front of her, Rayden braced for the next onslaught. The wounded Arguntier roared again and leapt for her.

Falling to the ground, Rayden swung her axe as the beast man passed by her. The blade cleaved the flesh at the back of its right leg, near the foot, eliciting a higher-pitched yelp.

She had no time to evaluate the strike, setting the pommel of her sword against the ground as the second Arguntier surged in the wake of its comrade and fell upon her. The sword driving far into its body, the creature shrieked in pain. Rayden gasped at the impact of the heavy creature's body.

The sword lodged in its body gave her a small gap to maneuver in. Using her legs, rotating her torso, and reacting fast, she executed a move that sent the creature rolling over.

Finding herself on top of the beast, she crashed her right fist into its throat. Raising her left arm, she chopped down hard, with her axe gripped firm. The blade landed square between the Arguntier's eyes, dousing its fiery gaze as life fled its body.

She evaded the other creature's next attack with little difficulty. Hobbled by its leg wound, the Arguntier could no longer rush her full force.

The wound not as severe as the one Rayden had landed on the troll she had fought, the Arguntier could still bear enough weight to come at her. In a rage, the creature staggered after Rayden, growling and gnashing its teeth.

She leapt over the dead troll, putting an obstacle in its path. The Arguntier propelled off its uninjured leg, hurdling over the troll carcass.

Loosing a screech of agony when landing upon the wounded leg, the Arguntier buckled, on the brink of collapsing to the ground. It jerked upright, doing all it could to prevent itself from falling, leaving an opening.

Rayden darted in and brought her sword across in a long sweep that opened a broad gash across the lower part of its torso. She jumped back over the carcass, turned, and looked to see the condition the Arguntier remained in.

Despite the pain wracking its body, the creature had rotated to face her. With a howl filled with rancor and anguish, the beast lurched forward.

Using its arms and unharmed leg, it surmounted the obstacle in its path. The creature moved faster than she had anticipated, scrambling over the troll corpse and flinging itself at her with a powerful thrust from both arms.

Before hitting the ground, the beast managed to slash with its right set of claws. Rayden twisted fast from the rapid strike, but a couple of the claw tips raked down the side of her right thigh, slicing through breeches and cutting into her skin.

Lifting her right leg, she kicked out hard. Her heel landed solid on the creature's head, eliciting a deep grunt. Stunned, the beast swayed a moment in the aftermath of the blow.

Rayden waded in, unleashing a flurry of strikes with both

sword and axe. When she ended her furious assault, the creature lay dead on the ground, both sets of claws and its head severed.

Chest heaving and heart racing, Rayden took a few moments to recover from the exertion. She pushed the searing pain in her leg to the edge of her mind.

Walking over to the body of the first Arguntier, she beheaded the creature with a couple of blows from her axe. Without knowing enough about the Arguntier, she could take no chances if the creature had the regenerative powers of a shapeshifter.

Sheathing her sword and securing her axe back at her waist, she took the less-maimed head of the first Arguntier and retrieved the troll head she had tossed at the outset of the fighting. She left the bloodied ground behind without delay, leaving the remains of the two Arguntier and the troll for the bellies of forest scavengers.

While not liking having to tread the night without a weapon in hand, she knew she had to lug her grisly haul from the night's ordeal along. Now, she had two heads to present to the Varganir; heads that would confirm her worthiness to them, and give loud testament and strength to her entreaty.

***

After moving a fair distance from the site of the encounter with the Arguntier, she arrived at a narrow stream. Halting at its banks and setting the two heads she carried down, Rayden tended her wounds, slaked her thirst, and rested in the cover of some brush close by, awaiting dawn's light.

Aching, bloodied, and weary, she was in no condition to face another troll or Arguntier. She hoped any forest creatures that could present a threat, like boars, bears or wolves, would be drawn to the three carcasses left behind. The stench of death from that area would undoubtedly serve as a beacon to an easy meal for any predatory beasts roving the woods.

To her relief, the rest of the night passed without disruption.

Listening to the steady flow of the waters nearby, Rayden dozed off into a light sleep until the morning.

The first rays of dawn a welcome sight, Rayden yawned and stretched, the tender scratches on her legs causing her to grimace. Getting to her feet and ignoring the aches throughout her body, she took in a deep, cleansing breath of the cool morning air, letting the grogginess from her slumber ebb away.

A brief span of foraging in the vicinity turned up a few berries and some edible mushrooms, though not nearly enough to assuage the hunger inside. With the stream too shallow and thin to offer any promise of fish, Rayden could only partake of its water.

A fair distance still remained before she reached Varganir territory. While any trolls in the area would have long since returned to their subterranean refuges, the Arguntier stood a deep concern. She had no idea how many more of the beasts might be in the area, but she knew well enough that they stalked the woods both day and night.

Wincing from the throbbing pain in her leg, and lugging a troll head in one hand and that of an Arguntier in the other, she started back for the territory of the Varganir. Between maintaining caution, accumulating fatigue, and continuing pain, the return took much longer, reaching late into the day.

Rayden knew she had reached Varganir territory when a pair of them stepped out from the trees to intercept her path. Dropping the heads, she snatched up her weapons before easing her posture.

"In Varganir land," one said, its eyes drawn to the heads she had discarded.

"Come," the other said, also fixing its gaze on the heads before turning.

She put her weapons back, picked up the two heads, and followed after the tall creatures. With their long strides, she had to pick up her gait to keep pace, an unwelcome task at the end of the laborious sojourn.

The Varganir led her to an area girded with towering pine trees, where a sprawling mass of Varganir had gathered. At their center stood Manak.

All fell silent and turned their eyes to Rayden as she approached, their attention quickly focusing on the grisly trophies she bore with her. The Varganir ahead of her parted aside, clearing the way toward their leader.

Walking into the center of the throng, and continuing up to Manak, she placed the heads of the troll and Arguntier down on the ground before him. She looked up, into the golden eyes of the hulking Varganir leader.

"I have slain a troll, as you have asked," Rayden announced. "I have also slain two of the creatures that are enemies to both Varganir and humans. The Arguntier, as one has named them. They are the creatures I spoke to you of, when I came to you.

"I brought you one of their heads ... to show you. These creatures are on the edge of your lands. I came upon them feeding on a troll they had killed. If they kill trolls, they will kill Varganir."

Manak looked for a moment at the troll head, but his gaze fixed upon the head of the Arguntier for an extended, silent period. Rayden did not interrupt, letting Manak take the sight and her tidings in.

"One Varganir killed in night ... not by troll," Manak said, breaking the quiet. "Body ... "

Gesturing with his lengthy claws, Manak made raking and stabbing motions across his own body, indicating tearing, goring kinds of wounds. He paused, staring at Rayden, and she knew he wanted to know she understood.

"The body of the Varganir was torn apart," Rayden said. "The attack looked like one of a wild beast."

Manak nodded his head.

"Then you know the Arguntier are a threat to your kind too," Rayden said. "Help us against these creatures. We must stand together. Varganir and humans must fight Arguntier."

"It is there ... with humans," Manak said. "It is here ... with Varganir. How can leave? These Varganir lands. Our hunting grounds."

"No humans will try to take your lands ... and if any human came to take Varganir lands, I would come fight them myself," Rayden said with a grim tone, looking Manak in the eye.

"You are strong human ... you have honor, like Varganir," Manak stated. "Your words true. I know this."

Rayden kept her face steady, though she realized the significance of the words. She knew she had more than passed the test given to her, in the eyes of the Varganir. She had gained high respect from the creatures.

She bowed her head. "I seek to be a friend to Varganir."

"Varganir friend of Rayden," Manak replied. His expression changed, a downcast look coming into his eyes. "But I must protect Varganir. Enemy is here."

"If we stand together against our enemy, you will protect the Varganir," Rayden said. "Many more Varganir will live if we fight Arguntier side by side. We will be stronger."

"Cannot give answer," Manak said, after a long impasse.

The words bitter to her ears, so soon after undertaking the Varganir test, Rayden could not fault Manak. His kind had now fallen under the threat of the savage beast men in their own lands. He had elderly and young to consider in any decision he made.

"I understand," Rayden said, trying not to let the disappointment show in her face. After a pause and taking a breath, she continued. "I must go back to my people. The Arguntier will attack humans soon. I must be there to fight them."

"Know you are Varganir friend," Manak said. He reached

forward and set his hand down, upon her right shoulder. She could feel the sharp claws pressing light against her tunic like so many blades, but wished such fearsome natural weapons would be defending the Gessa. "I must protect Varganir. We must fight here."

Rayden nodded, as the weight of her fatigue, wounds, and failed aims pressed in without mercy. She had done all she could do, and the cooperation of the Varganir had never been guaranteed.

Having come so far, and putting her life at risk, both in seeking the Varganir and undertaking the test given to her, the decision of Manak left her with a deep weariness in spirit. After everything that had happened, she would walk away with nothing achieved for the Gessa.

Leaving the heads with the Varganir chieftain, she turned about and made her way through the mass of creatures. Even though despairing in spirit, Rayden still carried her head high, knowing not one thing in her appeal to the Varganir could have been done any better.

CHAPTER 5

Rayden started back for the Gessa lands burdened in heart. A couple of the Varganir accompanied her to the border of their lands, but turned back when she reached the territory of the Arnan.

The large raven appeared in the skies again, guiding her by daylight through Arnan territory. Heading south, thoughts ebbed and flowed within her mind. She knew the journey back would be onerous with the things plaguing her mind without respite.

One recurring notion hammered at her. She had come a long way for nothing.

Having no idea of how they would receive her, she had risked everything in searching out the Varganir. Then she had accepted their test without hesitation, to prove her worthiness among them, and courted a brutal, violent death two more times in the encounters with the trolls and Arguntier.

Save for the wounds to her leg, she would return to Gessa lands in the same state that she had been in when she had departed. Rayden had nothing to bring the Gessa in the way of help.

If anything, returning so empty-handed could only bring more discouragement to the Gessa, during such a dark time. Clouded with fear and uncertainty, the Gessa teetered on a dangerous edge, and the last thing Rayden wished was to debilitate their spirits further.

Over and over again, she reminded herself that she had done everything possible, and that nothing in a person's life could ever be guaranteed. The things beyond her control she did not have to apologize for, or feel any shame in.

She had not fallen short in any area that she could affect. If anything, she had prevailed beyond all expectations.

Nevertheless, her spirit grew even heavier as the day proceeded. Her only solace the feel of the sword and axe gripped in her hands, she resolved to draw as much blood as possible from the Arguntier in the coming, inevitable fight.

Yet she could not deny the stark reality facing the Gessa. Even if the tribal warriors held a considerable advantage in numbers, they would still be no match against a sizeable force of Arguntier. In any kind of significant numbers, the beast men would be unstoppable.

Rayden eyed the dark bird flying overhead.

Angst clutching her heart, she spoke in a low voice, "Where can help be found now, Dreaghen? This journey availed us nothing. You know the Gessa will not survive the storm to come. Too much is sent against them."

Whether her words had been heard or not, she could not tell. The bird continued circling above and did not deviate from its pattern. Its lack of response prodded her ire.

"At the least I will be returning to them," Rayden muttered, with an air of defiance. "And I will be proud to die with them."

***

The raven departed from the skies as dusk approached. The shadows beneath the trees lengthening and broadening with the descending sun, Rayden began looking around for a suitable place to fashion a shelter for the night.

Her stomach carried a mild ache from hunger, but sustenance would have to wait until she had a place to conceal herself well for the duration of the night. She needed rest above all, having pressed hard from the outset of her journey to the Varganir.

With her body sapped, and her mind and heart weighed down, a little uninterrupted sleep would be a welcome boon before resuming the journey. She could go no farther for the time being.

Light continued to dim all about her, the shadows growing and deepening, the forest reaching the cusp of night. Rayden searched about with some exigency in the diminishing ambience, having little time left to determine a suitable resting place with the aid of daylight's last few rays.

Eyeing some nearby undergrowth, Rayden took account of an area where a tree had fallen, evaluating the best place to create her shelter. To her relief, she judged it would not take long to finish the task.

She walked toward the undergrowth, sliding her sword back in its sheath, intending to use her axe to cut some brush to take back to the fallen tree. Reaching down, she took up a handful and pulled it taut.

Throaty laughter echoed through the shadows from behind her. In an instant, Rayden pivoted and squared toward the sound, hearing shuffling footsteps and catching a flicker of movement among the trees. Letting go of the brush, she took up her sword.

"So far from home ... Rayden Valkyrie," a screeching, raspy voice called to her. "No priests here ... your friend in the skies is gone ... and darkness is stronger here."

A narrow face caked with filth peered around the trunk of one of the trees many strides away from her. Stringy, greasy hair and a scraggly beard ornamented a scar-ridden visage. One eye socket empty, the man's lone eye appeared to be solid black.

His fingers, ending in long, encrusted nails, clutched the bark of the tree. Hissing, spittle dribbled from his thin lips.

"Get away from me," Rayden demanded, angered that she would not be able to get any rest until the intrusion was resolved. "Or be left to rot. The choice lies with you. Make it quick."

"Rotting ... death," the man replied, breaking into a grating cackle. "So much death to come! The Master has given many the power over death! Death coils around all in these woods ... even now."

As he spoke, his voice began changing, taking on the strange, multi-layered quality of the madman she had encountered among the leagues of crucifixions lining the Boreus Way. Rayden had no illusions about what she now faced.

No demented outcast living in the wilds confronted her. Rather, something much worse and formidable faced her.

"His will. His way! My brothers, sisters, and our slaves in this world once more! Our world!" the man announced, his voice now sounding like a throng of beings. Laughing with an air of triumph, he stared at Rayden for a few moments, and then continued. "All roads lead to us! Everything ends ... in death!"

Rayden had heard the latter words spoken before, from the mouth of the crazed man on the Boreus Way.

"Test my blades, or shut your mouth!" Rayden responded.

Leaping from behind the tree, the man went into a low crouch, curling his fingers up like sets of claws. Snarling like a feral beast, he gazed toward her with a look of pure malice.

"You have caused us much trouble! But the Imperator carries out the will of the Master ... and will not be stopped!" the man shouted at her.

He hopped forward, frog-like, keeping to a crouch. Spreading his lips, he chortled again, the sound unnerving with its many layers.

"Stand back, or have honed iron send you fast back to your abyss," Rayden said.

The man sprang forward, vaulting far over Rayden's head and well out of the reach of her sword. Landing several paces behind her with perfect balance, he stood upright.

Rotating, Rayden kept her body facing the man, who had performed an astounding physical feat that no man or woman was capable of. Weapons poised before her, she braced for the man's next move.

Another chorus of laughter, sepulchral and devoid of mirth, broke out from the man. Staring at Rayden, he began lifting off the ground.

Rayden's eyes widened, her throat tightening in the grip of some unseen force. Dropping her weapons, she grabbed at her throat, her hands encountering nothing of substance where the force continued pressing on her windpipe. Within moments, each breath proved laborious.

Baring his dirty, broken teeth at her, he rose until he hovered far above her head.

"I can keep you here all night," he boasted.

Rayden continued to struggle, the act of breathing now a battle. With her thoughts on every shred of air that she could muster, she did not know how long the unnatural power held her captive. The tribulation extended long enough for night to take full dominion, silvery moonlight spreading through the trees from clear skies.

Rayden's adversary said nothing, a mockery of a smile resting on his face. A few glances showing no change in his expression told her the vile entity savored every moment of her suffering.

Suddenly, her tormenter broke his silence.

"You escaped one of my brothers on the Boreus Way!" the man told Rayden, the force upon her throat escalating. "Distance is nothing to us! We know everything that happens among our kind! All are of the mind of our Master!"

Gagging, Rayden writhed and strained against the increasing attack. Fingers still passing through whatever power clutched her tight, her efforts proved futile.

She knew she could not give in to panic, and had to keep her mind focused, but there seemed no way out of the dire predicament. Nearing the edge of unconsciousness, her vision began to waver, dark spots dancing in her eyes.

The invisible power holding her then lifted Rayden into the air and tossed her forward, as if she weighed little more than one of the many small sticks cluttering the forest floor. Landing on the ground several paces away, she managed to roll with the fall on instinct, though a grunt escaped her lips at the heavy impact.

Bracing on her hands, she gulped in the fresh air, filling her beleaguered, desperate lungs. Her vision steadied with the return of breath.

She lifted her gaze to the levitating figure, casting a hard glare in his direction.

"Your warnings avail the tribes nothing! They avail the wolf men nothing!" the man taunted her. "The Master has sent numerous slaves under the power of His servants here. The tribes and the wolf men are close to death, even now! They will be slaughtered!"

"They will fight ... they will never submit," Rayden said in a low, weary voice.

"They will be swept away," the man said, in a slow, measured tone. "While you die here alone, know that a great number of the Master's servants gather to slaughter your filthy kind."

Rayden knew few options lay before her. Whatever inhabited the body of the man before her could project powers far beyond her understanding, but it still dwelled inside of a human. A human body, one made of flesh and blood, had limitations, giving her the only sliver of hope at hand.

Her hand brushed along the ground. A few small rocks met her touch, one about palm-sized. Without a glance or change in her expression, she closed her fingers about it's jagged surface.

The man continued floating in the air. A maniacal grin spread across on his face.

"You will not go into the darkness fast or easily!" he declared. "You will get the end you deserve. You will suffer and beg for death, but I will not release you. I will hold you to life ... as you are eaten alive!"

He laughed, as a new clamor broke out in the wake of his words. A cacophany of high-pitched squeals and deep grunts accompanied the emergence of several dark, brawny forms.

A cluster of wild boars gathered just beneath the hovering man, and came to a halt.

Each one a dangerous beast, the wild boars eyed her hungrily. With sharp tusks that could shred flesh with ease, inflicting a mortal wound in one slash, the herd presented an insurmountable threat to Rayden.

Weapons out of reach and body weakened, she stood no chance against the feral beasts. Before they charged her, she had one last act available.

Steadying her breath and calming her mind, she clenched the rock in her palm tighter. Righting herself in a sudden burst of movement, she hurled the rock toward the levitating man with as much force as she could scrape up.

Racing through the air, the rock smashed into the right side of the man's head and opened a wide gash. The injury shattered whatever focus he needed to remain aloft.

Breaking into a free fall, the man shrieked, plummeting down into the midst of the boars. The power governing the creatures also appeared to have been severed, as the boars whirled about in an eruption of squeals and beset the lean figure with great savagery. A flesh-tearing frenzy ensued, the boars' quarry loosing one last, pitiful wail before falling silent.

Rayden wasted no time with the boars distracted. Getting to her feet and putting all she had left into the effort, she hurried for the nearest tree she could climb.

Springing upward, she grabbed a thick bough and hoisted herself up, sheer willpower summoning the necessary strength from her drained muscles. Continuing several branches higher, she finally came to a stop, far out of the reach of any boar.

Rendered a captive for the time being, Rayden listened to the crunching and cracking sounds from the boars consuming the flesh and bones of their prey. The creatures fed and rooted about until little more than a few scraps of cloth and a blood-soaked patch of ground remained of the man.

After quite some time had passed, the herd of boars, bellies full and hunger sated, finally moved onward. Rayden waited a little longer before climbing back down to the ground.

When her feet touched the forest floor, she trotted over to retrieve her weapons from where she had discarded them. Shaken to the center of her being by everything that had just happened, Rayden welcomed the feel of the weapons back in her hands.

She could not deny the truth. Had it not been for the diabolic figure's desire to draw out her death in a grisly manner with the boars, she would have died. She had been rendered helpless against the man's aberrant powers.

She had been fortunate, but once again had been confronted with the deadly threat of dark powers and the unseen world.

Night had deepened. Beams of moonlight sifted through the branches above, gracing the welcome stillness. The air had taken on a chill, but the taste of it unimpeded to her lungs made every breath soothing.

The ache in her stomach had grown, and a terrible exhaustion filled her, but the prevailing thought in her mind fixed upon gaining distance from the area. Blocking thoughts of food and rest, she resolved to continue onward.

Casting a glance at the dark ground where the madman had been eaten, an end that could well have been hers that night, she resumed her journey under the vast, starry skies.

CHAPTER 6

No unwelcome interruptions surfaced to mar the remainder of her journey back to the Gessa, which took a little longer with the growing weight of fatigue slowing her steps. Snatching up anything edible that she came across, Rayden fended off hunger with a few roots, berries and nuts, doing all she could to make use of every moment of the raven's guidance in daylight.

Sleeping lightly at night, Rayden gained little in the way of rest. From the threats of Arguntier to forest dwellers possessed by diabolical spirits, she could not dismiss any sound that broke the stillness of the night.

Each morning's light found nothing more than a sliver of revitalization in her depleted body. Even that diminutive amount of recovery proved ephemeral, well before the sun reached its midday zenith.

The hard ground left her body riddled with aches and soreness, to the extent that it took an extended amount of time to limber up. Despite the increasing betrayal of her own body, Rayden pressed harder when an assortment of familiar landmarks began to greet her eyes, letting her know she trod upon Gessa territory.

With the sun sinking on the horizon, the raven guide parted from Rayden for the last time. Lowering closer to the trees, it circled and loosed a few cries before flapping off. Watching the bird flying away, she whispered a few words of gratitude to Dreaghen for the aid he had lent her.

Reaching Eigon's settlement shortly after nightfall, Rayden found the chieftain sitting alone in the midst of his long hall. A fire blazed strong in the central hearth, saturating the interior with its warmth. A cauldron of mead stood full, a foamy layer cloaking its surface.

A look of relief crossed Eigon's face at seeing Rayden walking in. After giving her a welcoming embrace, he wasted no time in summoning two serving women to prepare some food for her.

Famished, Rayden accepted a cup of mead from one of the women. She took a seat on the bench where Eigon returned with his own cup full.

The women left and soon returned with a plate full of roasted wild boar. Rayden refused the plate of boar, despite her hunger, asking if any other kind of meat could be found. Both women looked surprised at her reaction, and Eigon had a puzzled expression, but said nothing.

One of the women took the plate away and found her some fish, gleaned from one of the many streams crossing Gessa lands. The other woman brought Rayden some bread and cheese, adding it to her plate.

Peeling off a large piece of fish, Rayden salivated copiously the moment she put it in her mouth. Chewing and swallowing it quickly, she replaced it with a larger chunk, savoring the taste after days of meager woodland fare.

While tending to her appetite, Rayden told Eigon of everything that had transpired on her journey to the Varganir. He listened to her account in rapt silence, interrupting only a few times to ask a question or clarify something.

None of the Gessa had such first-hand experience with the mysterious Varganir, and Rayden could see the astonishment growing in Eigon as she proceeded with her tale. Describing Manak, the test given to her, the hunt of the troll, and the encounter with the two Arguntier, she gave as much detail as she could recall.

Eigon's eyes widened when she spoke of the man inhabited by dark spirits, and how he had her at his mercy using supernatural forces. Talking of her suffering, she found herself running her fingers along her neck, memories of the extended strangulation vivid in her mind.

"The gods be praised for your fortune," Eigon exclaimed, when she told him of the boars, being dropped to the ground, and finding the stone that she hurled to maim her tormenter; and send him to his doom at the tusks and teeth of the wild boars. "We will sacrifice a bull in gratitude for your survival."

"It was a ray of good fortune, and it is even better to be freed from the unseen bonds of sorcery," Rayden stated, knowing Eigon shared her distaste for the mystic arts.

Rayden drank deep from the cup of mead in her hands, letting the dark memories ebb. The liquid in the clay vessel tasted even sweeter after the arduous journey she had undertaken. Draining the cup, she filled it to the brim from the large cauldron in the center of Eigon's long hall.

She returned to the bench and sat down again. Rayden grinned toward Eigon.

"Gessa mead has no rival among the tribes," she stated, before taking another long draught of the liquid. "And I have sampled the mead of many of them."

"No man or woman of a Gessa can ever fully slake their thirst of our mead," Eigon said, lifting a cup of his own and taking a drink.

"It has never tasted better, after stream water for a few days," Rayden said, letting out a satisfied breath and setting down the half-drained vessel.

"But no taste for wild boar?" he asked. "I've never known you to refuse wild boar. That surprised me."

"Not at this time," Rayden said, staring into her cup. She knew it would be a little while until she regained a hunger for boar, after witnessing the beasts kill and consume a man down to the last morsel, bones and all.

"It is a shame, for Jarut felled a large one this day, not far from the settlement," Eigon said. "It was incredible fortune, as our hunters do not stray far from the settlement with the threats looming."

Rayden returned to her plate, still piled high with bread, cheese, and fish. She had another bite of the fish, following it with a swig of mead. "This is a great feast, after the past several days."

"Regain your strength, rest, and eat whatever you choose," Eigon said.

"We do not have much time," Rayden said. "If I understood that fell being's boasts in the right way, I'd say an attack is imminent."

"All signs would agree with you," Eigon said, a grim look coming to his eyes. "Terian cast the **sticks** more than once. Every time she has told me we do not have long."

"The madman said large numbers are gathered," Rayden said.

Eigon nodded with a terse expression. "They are massing, in large numbers ... and from every sign are about to move from Runi lands in this direction.

"There is a lot of movement in the shadows very near our borders. We have lost many capable warriors to learn this."

"What is the state of the tribes?" Rayden asked. "Do any join with us?"

"I have sent messengers to many," Eigon said. "Some dismissed our warnings, some responded, and a few have sent large war bands here. We are gathering all of them outside the borders of Runi lands, keeping vigil in strength."

"Who responded with the sending of war bands?" Rayden asked, curious.

"The Arnan, the Cirni, the Rugara, the Marren, and the Lanassa," Eigon said.

"How many in the war bands each sent?"

"Each of them hundreds strong."

"How many Runi warriors survived the battle and the forest?"

"At least five hundred," Eigon answered. "Maybe six hundred."

"Then we stand thousands strong against our adversary," Rayden said. She then added, with a dour air. "And even that many may not prove enough."

"We have lost several good warriors to these unnatural beasts, since you left for the north," Eigon said. "Strong fighters who stood no chance against them. It would take thousands more before I could believe we could stop a force of the beast men ... these Arguntier as you call them."

Knowing what she did of the Arguntier, having fought three of them to the death, Rayden could not dispute the chieftain.

"If only the Varganir could have sent a war band," Rayden commented, with an edge of bitterness.

A dark frown crossed her face as she contemplated the Varganir's decision. All of her risk had come to nothing, a cold truth she could not dismiss.

"You did all that could have been asked of you," Eigon said. "The Varganir are doing no different than us. They are protecting their lands, and their kind."

"They would be good allies in a battle such as this," Rayden said.

"That they would," Eigon said, nodding. "But we cannot

regret what was never ours to begin with. At least we do have the warriors of several tribes standing with us now."

"That is a union of tribes that has not been seen in a very long time," Rayden said. "Or I don't remember the story of it."

"It never happened in my lifetime, nor the lifetime of my father, or even his father," Eigon said.

"It may never have happened before," Rayden said. "And if we survive the storm to come, then new paths have been discovered for the tribes to take."

"I would always see the Gessa remain Gessa, warding, hunting, and living well on their own lands, choosing their own fate," Eigon said. "But standing together against a common threat is wisdom, as much as remaining one of the Gessa is wisdom."

"You will find no argument from me on that," Rayden said, thinking of how strong the tribes could be if they all came together in a common cause. Even the Teveren Empire could be confronted, and perhaps even defeated, with an army created from all the tribes.

The door to the long hall opened. Alcedan and a couple of other warriors of Eigon's personal retinue entered. All looked fatigued.

"Alcedan, Migan, Torasek," Eigon greeted the men. "What tidings from the border?"

Alcedan looked from Rayden to Eigon, as he and the other two warriors made their way over to the cauldron. "A few scattered brawls, some tension, but a general peace holds between the war bands. All eyes keep watch on the forest's edge."

"Any word from scouts who have ventured into the forest?" Eigon asked.

"Nothing new," Alcedan replied. "The beast men keep to the forest, but, as we knew before, there is no doubt a large number of them are massed. No scout dares venture too far into the trees."

"Do we wait for them to move upon us, or do we march on

them?" Eigon said, shaking his head with a look of frustration.

"We do not know what the forest hides, and as long as the tribes keep from fighting each other, it is best to wait for them," Rayden said. "Fight them on open ground."

"I am in agreement with Rayden," Alcedan said. "There is little to nothing for them to hunt in the forest. Their hunger will move them soon enough. What they hunger most is in plain sight, in abundance."

Rayden thought upon Alcedan's words, in particular the ones about the Arguntier's hunger; a hunger that craved human flesh. The mass of tribal warriors would look to the Arguntier like a great feast, rather than any kind of opposition. The thought sickened her.

She picked at a piece of bread, wetting it in her mead cup before chewing the softened morsel. Feeling a little vitality and strength returning to her limbs, she followed it with another piece of fish.

The other three warriors went about getting cups and filling them with mead. In moments their beards glistened, where some of the liquid had escaped the vessels and trickled down from the sides of their mouths.

Alcedan smacked his lips, and loudly exhaled. "So good, after such a long day."

"I'm famished," the one called Torasek stated. "I'm going to pay a visit to Jarut. When we returned I heard a tale about him and a large boar he found in the woods. I hope it speaks truly."

"The tale is true," Eigon stated. "The gods gave him the fortune of encountering a brute of a boar, just outside the settlement."

Rayden kept the thought to herself, but doubted the boar the result of a god's beneficence. Like the Snow Lions driven down from the heights of their natural domain, the boar had roved near to the settlement rather than become quarry for the

Arguntier.

Torasek grinned. "Then I should visit Jarut, before this tale spreads too far."

"Probably wise to do so," Eigon said, a trace of good humor surfacing through the weariness in his voice.

"For my part, I'm just looking forward to a night's sleep," the black-haired warrior named Migan remarked. Lifting his cup, he drained its contents, and then moved over to the cauldron to refill it.

"A full night's sleep is a treasure during these times," Alcedan said.

"A treasure I would like to find, if it existed," Migan said. "I find myself far too restless these days."

Rayden caught the flicker of fear in the warrior's eyes.

"It has been some time since I had a full night's rest myself," Rayden said.

"You should try and seek a full night of rest tonight, Rayden," Eigon said. "The watch over the settlement is covered, and I don't know how many more chances you will have to get any rest in the days ahead."

"You give me good counsel, and you should take your own counsel, if you can. Tonight may be the only chance any of us has, and even that is uncertain," Rayden said, the thought stark and sobering.

She knew scant warning would come when the Arguntier emerged from the forest's shadows to unleash a massacre. There would barely be time for the warriors to line up and face the ominous tide when it rolled into Gessa lands.

"I will try," Eigon said. He looked to the other three warriors. "Go to Jarut, and fill your bellies. We need you three strong."

Alcedan nodded. "I will visit with those on watch while we are out, and make certain all know to keep their vigilance."

"I doubt any of them are faltering in that," Eigon said. "The storm cloud looms over all of us, and the first drops of rain have begun."

After pausing to drink another cup of mead, Alcedan and the others left the hall, leaving it draped in silence once more. With Eigon's personal retinue of warriors maintaining a watch over the settlement, few would be slumbering in the hall that night, at any given time.

The emptiness of the chieftain's hall added to the unease permeating the air. Looking around the hall, Rayden wished it could be full of sloshing mead cups, bawdy jests, boastful tales, and the camaraderie present among warriors bound by oath.

"We are on the brink of a fight like no other, Rayden," Eigon said. "Against something whose purpose we do not understand."

Swallowing another hunk of fish, Rayden looked back to Eigon. "There is no need to understand darkness or wickedness. They are akin to flames burning out of control ... in a fire that consumes everything in its path. They need only be doused."

"I never thought that my greatest battle would come in the dusk of my life, against a foe so murderous and devoid of honor," Eigon said. "The more I learn from you and see with my own eyes, the more I understand we are fighting for our very existence ... not of the tribes, but I fear of something much more ... of human kind."

"That is why there is nowhwere to run to," Rayden said, resolute. "We must ready ourselves to meet them on an open field of battle. Be patient, and let these monsters come forth. I do not think it will be long."

CHAPTER 7

Two days later, a few Gessa scouts came running to Eigon's hall in the gloaming of dusk, the sun dipping on the western horizon. Winded and caked with sweat, the men had pressed their bodies to the limit.

The scouts carried dire tidings. The Arguntier had begun to move in large numbers toward the border of Gessa territory. The scouts estimated that the core mass of the creatures would reach the edge of the forest just after nightfall.

Warriors from the settlement took up their weapons and rushed in haste to join the others gathered in the open swathe of land adjacent to the forest. Word spread fast among the tribal encampments.

Warriors from the Gessa, Runi, Arnan, Cirni, Rugara, Marren, and Lanassa streamed to the looming battlefield. Forming a great line facing the forest, the grim-faced warriors eyed the trees beneath overcast skies. Tendrils of wind whipped through their ranks.

The sharp, icy blasts, like lashes from abyssal spirits gathering in anticipation of blood, chilled Rayden where she stood at the center of the great line, among the Gessa. Were they facing a human army, Rayden would have deemed their chances strong.

Never before had she seen so many tribal warriors gathered in unity. Several thousand had massed on the battlefield; not as adversaries, but as allies.

The wall of tribal warriors stood as the only barrier between the fell creatures and large numbers of elderly, women, and children. There would be no spoils of war if the Arguntier prevailed, in the manner of a human army like that of the Teverens; with looting and the taking of slaves.

Slaughter alone awaited the most vulnerable of the Gessa, should the battle be lost. Rayden, Eigon, and other leaders among the tribal contingents had made certain to impress that cold fact on the minds of the warriors. No mercy would be given from the Arguntier.

Rayden knew it would be the only thing that would keep many warriors rooted in place, when they first set their eyes upon the monstrosities coming out of the forest.

Save for the sounds of gusting winds, the battlefield remained cloaked in silence. A pensive atmosphere permeated the night air. All knew it would not be much longer before fighting commenced.

An eerie cacophony filled the air, pouring from the shadows beneath the trees. The enveloping sound chilled Rayden's blood, prompting her to tighten her grips upon her sword and axe.

The feel of hilt and haft gave her a little comfort. Having sharpened iron at hand to wield against the horrors soon emerging from beneath the dark boughs, Rayden also held the confidence of having overcome three of the creatures in combat. In that aspect, she stood alone among the thousands of tribal warriors who would be facing the fearsome beasts for the first time.

The unsettling prelude did not last long.

Racing out of the trees, a broad line of Arguntier charged toward the tribal warriors. Like a hunting pack descending upon a herd of prey, the creatures bounded across the ground with killing intent and slavering jaws. Roars, barks, snarls and growls joined in a hideous din, surging with their approach.

The three that Rayden had faced required her utmost skill to overcome, and now well over a thousand of the creatures rushed toward the tribal lines. The ground between human and Arguntier shrinking rapidly, the warriors could do no more than hold their ground and brace for the inevitable collision.

Blood and flesh flying in all directions, the beasts tore into the ranks of the tribal warriors. A macabre serenade to the ash gray skies above, the screams and shrieks of terrified warriors in agony erupted up and down the line.

The line of warriors broke apart in moments, and a chaotic melee spread fast across the battlefield. Sword, spear and axe wielded in desperation, tribal warriors fought opponents far superior in speed and power. The numbers of human dead mounted quickly.

Rayden witnessed a man disemboweled only a few strides away, the talons of the beast assaulting him driven so deep they extended out his back. Gurgling, gagging up clumps of blood, and eyes wide with shock, the man toppled forward, falling into his monstrous slayer. The creature snarled, shoving the man aside, and tearing its claws free in a spray of blood.

The sight of their comrade's guts being torn out evoked a frenzied response by two tribal warriors. Rage overcoming their fear, they hacked with fury, their swords cutting into the beast. A third warrior drove his spear deep into the creature's back from behind.

Though riddled with wounds, the Arguntier did not fall right away. Swiping at one of the sword-bearing warriors with astonishing speed, it ripped the man's head off in one blow.

At last, the beast crumpled to the ground, but not before a couple of its ilk fell upon the two remaining human combatants.

The warriors stood no chance. One had his throat shredded in the crushing jaws of one Arguntier. Suffering several rapid, mauling strikes that left his face, chest, and stomach in tatters, the other warrior endured a savage mangling before the mercy of death overcame him.

Rayden could do nothing for the men. Grave peril loomed. Only fate spared her from another beast's attack, as it crashed into a spear-bearing warrior just to Rayden's left, slamming him into the ground.

Spinning around, Rayden attacked, unleashing strikes with both sword and axe on the beast's exposed side and back. Jumping back as soon as she completed the blows, she avoided the claws of the beast, tearing through the air where she had stood an instant before.

The warrior who had been taken to the ground, disarmed of his spear, drew a single-edged knife from his waist and slashed across the face of the beast. The attack pulled the beast's attention from Rayden, and it engulfed the hapless man's face within its jaws.

Rayden hacked into the creature's thick neck with her axe, but not before the thing had torn the flesh off most of the other warrior's face. The man quivered and shook, in throes of tremendous agony, before going still.

Leaping over the dead Arguntier and warrior, Rayden went to the aid of a warrior with a distinctive top knot of hair; the mark of a warrior of the Cirna tribe. An Arguntier with a broad muzzle that reflected the look of a massive war dog had turned from where it had just slain three other Cirna in a brutal fashion, a few of their mangled limbs scattered about the area where it stood.

Growling and baring its fangs, the creature squared toward Rayden and the Cirna warrior. Blood coated its face, chest, teeth and claws; none of the gore its own.

"Strike high, now!" Rayden shouted.

The warrior thrust his spear at the beast's face. The creature batted it aside before it struck, but in doing so left an opening low. Rayden lunged in, ducking and slashing at its left knee, opening a broad, deep gash.

The beast howled in pain and swatted at her, missing Rayden's head by less than a handspan. The Cirna warrior took advantage of the beast's distraction. Jabbing his spear up into the creature's maw, he put his weight behind the blow such that the tip barreled through the back of the creature's skull.

The creature tilted its head back, making choking sounds and grabbing at the embedded spear. With its throat exposed, Rayden moved in fast and slashed hard, the sharp iron cutting through the flesh of its neck and loosing a torrent of blood down the front of its body.

The creature sagged, went slack, and fell to the ground.

Rayden picked up a spear from the ground that had belonged to one of the slain Cirna, and tossed it to the warrior. He looked her in the eyes for a moment, gave a quick nod, and looked about for the next threat of attack.

Turning in place, keeping a fighting stance and weapons up, Rayden braced for the next onslaught. Arguntier raced about everywhere she looked, but none yet charged her, nor were any close enough to attack.

Despite Rayden's slayings, the course of the battle headed along a dismaying path, the tribal losses continuing to mount. Those who could join together in tandem to combat their massive adversaries gained a better chance to survive a little longer, while those finding themselves isolated against an Arguntier did not stand long.

Though terror filled the eyes and faces of many of the tribal warriors, Rayden could not see any signs of fleeing. The various contingents that had come to stand with the Gessa continued to fight back wherever they stood, despite the dismembered, maimed bodies of fellow warriors strewn all throughout their midst.

A few had gathered into larger clusters, and many pairs and trios had formed all over the battlefield, but a great number of warriors found themselves on their own, with Arguntier bounding and leaping all around them. For any warrior standing alone in the open ground, an attack could come at any moment, from any direction.

Swirling chaos enveloped Rayden. A host of cries bestial and human intermingled, forming a song of death that rose above the tempest like an incantation to a sepulchral deity. Blood flowed in abundance, with every moment rendering more patches of ground hazardous for the footing of those still alive.

Looking about, Rayden saw a leopard-headed Arguntier rushing up from behind a pair of warriors locked in desperate battle, using long spears to fend off an attack from a hulking Arguntier with a boar-like head. The charging Arguntier leapt, vaulting through the air and engulfing the unaware warrior, a crimson spray erupting under a barrage of claws.

The other warrior, distracted at the sudden attack on his comrade, took his eyes off the other Arguntier. In a burst of speed, the creature lunged in, swatted the spear aside, and decapitated the remaining warrior in one vicious, upward swipe.

Seeing the combined attack on the part of the beasts, Rayden knew the massacre would only accelerate.

Then, an unexpected development in the battle took place.

A chorus of howls filled the air, deep and sonorous, shrouding the battlefield and raising the hairs on the back of Rayden's neck. Moments later, a shadowy, winged form soaring overhead drew her eyes upward.

Astonished, Rayden fixed her gaze upon a large raven drifting across the night skies, far above the battlefield. Her eyes lingered upon the bird, realizing at once the nature of the creature.

The howling surging in volume, the edge of the woods erupted with movement. Dark, muzzled, two-legged shapes burst from the shadows in great numbers, fangs bared and golden eyes blazing with savage fury.

Racing toward the maelstrom in powerful, lengthy bounds, the Varganir charged the battlefield. The Arguntier reacted in swiftness, those not engaged against human warriors turning to face the oncoming wave.

The wolfish beings descended upon the bestial horde, up and down the battle lines. Jaws snapping, and claws slashing and gouging, the combatants began spilling each other's blood. Watching the huge creatures tearing into each other, Rayden judged the Varganir capable opponents for the Arguntier.

"Together! Gather together!" Rayden shouted at the top of her lungs, waving to the warriors scattered about in the sprawling melee to regroup.

Given a reprieve from inevitable slaughter, the warriors needed no encouragement. Rapidly, fighters from all the tribes streamed in toward Rayden.

Alcedan manifested soon after, adding his voice to hers. In his wake came others she recognized, including Jarut, Renna, Torasek and Gerran. Within a short span of time, other warriors of higher rank joined their assemblage, hailing from all the tribes, anchoring a growing, concentrated throng.

Several Arguntier rushed them from all around, and many warriors fell, but the cohesion in the massed group held. Either hewn down or fought off, the monstrous attackers failed to break into the dense circle of tribal warriors standing shoulder to shoulder.

Gradually decreasing in number, beset with the influx of Varganir from their back, and unable to break the regrouping tribal warriors apart, the Arguntier conceded the field of battle. Throughout the melee, the beasts began falling back toward the forest, heading for the refuge of the shadows.

Before many of them had gotten far, another mass of howling rose into the night. The new series of howls carried a different tone from that of the Varganir.

Looking in the direction of the forest, Rayden's eyes widened. Spanning the treeline marking the open swathe of ground, a dark, gray wave flowed into view.

Hundreds upon hundreds of large wolves hurtled toward the retreating Arguntier, blocking their path of escape. The Arguntier came to a halt, finding themselves trapped in a perilous state; between the Varganir and humans to their backs, and the rolling tide of wolves closing the distance from the front.

In full stride and force, the wolves assailed the Arguntier. Many clamping down on legs, others leaping high, slamming into their adversaries and snapping jaws tight upon throats and arms, the wolves' ferocity captivated Rayden.

No single wolf a match against one of the Arguntier, the lupine horde proved deadly when attacking in cohesion. Overwhelmed, many Arguntier were taken swiftly down to the ground.

Wolves swarmed the Arguntier who fell. With arms and legs seized fast between powerful jaws, the Arguntier could do little to stop wolves from ripping at their throats, midsections, and other exposed areas.

While the human warriors held back from entering the raging fray of wolves and Arguntier, the Varganir hurried to join their four-legged allies. Falling upon their enemy at the side of the wolves, the Varganir added their strength to the furious struggle.

The fighting did not come without great cost to both. Many wolves and Varganir suffered grievous, mortal wounds from the Arguntier, who still proved lethal, even in the final throes of death.

Whittling down in number and unable to evade the combined assault of the wolves and Varganir, the remaining Arguntier lashed out in a crazed wrath. Lethal whirlwinds, they scattered both wolf and Varganir alike, spreading the fighting all over the expanse of ground.

Rayden's breath caught in her throat. Not far from where she stood, one of the Arguntier, a towering, massive, bear-headed brute, grabbed up a wolf in each of its giant hands, while stomping down on a third.

With tremendous force it smashed the wolves together, before hurling the broken, dead bodies at an oncoming Varganir. Swinging an arm back, it hammered aside a lunging wolf, and advanced on the Varganir.

With one swipe, the beast opened the guts of the Varganir, following with several more mauling strikes that shredded the unfortunate creature's front side. Another Varganir slammed into the beast from behind, managing to knock it to the ground.

The Arguntier whipped its bulk about, throwing the Varganir off. Hitting the ground hard and scrambling to get to its feet, the Varganir bared its fangs at its assailant.

The bear-headed monstrosity had also gotten back up, trudging forward to press an attack.

Time froze for an instant, as recognition pierced Rayden. Not long before, she had stood before the wolfish being, receiving a bleak verdict at the culmination of an arduous test, one that had nearly cost Rayden her life.

Though the largest of the Varganir that Rayden had seen, Manak looked to stand little to no chance against the massive creature advancing on him. Embroiled in furious combat, the closest wolves and other Varganir could not come to Manak's aid in time.

Rayden broke out from the circular throng of warriors, ignoring the shouts directed at her from many of them. Bounding across the ground with all the speed she could muster, she concentrated on nothing other than the bear-headed creature in front of her.

The huge Arguntier reached Manak.

With a grating roar, the Arguntier took a swipe at Manak. Leaning back, Manak escaped the creature's sharp claws, but his assailant swept its arm back in a heavy blow that caught the Varganir squarely on the side of the head. The force sent Manak sprawling onto his back.

Rushing up from behind the Arguntier, Rayden looked on in horror. The Varganir chieftain did not move when the Arguntier stepped forward, looming over him and roaring. The bear-headed monstrosity reared back, its right claws poised to maul the defenseless Varganir.

Rayden propelled off her right leg, leaping forward. Hurtling through the air and thrusting with all her might, she drove her sword into the middle of the Arguntier's back. The beast threw its head back, bellowing in anger and pain.

Letting go of the sword, Rayden grabbed up a fistful of its coarse fur and yanked down hard. Lurching upward, she chopped down with her axe, landing the blade in the middle of its back.

Keeping the grip of her right hand tight, she continued her frenzied assault. Again and again she hacked away, iron cleaving into flesh and bone.

The Arguntier flailed and turned about, shrieking and trying to shake its relentless attacker free. Crying out, and with the muscles of her right arm strained to the limit, Rayden continued the barrage of strikes with her axe.

Rayden's axe opening a growing cavity in the beast's back, blood, bits of flesh, and fur flew. In a desperate attempt to stop the onslaught, the Arguntier threw itself onto its back.

Rayden let go, hitting the ground and rolling to the side, an instant before being crushed beneath the Arguntier against the hard ground. The creature howled when it slammed down, the sword blade lodged in its back driven even deeper.

When the beast lifted its torso up, and rotated toward her, Rayden greeted the Arguntier with an axe between the eyes.

Blood streaming down both sides of its muzzle from the fissure, the beast's eyes widened. Then, its body went slack, a long, rattling hiss coming from the depths of its throat. It slumped forward, muzzle oriented down, and became still.

Stepping atop the wide back of the creature, Rayden leaned over and pulled her sword free, and then ripped her axe free of the beast's head. Moving away from the Arguntier, she turned her attention to the unconscious Varganir lying nearby.

Kneeling at the side of Manak, she could tell he yet breathed. Relieved, she looked for any signs of bleeding or other injury.

Out of the corner of her eyes, Rayden caught movement toward her, first on her right side, and then to her left.

Rising to her feet and straddling Manak's prone form, Rayden raised her weapons up. Eyeing the two Arguntier coming in on either side of her, one with the head of a jackal and the other with the visage of a hyena, she girded herself.

The jackal-headed beast growled, while high-pitched sounds resembling laughter came from the other.

"I'll have no covenant with jackals and hyenas," Rayden said, a cold grin spreading on her face. "Know this lion does not abandon friends. Come, and do what you must."

A calmness descended over Rayden, her only thoughts on defending Manak against two adversaries about to attack her at once, from two sides.

The two Arguntier had only advanced a couple of paces when one fell under a swarm of wolves, and the other found itself taken to the ground by a pair of Varganir. Rayden looked about, seeing no more Arguntier nearby.

The battle coming to an end, the few remaining Arguntier fought to the death against the wolves and Varganir. Rayden kept her position over Manak, not about to leave him until the fighting concluded.

A low groan came from Manak. Rayden moved back to his side, keeping wary of her surroundings, though she did not hear the sounds of any more Arguntier in the air.

Eyes flickering open, Manak stared up at her. Bracing on his arms, the Varganir raised his torso up until he came to a sitting position. He looked at the corpse of the bear-headed Arguntier close by, with its back and skull exhibiting the wounds delivered from Rayden's weapons.

"You ... kill?" he asked in a low, strained-sounding voice.

Rayden nodded.

He looked toward the bodies of the two Arguntier that had just been slain, and then turned his head to Rayden. "You ... kill two more?"

"No, your wolves took one, and other Varganir killed the other," Rayden said.

"You did not leave," Manak replied,

Rayden shook her head. "No, I would not leave a friend."

Manak stared at her. "Two ... would have killed you."

"I know," Rayden said.

Manak's golden eyes remained fixed on Rayden a few moments longer, though she could not read whatever thoughts came to his mind.

Around them, the fighting had ceased. A few wolf growls, the distant voices of human warriors, the groans of wounded, and voices of Varganir from close proximity accompanied a subdued atmosphere.

Rayden gazed about. "The fighting is over. No Arguntier left this field alive."

"We stand with humans ... this day," Manak said.

"And humans stood with the Vargnir," Rayden replied, with a smile.

Manak, with a little difficulty, got up to his feet. The Varganir gathered around them, many with the fur about their muzzles soggy with blood. A number exhibited wounds, including many who had suffered deep lacerations and broad gashes.

Nearer to the woods, the surviving wolves massed. Though keeping their eyes on the Varganir, the creatures did not approach.

Farther away, the tribal warriors looked on with expressions of wonderment and apprehension. Though most kept their distance, a few had begun edging forward, Alcedan among their number.

A few of the Varganir cast growls in the direction of the human warriors, and tension began rising in the air.

Rayden raised her hand to Alcedan, signaling that no threat loomed. Alcedan nodded, and had the other warriors keep their distance.

"Friend of all Varganir," Manak said. With a little awkwardness, he rendered a bow to her. "I ... give you thanks."

Rayden gave a bow in return to the Varganir chieftain. "You have my thanks and my friendship. All the humans standing on this field owe their lives to the Varganir."

"Varganir owe lives to humans," Manak said. "All would die ... if beasts not killed."

"It was a threat to all of us," Rayden said.

Manak looked around at the Varganir now surrounding them, and then gazed out toward the mass of wolves outside the forest edge.

"Must return to lands," Manak said. "Must take our own."

Rayden knew what he meant. "We will stand back until it is done."

Manak nodded. "You are welcome in land of Varganir."

"As you are here," Rayden said.

The huge creature took a step forward. Though a little awkward, Manak gave Rayden a human-style embrace, his long arms enveloping her.

Rayden stepped away, the Varganir behind her parting to give her a path to her fellow humans. Walking through the throng of tall beings, she did not fail to notice many lowering their eyes and heads, showing a genuine respect to the human who had braved their lands and then defended their cheiftain.

Rayden made sure the human warriors kept back from the area where the Varganir and wolves had fought the Arguntier. The Varganir moved in and began taking up their own wounded and dead, including the wolves. Watching the creatures lifting up the bodies of their comrades and allies, Rayden sorrowed for the creatures.

A battle, no matter how victorious, exacted a terrible cost.

In silence, the Varganir departed from the field of battle. The wolves fell in with them, as they all left the open ground and disappeared from sight into the trees.

"A chance for a new age between humans and Varganir has been won," Rayden said to Alcedan, staring toward the quiet forest. "For all those who have given their lives this day, we must do what we can to see a new age take root, from here forward."

Alcedan met her eyes and nodded. "The blood of both our kind has been shed in abundance, and the victory belongs to both."

Rayden looked back over the battlefield, strewn with the bodies of humans and Arguntier. She braced herself for the inevitable revelation of who had fallen that day, knowing that she would soon be mourning many she counted as friends.

Survival her reward, a grim aftermath loomed.

***

The surviving warriors from all the tribes who had fought spread out across the battlefield, looking for human survivors among the vast carnage. Making certain no Arguntier drew breath, they drove their weapons into the bodies of the creatures wherever they lay.

Rayden joined Alcedan where he and many other warriors had gathered in a circle. Sorrow gripped her the moment she saw what had drawn them, seeing Eigon lying upon the ground, devoid of life's spark.

Reminding herself that she viewed only a shell, or husk, and not the man, Rayden did her best to maintain composure, though she could not hold back several tears that tumbled from her glisenting eyes.

Eigon had died the way he wished, standing on a field of battle, sword in hand, fighting for his people.

Rayden struggled to avert her focus from the grievous wounds he had suffered. She took note of his bloodied sword and the corpse of one of the beasts lying nearby. Eigon had opened the creature's throat, most likely after receiving the mauling strike that raked deep, gory furrows across his gut.

She closed her eyes and remembered the first day she had met Eigon, a much younger chieftain who had given her a warm hug and spoken in gentle tones when she had found herself in a cold, harsh nightmare as a child. Through the years she had seen him show such compassion to many others, while leading the Gessa with wisdom and strength.

Rayden had encountered a few rulers with good hearts on her travels, but Eigon's shined brightest of them all. Another void formed in her spirit, one that would carry a deep ache.

Eigon had been a man who had become part of her. In losing him, she lost a little more of herself.

"May you walk in the sun of Elysium," Rayden whispered, her eyes bright with tears, looking upon Eigon's face. "Thank you for all you have been to me, all these years. I will do all that I can to live out my life in a way that honors you."

Though a great many had been left heavy of heart seeing Eigon's body, it did not take long before Gessa warriors began calling for a new leader of the tribe to be chosen, right on the battlefield. Several began acclaiming their choices, and the commotion drew in all the Gessa warriors from around the field.

A multitude forming, the leaders of settlements moved to the forefront, their voices carrying the greatest weight of influence. Farther away, a great many of the warriors of other tribes stopped whatever they were doing and looked on with interest and curiosity.

Shouts rang out for many strong warriors among them, but two in particular carried into the air over the battlefield far more than the rest. It soon became clear that Rayden and Alcedan stood as the most popular choices of the tribe.

Then, even that balance began to tilt. Those who had acclaimed other warriors, seeing the choice narrowed to two, began to choose between the man and woman at the center.

A greater majority of those choices hailed Rayden, until it could not be disputed that she held the highest amount of support. Most every settlement leader acclaimed her. Even Jarut, who had exhibited tension with her on the hunt, called for her to lead the Gessa.

No woman had ever been acclaimed chieftain of the Gessa. The honor without precedent, Rayden found herself filled to the brim with powerful emotions at the outpouring of respect from warriors who had more than demonstrated their mettle in courage and blood.

Looking over to Alcedan, part of her expected a dispute. Other than Rayden, he held the strongest amount of support. In addition, he had been the one living among the Gessa, day after day, year after year, not her.

She had been summoned by Eigon to aid with the encroaching aggression on the part of the Runi. No indication had been given that she would stay. If anything, most could assume she would be heading onward one day, once the conflict came to an end.

Rayden understood if the fast-developing situation chafed on Alcedan and wounded his pride. She could only hope that it did not drive him to recklessness.

If things came to blows, she would have a wounded heart in fighting him, but she would meet any attack with sword and axe.

The look in his eyes spoke loudly. Disappointment reflected there, but she could see that he would accept the decision of the tribe.

His willingness to submit to the will of the majority in the tribe became accented a moment later. Holding her eyes, he gave a slight nod of his head. No vitriol or ill intent could be found in his gaze or expression.

The moment brought her everything Rayden needed to see, to make the choice that followed. She looked into his eyes a moment longer, finding surety in her assessment, and then thrust her sword high into the air.

"Warriors of the Gessa, I would speak to you now," she called out, drawing all eyes to her.

A hush rippled outward from where she stood, until the mass of warriors in the vicinity had given her their full attention.

"We have fought together. And we have seen far too many good, courageous warriors fall on this field," Rayden exclaimed, sweeping the multitude with an iron gaze. "There is something to be gained in this hour of victory over an evil that would seek to destroy Gessa, Arnan, Cirni, Rugara, Marren, Runi, and the Lanassa alike, to the last.

"The warriors of seven tribes stood together to defend their people on this field of battle. Several fingers close to make a fist. All of you have seen this day that seven tribes can come together, and forge great strength.

"I must soon return to the south, to seek the destruction of an even greater evil. A worthy, honorable warrior stands among you ... one with the wisdom and discipline to lead you well. One who can continue the path that Eigon led you on."

Rayden turned in a deliberate fashion, and pointed her sword straight at Alcedan. Surprise reflected in his eyes, and not a little confusion.

"I give my acclaim to Alcedan, to lead the Gessa and build upon what Eigon has given to all of you," she declared. "Eigon gave you a treasure beyond any jewel, or any piles of silver and gold. You are a people who have been guided along a path of wisdom, fortitude, and resolve ... you have not been led into acts of cruelty and barbarity ... you have grown strong and are a beacon to others.

"Alcedan must now take you forward on that path, and in my heart I know he is capable of greatness. I call upon him now, to live up to what I see in him, in this dark, trying hour."

Rayden paused, looking out over the faces of the Gessa warriors, many of whom she knew well. She raised her sword up again.

"Join me now, and acclaim Alcedon as the new chieftain of the Gessa!"

From settlement leaders to warriors at the back of the multitude, weapons began rising into the air to join Rayden's blade. More and more added to their number, the voices of the warriors calling out the name of Alcedon.

Rayden listened to the swelling cheer with gladness, her heart brimming with conviction that Alcedan would continue what Eigon had begun. She also had no desire to settle and lead a tribe, no matter how unprecedented the choice of her had been.

Rayden's path led in a different direction, but she wanted to be sure the right individual followed Eigon as leader of the Gessa. Her instincts told her Alecadan possessed the qualities needed, if not the range of experience ideal for guiding an entire tribe.

Consensus behind Alcedan, the Gessa had a new chieftain.

Accepting praise from surrounding warriors, Alcedan made his way over to Rayden.

Leaning in and speaking in a low voice meant only for her, he said. "I would have gladly recognized you as our chieftain. You are the best choice among our people. I will never forget what you have done here, and I will give everything I have in me to live up to your faith in me."

"I know you will," Rayden answered.

The two embraced, and then the Gessa spread out to begin attending to the dour task of gathering up their dead. All the warriors who had fallen would be given to the fire and honored, while the corpses of the Arguntier were left to rot, wherever they lay.

***

The meat of sacrificed bulls hissed and popped in the embrace of flames. Gessa warriors feasted under the deep night sky, a number of warriors from the other tribes among them.

The late night air held an atmosphere filled with a blend of emotions. While mourning the fall of Eigon and so many friends, brothers, sons, and fathers, the warriors also celebrated survival and victory, and the rise of Alcedan as the new Gessa chieftain.

Ale and mead in copious amounts flowed down the throats of men and women. Rayden indulged in both meat and drink, eager to feel a sense of living after facing so much darkness and death that day.

She moved about, partaking in the camraderie of warriors

around the fires. No matter how skilled a warrior might be, or how much status one of them held, all the warriors stood as equals in the firelight, sharing a bond forged of blood and battle.

More than once, she lent her voice to songs being sung in praise of fallen warriors, though she choked up a little at a powerful one honoring Eigon. Following that song, she downed another cup of mead, wanting to try and forget pain for just a little while.

Rayden received warm welcomes and praise wherever she roamed, though inside she wished she could be anonymous; just another warrior grateful to live another day. She accepted the accolades with a humble air, returning praise to the warriors she recognized and had seen on the battlefield.

The ale and mead empowered a sense of well-being. Her thoughts took mercy upon her, turning to the moment rather than dwelling upon all the difficult things that had happened, and worries toward the future.

Emptied for a little while from sorrow and concern, she allowed a more primal urge to draw her focus. A hunger needed to be fed; one that would remind her that she yet lived and could even thrive.

Rayden locked eyes with a tall, broad-shouldered warrior of the Rugara she had drank some ale with earlier in the night. No craven, his exploits had been related to her of how he had stepped into the path of an Arguntier rushing up behind another warrior, and hewn the creature down with two sword strikes.

A grin came to his face, as another rose upon hers. Desires left unspoken, invitation and intent stood clear enough.

Striding forward, Rayden gripped the warrior strongly on the arm and pulled him away from the fireside. A startled look crossed his face for a moment, finding himself being tugged in the direction of the trees, but his expression eased soon enough.

She paused only to spread her cloak on the ground and add

his to hers. Taking up a fistful of his hair, she pulled his head back and thrust her tongue deep into his mouth.

Tongues intertwining, she let herself immerse in the moment. Heat spiraling from within, she pulled him down on his back, atop the cloaks.

In rough fashion, she pulled his tunic and other clothing off, revealing a muscular body. She took her own garb off, relishing the cool touch of the air all over her skin.

Reaching down, she brought him to a level of hardness rivaling the trees surrounding them. When he tried to roll her over, she forced him onto his back, and took control, mounting him.

Burning with the fires of being alive, Rayden joined with the warrior who had shared the battlefield with her that day. In ebbs and flows of intensity, Rayden embraced every moment of passion with fervor; and a harmony of mind, body, and soul.

She rode the warrior through several waves of intense pleasure, throwing her head back at the crescendos and pressing tight with her thighs. When the fires inside her had been consummated, the warrior utterly spent, Rayden leaned down and gave him another extended kiss.

Sweat beading all over her skin, she slowly rolled to her back and stared upward. The sounds of his breathing slow and peaceful, the warrior succumbed to exhaustion and fell asleep.

Savoring the tranquility and glimmer of the stars, Rayden listened to the winds passing through the leaves above. A sense of timelessness passed over her, bringing along with it a feeling of weightlessness, akin to floating upon the waters of an ethereal ocean.

***

Dark as the shadows pooled about it, beneath dense foliage allowing only a fraction of the moon's rays through, the winged emissary loosed a cry that grabbed Rayden's attention. Fixing its black eyes upon her, it cried again, the sound carrying an air of insistence and intent.

Rayden looked over and saw that the Rugaran warrior still remained in a deep sleep. Keeping quiet, she donned her clothes and leather boots, leaving her cloak beneath the slumbering warrior.

The bird flapped its wings and took to the air, circling about and leading her back to the battlefield. In the depths of night, devoid of any living presences, the stillness gave off an unsettling milieu.

The bird landed near one of the dead Arguntier, one with a dog-like head.

Rayden walked over and gazed down upon the carcass of the bestial invader. Looking at its extensive jaws, and the lengthy claws it possessed, in a body of such height and mass, she regarded it in the light of unwavering reality.

Rayden did not wish to think what the fate of the Gessa would have been had not the aid of the Varganir arrived to help the tribes avoid what would otherwise have been certain genocide.

She did not flinch when the shimmering, translucent form of Dreaghen manifested to her right, looking as if formed out of moonlight.

"Thank you for guiding the Varganir to the battlefield," Rayden said, thinking of the raven she had seen right before they emerged from the forest.

"The Varganir bore little love for humans, and even less for human sorcerers, but a certain warrior opened their ears to listen to wisdom," Dreaghen replied.

"I had believed my journey availed nothing," Rayden said.

"You planted a seed that sprouted and grew fast," Dreaghen said. "I merely offered my help in guidance, and reminded them that the Arguntier had gathered in force against you ... a force that would come visit the Varganir once it had finished with humans. But make no mistake, my words would have rang hollow had it not been for what you had done."

"You still have my gratitude, sorcerer," Rayden said, finding that she liked the mysterious figure a little more.

"And you have mine," Dreaghen said.

"I know you do not appear for purposes of idle chat," Rayden said, smirking. "Why did you rouse me from the first night of good sleep I could have gained in a long time?"

"It could not wait. I have unraveled the mystery, and it portends something dire about the Teveren Imperator," Dreaghen said. "Let me show you the proof of what I believed before, first, before we speak more on that."

Dreaghen began chanting in a language Rayden did not understand. At first, nothing happened, but as the chant continued slow pulses and movements occurred all along the corpse of the beast lying before her.

Catalyzed by Dreaghen's power, a shifting of form began transpiring in the carcass. Having witnessed the body of shapeshifters ebb back into human forms more than once before, she found herself both apprehensive and astonished at what took place before her eyes.

The body's metamorphosis held no human form at its culmination. Back and leg structures altered, changing the body from two-legged to four.

When the shifting, cracking, and pulsing became still, a massive canine beast lay upon the ground before Rayden. Coarse, dark fur covered a body rippling with pronounced muscularity. Eyeing its long legs and broad paws, she had no doubts of the creature possessing great speed; just as its wide muzzle and thick neck testified to bone-crushing jaw strength.

"As I thought, and had told you before, these were

just animals in their origin, all along," came the voice of Drehagen, lower, and imbued with a weary edge. "I have suspected such, for some time. And with this one, they had a far reach to find such a host. These are the largest predators roving the Great Plains ... far, far to the north and east." "Then what made it into the thing it was, on this battlefield?" Rayden asked, staring down at the brawny, huge canine form. She could only imagine encountering such a monstrosity on open plains.

"A spirit of the damned held dominion over this creature," Dreaghen said. "A spirit of the most brutal kind. Spirits filled with a hunger for violence, cruelty and killing. Even worse, these spirits carried the madness of the abyss within them. No damned soul can avoid being tainted with the greatest darkness ... the infinite blackness in the realms beyond that swallows such wicked souls."

"Then they could change form ... from that of an animal, to one such as we faced," Rayden said, drawing the obvious conclusion.

"The power of darkness gave them the ability to change form," Dreaghen confirmed. "Combine the mind of a spirit filled with bloodlust, madness and an endless craving for killing with the mind of a feral, fearsome predator ... and you have the type of creatures that you and the tribal people faced."

"But to create hundreds of these dreadful things," Rayden said, lifting her eyes to take in the battlefield, still laden with the bodies of the creatures. "The power that reflects ... to have them act together ... to carry out aims. These things had a leader ... one that overshadowed the madness you speak of. They did not act as wild beasts or raving mad beings. They were encircling the tribes, and they attacked here in force, like an army. Something else governed them, and is at hand."

"Which makes me fear what the Imperator is preparing

in the heart of the Teveren lands," Dreaghen said. "It may be something well beyond my ken to fathom."

Rayden looked to the skies, disquieted at the thought. "Then it would be even farther from my ken."

"Both of us must try to learn what we can, by whatever means we can," Dreaghen said.

"Agreed," Rayden said. "Our fight is far from over."

A horrendous cataclysm had been averted, only to have an even greater one threaten just ahead.

"I shall do what I can to aid in this fight," Dreaghen said.

"As will I," Rayden said, looking over to the sorcerer.

With a somber look on his face, he nodded, and faded from sight. Rayden looked around at the Arguntier corpses, recognizing one more task that needed to be done before the next steps could be taken.

CHAPTER 8

Knowing with certainty what the creatures had been, and what had transformed them, Rayden took it upon herself at dawn's light to gather everyone she could for a task she deemed necessary.

Alcedan did not hesitate in giving his support to her aim, resulting in the cooperation of most all the men and women of the Gessa throughout the morning. A large number of warriors from the other tribes also gave their assistance in the laborious effort.

Stacked about with wood, the bodies of the Arguntier were dragged and piled into great heaps, and then set afire. Masses of smoke rising into the skies, a noxious stench filled the air.

Though Dreaghen had given no warnings of anything happening with the corpses, Rayden did not want to take any chances with a creation of dark sorcery. She had more than enough experience with dead things being reanimated.

A forest of flames devoured the bodies of the abominations, consuming all lingering concerns within Rayden's mind. She stood vigil and watched the fires until they finally died down, and the winds began scattering the piles of ash left behind.

* * *

Rayden found Alcedan standing in the middle of the battlefield, staring west toward the forest. The look on his face held the kind of weight usually found on a man or woman much more advanced in years.

Wind swept across the open field, as if seeking to brush away the memories of the carnage.

Alcedan looked over to Rayden as she approached. The ghost of a smile came to his lips.

"I thought I might find you here," Rayden said.

It had been several days since the great battle. The other tribes had returned to their own lands, and most of the Gessa had dispersed to their settlements; save for a few such as Alcedan.

"I am tethered to this place, no matter where I may go," Alcedan said. "A part of me will always be here."

Rayden nodded. "The terrible price a warrior pays, over and over again."

"I didn't think he would die," Alcedan said, looking away to the forest, likely to try and hide the glistening she caught in his eyes. "Not like that."

Closing her eyes for a moment, Rayden thought of Eigon, the man who had given her sanctuary as a child. A wave of sorrow clenched inside, as it had every day since the battle.

"With great men like him, it is hard to accept that they can ever die," Rayden said, in a low voice. "It is hard to believe a man with so much honor would be made to suffer such an end. It is a difficult truth that so many of the wicked die in peace, in their sleep, while many of the good are put through great trial and agony before dying."

"And yet the gods do nothing about that," Alcedan replied, a bitter edge to his voice.

"I do not know the mind of the gods," Rayden said. "But

perhaps the end of this life is not where the final account takes place."

"As unjust as this world is, it is hard for me to think of an unseen world having the justice that is absent here," Alcedan said. He then shook his head. "No ... no ... it is not for me to question the ways of gods."

"I never stop questioning," Rayden said. "We all find ourselves in this uncertain, often merciless world. It is hard to reconcile what we see, with what we are told. I would think an immortal god could suffer a few questions from mortals caught in the strife and turmoil of a handful of years."

"What now, Rayden?" Alcedan asked, his face looking more like an anxious young man, than a chieftain of a strong tribe. "We have survived here, but you have spoken many tales of a great shadow to the south. One even greater than the threat we faced here."

"A greater threat for certain, and the source of what we resisted here," Rayden stated, her tone grim.

"What do these Teverens seek?" Alcedan said.

"To subjugate, to enslave, to rule without rival," Rayden said. "It is a disease afflicting many of the powerful in the world. They carry a hunger that can never be filled."

"A messenger came from the Borreni, just this past night," Alcedan said. "They find themselves in a dire situation. The shadow to the south that you spoke of is spreading into their lands. They speak of border raids, of slaves taken, and entire settlements put to fire."

Located on the southernmost edge of tribal lands, and bordered to the west by the Tega, the Borreni stood on the cusp of the Teveren Empire. It came as no surprise to Rayden that the Imperator had already begun to move upon tribal lands; the first few rain drops of an imminent downpour.

"You will have to face this shadow, whether you go to it or

wait for it to come to you," Rayden said.

"I know so little of it," Alcedan said, the youth showing in his expression once more. "I have not traveled where you have. These Teverens are unlike any tribe."

"It would benefit you to understand more of their nature, and what they would do in all the tribal lands," Rayden said. "It is also best for you to see Teveren wickedness with your own eyes."

"How can that be done?" Alcedan said.

"We go there, without delay," Rayden answered. She added, with a rueful air, "It will not take long to find what you need to see."

CHAPTER 9

Rayden, Alcedan, and a few warriors from his new household retinue traveled southward, taking a similar route to the one she had taken when summoned north by Renna and Pallan. Hunting and foraging along the way, the group kept their strength up and maintained a brisk pace.

Reaching Tega lands, they proceeded to the hall of Grogner. The Tega chieftain received them amiably enough, though concern deepened on his face as he listened to their words.

Upon hearing of the battle in the north with the Arguntier, and Eigon's death, he asked the new arrivals to stay a night before continuing their journey. Rayden anticipated the slight delay and did not mind the invitation, knowing the Tega chieftain would be generous in his accomodations.

As she expected, Grogner held a sumptuous feast for them that night in his long hall. Mead flowed and the meat of a sacrificed bull was served; to honor Eigon, and seek the gods' favor for Alcedan.

Rayden and Alcedan were seated in the places of honor nearest to Grogner and his wife Carratha. The two ate and drank to their fill, while answering the chieftain's many questions regarding the events in the north.

Learning a little themselves, Rayden was pleased to hear that the settlements of former slaves had integrated well in Tega lands. Grogner expressed great satisfaction in the relations between his people and the new populace, and that the settlements had done whatever had been requested of them in helping to keep a watch on Tega borders.

No Teveren raids had occurred yet, but Groger believed they would be attempted soon. Tidings of the Borreni's misfortunes had the Tega in a full state of alertness.

Many priestesses among the Tega had reported visions of a coming storm. Those casting the sticks spoke no differently, telling of a dark threat to the Tega rising in the near future.

Late in the night, Grogner and Carratha finally took their leave. Rayden, Alcedan and the others in their group were given places in the hall for sleeping.

While a few of their number remained awake, talking and drinking with a few of Grogner's household warriors, Rayden and Alcedan took advantage of a chance to get a night's rest. Settling onto a straw-stuffed palette in the warm hall, surrounded by warriors, and having a roof over her head, Rayden soon drifted asleep.

***

A woman with dark, flowing hair broke into a run at the sight of Rayden striding toward the new settlement populated with former slaves of the Teveren Empire.

"It would seem our paths cross again," Doros greeted, after they embraced.

Rayden looked into the unusual, cat-like eyes of a woman she respected and deemed a friend. Her grin widened.

"You are still here?" Rayden asked.

"I have not resumed my own quest," Doros said. "Too much has been happening here. The Teveren snake coils around us."

"We will see to cutting the head off that snake soon enough,"

Rayden said, a steely glint in her eyes.

"I desire to see that, given what I have witnessed," Doros said. "They have begun border raids."

"As I have heard," Rayden said.

"I would see this Teveren matter settled before I venture onward," Doros said.

"Then may it be that I can go with you, when you do pursue your quest" Rayden said.

"It may be that we can visit that warrior queen of the Western Isles," Doros said, grinning.

"I would like that, very much so," Rayden said. "Though I cannot remember the last time I traveled somewhere just to see something for myself."

"Maybe it is time you undertake such a journey," Doros said.

"Maybe so," Rayden said. Then, she laughed. "Besides, I can think of no one better to go to the Western Isles with than you. We will need to cross some water."

"The waters of an ocean too ... a welcome challenge," Doros said. "After all, I have only had some lakes and streams to ply in our time on these Tega lands."

"I trust that it has gone peacefully, between the Tega and the new settlement," Rayden said.

Doros nodded. "Between us, yes. All minds are turned toward the south, and the growing shadow of the Teverens."

Rayden looked toward the sprawling mass of huts and enclosures. "It would seem much has been built here."

"It has taken much labor to clear land and build dwellings," Doros said. "It will take more time to bring a harvest from the land, but the forest is filled with an abundance of game, and the lakes and streams team with fish. We have been able to keep everyone fed."

"I'm sure your bow has helped in that," Rayden said.

"It has provided meat for a great many," Doros said.

Rayden stared toward the dwellings, looking for a certain young boy she had missed greatly. Some young children ran about at play, but no sign of Hamilcar could be found.

"You are looking for Hamilcar?" Doros asked.

"I would like to see him, though I do not have long here," she said.

"He is away with Crassor, on a hunt," Doros said. "He will be back by nightfall."

"When I have to be moving onward," Rayden said, dispirited with the news of the boy's absence.

"I am sorry," Doros said. "I know how much he means to you."

"Sometimes I feel my life is not my own," Rayden said, thinking of the summons that had pulled her north, to confront the Arguntier.

"I do understand," Doros replied, placing a hand on her friend's shoulder. "And know that we all understand why you had to leave and go to the Gessa."

"I am honored to count you a friend," Rayden said.

"Speaking of your friends ... ", Doros said, looking past Rayden.

With rapid strides, a tall, broad-shouldered man with a thick beard approached them. Grinning wide, he took Rayden into a tight hug.

"Annocrates, the sight of you gladdens me," Rayden exclaimed.

"Seeing you again is like the sun in the morning," Annocrates replied. "We have all missed you, including the boy. I regret to say he is on a hunt today, under the eye of Crassor."

"Crassor may be thick-headed and unpleasant, I doubt there are many better suited to show him the ways of hunting," Rayden said, thinking of the irascible warrior. While she had often found herself at odds with Crassor, he had proved to be a warrior she would not hesitate to have at her side in a battle.

"Crassor is a temperamental ox, but he is our ox," Annocrates said, chuckling. "The boy may not enjoy Crassor's wit or charm, but he will learn to hunt well. Of that I am certain."

Doros laughed. "I did not think I ever would hear the words wit or charm when speaking of Crassor!"

"He has his ways, but he is a warrior loyal to those who he counts as his people," Rayden said. "His people are now those of this settlement."

"Very true, and he would seek to cut anyone in half who would try to harm us," Annocrates said.

"That outweighs his shortcomings in wit and charm," Rayden said. "So how fares Hamilcar?'

"The boy does well, and will be very eager to see you," Annocrates said. "There is not a day that goes by when he fails to mention your name.

The news came as both a relief and heartache. A part of Rayden carried worry that the boy would harbor ill-feelings for her sudden departure. Yet given how much she wished she did not have to leave him behind when summoned by Eigon, it stung to hear that he spoke of her each day.

"He truly understands why I had to go?" Rayden asked, wanting confirmation from the man she had entrusted the boy to.

"At first, he was very upset," Annocrates said. "But it was more from missing you, than what you had to do. He understands why you had to leave."

"There is so much to tell of what happened in the north," Rayden said, looking from Annocrates to Doros. "You both will find it hard to believe much of it, I fear."

"I doubt that," Doros said. "These times are like sailing into unexplored waters."

"What brings you back to us?" Annocrates asked.

"The Teverens, and the need for the new chieftain of the Gessa, Alcedan, to understand their threat," Rayden said.

"New chieftain?" Annocrates asked.

"Eigon fell, in battle against unnatural creatures," Rayden said. "The creatures that were the reason I was summoned."

"I am sorry to hear of this," Doros said.

"As am I," Annocrates said.

"He fell defending the people he loved," Rayden said. "Would that all warriors could meet death in such a way."

"I could ask for no more myself," Annocrates said.

"Nor I," Doros said.

"I am convinced the Teverens were behind the evil that fell upon the Gessa lands," Rayden said. "Alcedan must see what price the Gessa would pay should the Teverens sweep north."

"It will not take long for you to show him that cost," Annocrates said, his mood darkening. "They raid into Borreni lands, and it will not be long before they raid into ours."

"They are less than a day's march from where we stand," Doros said in a grim tone. "As Annocrates says, it will not be long before they begin entering Tega lands."

"A messenger came to Alcedan, telling of the raids into the lands of the Borreni," Rayden said.

Doros nodded. "Settlements have been burned to the ground, slaves taken, and others slaughtered. A strong force of Teverens is encamped on their borders."

"I must take Alcedan into Borreni lands, without delay," Rayden said.

"I would go with you," Doros said.

"As would I," Annocrates said. "When they have finished with the Borreni, the Teverens will be in our lands. Perhaps we can learn more."

"We will not be taking a large war band, just Alcedan, some warriors of his new household, and myself," Rayden said.

"We will bring a few from the settlement," Doros said.

"Leave Crassor and those of his mind-set behind," Rayden cautioned. "We go to scout the area."

"Understood," Annocrates replied.

***

Coils of smoke beckoned to Rayden with dark promises of finding what she had come to seek, inviting her to come closer, if she dared. Not born of the fires of any hearth, the cluster of tendrils snaking upward boasted of war and violence.

Rayden hurried toward the ascending smoke, the rest of the group increasing their gait to keep up with her. Making their way to the top of a hill, Rayden, Alcedan, Doros, Annocrates and those with them found an overlook to observe a distressing sight below.

Huts blazed and bodies littered the ground. Most of the dead looked to be men, though the corpses of a few boys lay among them. Weapons still rested in a few of their hands, indicating that recent fighting had taken place.

A line of frightened-looking people faced a number of well-armed figures. Their helms and segmented armor gleaming in the sunlight, the soldiers had the women, children, and a few elderly men surrounded.

An old woman huddled with a young one, the latter's clothing in tatters barely sufficient to cover her nakedness. The pair's heaving sobs and downcast eyes kindled a furor within Rayden.

She knew the young woman had endured the horror that so many women did at the hands of a conquering force; a violent invasion of the most intimate and vulnerable realm, whose effects would persist long after the physical pains had ebbed.

The older woman, likely the mother, would suffer a different kind of tribulation. Having been helpless to protect her daughter, the old woman would carry a lifelong burden that no words could console.

Rayden's hands found the hilt of her sword and haft of her axe, tightening upon them. Watching the two suffering women, everything within her wanted to charge down from the hill and exact a blood-heavy vengeance on the soldiers around them.

Reining in her fury, Rayden continued with her observation.

One in the long garb of a priest, and the other in a tunic and cloak, a couple of men took slow steps together at the forefront of the captives. Eyeing the Borreni survivors with scrutiny, the two men exchanged a few words among each other.

Two groups were formed from the mass of captives. Both had shackles and chains placed upon them.

The larger of the two went with the cloaked man. The smaller group, containing about half of the children, were taken away under heavy escort with the priest figure.

Rayden's gut clenched watching the faces of the Borreni streaming with tears, a hapless lot shuffling on their way into a future of bondage in a foreign land. She let the images of the enslaved Borrenni become etched in her mind, each one girding her resolve to confront any obstacle until the Teveren Imperator's power was shattered.

Both groups headed southward. Having been unassigned to either contingent, a handful of elderly men and women still remained behind.

A tall soldier in more ornate attire than the others, with a high, horizontal crest of horsehair atop his helm, gave a nod toward a few soldiers to his right.

Withdrawing their short swords, and without hesitation, the soldiers moved in and began slashing open the throats of the sobbing, begging captives. The piteous cries of the doomed captives wrenched at Rayden's heart, though distance rendered her unable to do anything to save them.

Looking over at Alcedan, she could see raw anger boiling within his eyes, mixed with a deep sadness. His gaze told her everything.

She knew he understood the nature of the shadow now spreading into tribal lands; and what fate the Gessa would meet at Teveren hands, should the Imperator prevail.

With the last of the elderly captives lying dead, the higher-ranking soldier shouted orders to the others. In moments they had gathered into an orderly column, before marching in the direction their comrades had taken.

"Now, it is time to get a look at their encampment, and then we can decide what to do," Rayden stated in a firm manner, getting the attention of the others and moving out from their hilltop perch.

With somber expressions, Alcedan and the others followed her in silence, none uttering a word.

Following the large Teveren contingent at a distance, Rayden and the others kept to cover. The slower pace of the newly-enslaved encumbered the progress of the Teverens, and it took well over half a day's march to reach their main encampment.

Nestled among a cluster of high hills, the rectangular encampment could quarter around a thousand soldiers with ease. Arranged in the meticulous order typical of the Teverens, several lines of elongated tents formed a great square, at the center of which stood a couple of larger pavilions.

Around the perimeter, an earthen ditch had been excavated, the debris from which used to build up a high rampart. Latrine trenches situated away from the main rows of tents had been dug inside the ramparts.

The smoke from several cookfires wafted skyward. Honing blades, conversing, practicing at weapons, or standing sentry, a considerable number of Teveren soldiers were in view, all throughout the encampment.

A throng of pack mules occupied a section of open ground in the northeast quarter of the camp. Rayden could see no evidence of the kind of horses used for mounted combat.

The presence of strictly baggage animals eliminated the possibility of a cavalry element, giving Rayden less to weigh in regard to a possible assault.

The return of the Teveren contingent raised a little commotion. Soldiers in the camp greeted their returning comrades, while the one with the horizontal crest headed toward the largest pavilion in the center.

It did not take long for the slaves to be ushered to a holding area set deeper in the camp, and the soldiers from the raid to disperse among their tents.

"We can summon more than enough warriors to storm that encampment," Annocrates said. "Just from our settlements alone."

"I would think the Borreni would want to join in any attack," Rayden said. "It was their dwellings burned, their blood spilled, and their people put in chains."

"We can get a messenger to them," Doros said. "It is said they are not a numerous tribe, but I know they would welcome a chance to fight back against the Teverens."

"When should an attack happen?" Annocrates said, turning to Rayden.

"The Teverens will not wait here long, with that many new slaves," Rayden said. "They will break camp and march soon. We should strike them at night. No later than the next day or two.

"If we can muster the numbers, we can take them swiftly if we press the attack on all sides at once. Throw them into confusion fast and the battle is won."

Turning, she studied Alcedan's face as he gazed upon the Teveren encampment. She knew he had not seen anything like it, with its uniformity of arrangement.

"So much iron ... every man of theirs is clad in helm and armor?" Alcedan asked in a low voice, glancing over to Rayden.

"Yes," she answered. "And what you see down there is not a full legion. What you see is a detachment. A Teveren legion is much larger than the force in that encampment."

Alcedan said nothing in reply, but she could see the astonishment in his eyes. He had seen the Teveren cruelty and hunger for mastery of others. Now he witnessed a hint of their power. She needed him to understand both lessons.

"They bring several of these ... legions ... into battle?" Alcedan asked.

"Sometimes one, sometimes more than one," Rayden said. "The day they march on the north, they will combine many into the invasion."

Alcedan looked from Rayden back to the encampment, but not before she caught a shimmer of anxiousness in his gaze.

"Do not forget, Alcedan ... they are of flesh and blood, and nothing like the Arguntier we faced together," Rayden said. "The Teverens are human in every way. No different than you or I. They can be beaten. The settlement of former slaves in Tega lands stands strong testimony to that."

"If they had a hundred warriors for each one of ours, I would still fight them," Alcedan said. He looked back to Rayden, a fire kindled in his eyes. "I would like to begin that fight now, and I know our people cannot remain idle and wait until these Teverens march upon them."

"Then let us spill Teveren blood, and see every captive from that settlement freed," Rayden said, keeping her face firm, though inside she celebrated Alcedan's response. Turning her attention to the others, she declared, "We will go now to summon the others. How far is it to one of the larger Borreni settlements?"

"Not far from the path we took, to the north and east just after crossing into their lands," Doros said.

"Then hasten to them," Rayden said. "More than a few of the warriors there will show interest in joining us."

"We will lay their camp to waste," Annocrates said. "They must answer for what they do."

Rayden set her eyes upon the Teveren camp, glaring.

"They will answer with their blood, Annocrates," Rayden said. "We will have the advantage in numbers, and they will have no warning. They will not be able to form up in the lines they are trained for.

"We will hit them from all sides ... in a great storm that no Teveren can escape."

***

A swarm descended on the Teveren encampment out of the night. Preceded with a hail of javelins at all four of the camp's entrances, sentries barely had time to shout before the attackers took full control of the portals.

Rushing through the openings in the earthen rampart on all sides of the camp, the force of former slaves and Borreni warriors flooded the encampment. Teverens stumbling half-awake from the tents nearest the ramparts in response to the swelling cacophany met swift deaths.

Distance no longer keeping the Teveren soldiers free of her axe and sword, Rayden channeled her boiling fury into each and every blow. One after another Teveren falling to her blades, Rayden pushed deeper into the encampment, leaving a trail of dead in her wake.

Around her, fires blazed from tents set afire, casting a reddish glow over the chaotic melee. Men cried out in alarm and weapons clanged.

Caught unprepared and overrun, and unable to don their armor, Teverns fought in plain tunics against the horde of former slaves and Borreni flowing through the lines of tents. Many

Teverens resorted to using whatever they could grab up, making use of helms, entrenching tools, pots, pans, iron flasks and anything that could be wielded against the maurading attackers.

Attacked on all four sides of the camp at once, and heavily outnumbered, the Teverens fell into confusion and disorder. Unable to muster solid lines of defense, the soldiers were prevented from fighting the kind of battle they had been trained for; just as Rayden intended from the outset.

Leaving the swirling melee among the tents, Rayden hacked and slashed her way toward the large pavilion at the center of the camp. Teverens kept rushing at her, with two of the most skilled she had encountered in the fighting attacking within view of the pavilion's entrance.

Cutting the pair of swordsmen down, Rayden knew she neared the quarry she sought.

The last adversary to charge her was a massive, thick-bodied war dog.

Rippling with muscle it bounded across the ground, its dark form outlined in the glow of fires. Rayden came to a stop, waiting until the last possible moment before the beast barreled into her.

With a quick shift forward that caught the war dog an instant before it leapt at her, Rayden delivered a powerful thrust of her sword between the beast's broad, open jaws. The war dog's own momentum magnified the impact of the impaling strike, the iron tip exploding out the back of the creature's head.

Her axe followed without delay, arcing down fast, the force driving the blade into the midst of the beast's skull. The war dog collapsed to the ground, dead.

Raising her weapons and stepping over the body of the war dog, she eyed a lone figure in full battle garb, positioned next to a standard planted before the pavilion's entrance.

With its spear-blade tip, tassels hanging from a short transverse bar beneath, and an array of four silver discs running down the shaft below, the standard heralded the power and authority of the entire encampment; an authority wielded by one man, with brutal efficiency.

Unlike the other Teverens, the man a few paces from Rayden made no move toward her.

A horizontal crest of feathers adorned a helm with cheek guards, the latter featuring embossed bear heads in mid-roar. Golden in hue, a magnificent scale cuirass and an outer harness of leather protected his torso, the circular iron discs atop the intersections of the harnessing displaying an assortment of silvered images of horses and eagles. Rows of short leather strips ran along the bottom of his cuirass and at the ends of its short sleeves.

An eagle motif continued on the silvered greaves protecting his legs, with the embossed head of the bird at the knee and feathered patterns running down the rest of their length.

His large, rectangular shield curved back toward his body on both sides. The facing, painted white with red strips along the sides and down the middle, held an iron boss in the shape of a wolf's head in the center.

From the unique nature of his armor and helmet, Rayden knew without doubt that the man before her held the highest rank in the camp. He stood his ground, gripping a sword of the Teveren style, but terror filled his eyes.

Rayden took a step toward him, a judgment of death reflecting in her eyes.

"Spare me, I will surrender," he said, his voice sounding like a bleat to Rayden's ears.

The inferno within Rayden surged.

She loathed the kind of men he commanded. The Teveren soldiers, in carrying out his orders, had cloaked themselves in the wickedness inflicted upon the small Borreni settlement.

All could have refused to engage in such evil, even if that

choice came at a cost. Every one of them deserved to answer for their brutal crimes; and they had at the ends of sharp iron blades.

But their commander bore the greatest responsibility of all. His authority had set the tragedy into motion, with full, conscious intent to kill, burn, and then enslave.

Rayden thought of the elderly men and women falling to the ground with their lives flowing out of them in the blood pouring from their gashed throats. She thought of the young woman in shredded clothing, being cradled in the aftermath of a horror that would leave interior scars for the rest of her years.

She thought of the fear gripping the women and children who had been placed in chains for the first time in their lives. Mourning the death of loved ones and filled with despair, they stared into the murk of a hostile, uncertain future.

Rayden's anger burned white-hot.

"I will spare you the quick death that your men had," Rayden answered, in a voice cold and firm. "Yours will last longer."

"I ... I am a man of means, I can have a large ransom paid to you, for my return," he replied, speaking fast, beads of sweat breaking out on his forehead.

"Return? To where do you think you will return?" Rayden asked in a calm voice, taking another step toward him.

"I live in the Imperial City," the man said, a glint of hope reflecting in his eyes at her question. "I come from a family of prominence. One that has places in the senate itself! I can arrange a great sum to be paid."

She doused any shred of hope in the man a moment later. Flashing him an icy smile, she said, "My road already leads toward the Imperial City. I would seek you out, to make certain you answered for those you violated here. But there's no need for you to return and delay the inevitable. You will forfeit your life here."

Rayden advanced upon the man, who cried out and slashed

at her in a wild manner born of desperation. Rayden swatted his panicked attempts aside with ease, opening up wounds on his arms and legs with her own blades.

Each gash and cut she inflicted brought a shriek of pain from the Teveren. His movements began slowing.

A couple of times he rushed forward, intending to slam his shield into her. She easily dodged and sidestepped the clumsy attempts, countering and taking full advantage of the openings he exposed.

Continuing with her onslaught and whittling him down, she held back from delivering a killing blow. Reduced until he stood disarmed of both sword and shield, he could no longer hold his arms up, or even stand upright.

Defenseless, bleeding from a myriad of wounds, and weeping, the Teveren commander sunk down to his knees before her. His gaze fixed toward the ground, he said nothing.

"I've had my fill of the filth of your presence," Rayden declared, her voice taking on the timbre of a snarl. She brought her sword back. "For all those who died and suffered at your authority, your wicked life ends now!"

With one vicious blow of her sword, she beheaded the Teveren. The man's body remained upright for a moment, and then toppled to the side.

Rayden stared down at the headless corpse, catching her breath. Shouts, cries, and the sounds of fighting still carried into the night from deeper among the tents, but around her stillness reigned.

She took no satisfaction from the slaying of the Teveren commander. His death would not bring back those who had been executed, nor would it restore the dwellings left in ash. It merely ensured that the Teveren would no longer be able to condemn others to such tragic fates.

"This night, true justice has been meted out," Doros stated, coming up from behind Rayden.

"And we are the means of it." Rayden turned and looked to her friend, thinking again of the Borreni huts engulfed in flame, and the old men and women who had their throats slashed without mercy. "Had we done nothing, their evil would have grown and strengthened, and the suffering of those enslaved increased. Every Teveren death here is well-deserved."

"If only we could resurrect these beasts, to kill them once more," Doros said, her long dagger gleaming in the firelight and the heat of combat yet simmering within her eyes.

"With these Teverens, I agree with you," Rayden said, eyeing the opening to the pavilion nearby.

The sounds of battle ebbed, until only the shouts of boisterous victors and cries of the wounded remained.

Annocrates trotted up, breathing heavily. His blade slick with blood, he paused to steady himself.

"No Teverens are left," he announced. "The only others alive in this camp are the women and children they were to enslave. They all have been freed, but there is no joy among them."

The man's face shadowed over with a downcast expression. Alcedan walked up to join them at that moment, his face and tunic spattered all over with blood. Like Annocrates, his blade had been coated in the blood of the enemy.

"Their freeing comes with great sadness," Rayden said. "And fear. They have all lost their homes, and many who they loved, the ones who protected them."

"There is no comfort we can give them," Annocrates said.

"Yet we can stand at their side," Rayden said. Her mood darkening, she looked to the southern horizon. "This is why we must march against the Teverens ... so no settlement suffers such a vile fate. All who seek to become the masters of others deserve to be ground into dust."

"And we shall bring them down," Doros said. "The Imperator

and all those with him."

Rayden nodded. "That we shall, or die in the attempt."

"We can do no more here," Annocrates said. "Do we head back now?"

"Yes, though I am going to take a look around here, by myself," Rayden said. "Take up weapons from the fallen soldiers. They can be wielded against Teverens later. Then take the survivors from the settlement back with you, and see that they are cared for."

Doros and Annocrates nodded. Rallying other warriors, they set to rounding up the women and children who had been doomed to enslavement at the hands of the Teverens.

Rayden walked toward the pavilion opening, keeping her weapons at hand should any Teverens have taken to hiding during the fighting. With silent steps, she crept through the opening and entered, pausing a moment to let her eyes adjust.

Illuminated by firelight from braziers, the interior held flicking shadows, but nothing that could hide a soldier waiting to ambush her. Nevertheless, she paused to take careful assessment of the area, scanning every detail from one side to the other.

Rugs, low couches, chairs, chests and other accoutrements indicated the quarters of one of high status and wealth. A table anchored the center of the room, still displaying a large map upon which a few small figurines rested.

Though Rayden wanted to study the map and see what she could glean from the figurines and their placement, she kept her gaze moving to the right.

Piercing golden eyes stared back from the shadows, meeting her eyes in a union of lionhearts. Looking upon the majestic leonine visage framed by a grand mane, Rayden's breath caught in her throat, echoing the astonishment gripping her.

In an instant, she knew the great lion trapped within the cage to be the same one she had seen upon entering the Divine City in the Mystic Kingdom, during her long journey with Ammanus toward Kartajen. The creature had undoubtedly been taken across the seas and sold to the wealthy Teveren who commanded the force they had just overcome.

Fear and loneliness still reflected from the creature's luminous eyes. The lion showed no agitation at her presence, and a part of Rayden believed that the beast somehow recognized her.

She could not leave the regal creature caged. Leaving it to a fate of slow starvation or being killed outright, by whomever came upon the cage later, were not outcomes she could live with.

"You are a king ... and no king should remain treated as a slave," Rayden said to the lion in a calm tone. "One more living being remains to be freed in this wicked camp."

Striding over, Rayden set her axe to the wood around the main lock of the cage. Splinters flew, and in moments the lock no longer secured the opening to the cage.

Having backed up in the small interior space while she hacked at the lock, the lion growled. Rayden grabbed the cage door and looked once more into the eyes of the lion.

"I am setting you free, I want no harm to come to you," she said, in a gentle voice. She knew it could not understand her words, but perhaps it could somehow perceive her intent. "But neither do I wish to be harmed by you. Humans have been cruel to you, and if you seek vengeance I would rather it not be the one who freed you who suffers such wrath."

She paused, and took a deep breath.

"Now go ... and be free once more, king of beasts," she said. "The world is yours to roam once again."

With slow, backward steps that kept her facing the cage, Rayden opened the door to the enclosure. She kept moving away, orienting her path toward the entrance of the tent.

The lion remained in the cage, though it paced toward the opening when she reached the front of the tent. Rayden smiled, and a ray of joy shined within her, seeing the lion take a cautious step out of the cage.

The broad paw setting upon the ground beyond the cage door represented its first step from bondage into freedom; a freedom it had not known for a very long time.

Turning, Rayden moved out of the lion's sight, exiting the pavilion before quickening her pace. Breaking into a run, she headed through the destroyed camp and into the night.

From the depths of her heart, she wished the lion an abundance of days and ample game in the forested hills surrounding her.

CHAPTER 10

Before Rayden had gotten far on her way back to the lands of the Tega, a stark anomaly in the landscape drew her attention. Just to the north of the Teveren encampment, and silhouetted against the night sky, a large pavilion crowned a hilltop.

Close in size to that of the Teveren commander, its form had the same shape. The reddish flickers of several torches dotted the area in front of the pavilion.

Wondering why such a sizeable pavilion would be erected on its own, apart from the Teveren camp and in such an unusual place, Rayden found she could not ignore the structure and continue onward. She chose to divert from her path, and find out what she could about the pavilion.

Rayden angled toward the hill and picked up her pace, reaching the base of its slope before long. Climbing upward, she approached the structure with caution, listening for sounds and watching for any movement.

Keeping to the shadows and trees, she proceeded until the front of the pavilion drew into sight. Coming to a stop and remaining concealed, Rayden took a little time to make a careful assessment of the area.

Five tall wooden posts had been set in the ground before

the pavilion. The posts had been arranged such that each of them formed a point along the course of a great circle. From high on every post dangled a pair of shackles affixed to an iron ring.

Rayden stared at the area inside the quintet of posts. A broad pool of shadow, dense to the degree that it appeared solid black, covered the entirety of the space. Nothing could be made of the ground the shadow cloaked.

The area inside the posts held a strange quality, one that Rayden could not put her mind to. Disconcerted, she looked about for signs of those who had erected the posts and pavilion.

Flames from the torches outside of the posts billowed in the night breezes, but everything else on the hilltop remained shrouded in an uneasy stillness. The absence of guards around a pavilion suitable for a Teveren commander perplexed Rayden.

Taking a few steps forward, Rayden started toward the pavilion entrance. Answers would have to be sought inside the structure.

She looked back to the swathe of darkness inside the posts. The fires and the pavilion itself did not explain the black area. To her eyes, no light source or object within view could have cast the shadow.

As with the area outside of the posts, the ground should have been illuminated well enough from the bright moon above. No clouds blocked its silvery light, a cascade of unobstructed luminance that failed to penetrate the dark area.

Stepping forward, and keeping to the outside of the posts, she could not take her eyes from the ring of shadow. Every instinct within told her to keep a firm watch upon the space.

The entrance to the pavilion drew nearer, one stride at a time. After several more steps, Rayden stood between the wooden posts and the pavilion.

Nothing stirred, but the unease within her continued to mount. A sense of imminent danger permeated the air, and she kept her weapons at the ready.

Rayden froze in place.

In sudden fashion, the sprawling pool of darkness set into motion and began flowing toward her. It swept beyond the boundary of the posts, causing her to take several steps backward.

Light from the surrounding torches did not affect the advancing shadow. If anything, the mass of darkness affected the flames, the light from the torches nearest to it ebbing and dying down, as if being strangled.

Rayden edged away from the pavilion entrance, making sure she did not get caught between the shadow and anything that might emerge from within the structure.

A change took place within the creeping darkness.

Lifting from the ground and rising to a height a full head above Rayden, the center of the darkness extended upward in a host of narrow tendrils, each of the latter resembling coiling, black smoke. Though slowing, all of it continued moving in her direction.

Backing away from the dark apparition, Rayden kept her sword and axe in front of her, though no forged weapon could injure the kind of threat manifesting before her.

Twisting and billowing, the tendrils from the ground began coalescing, forming into a massive torso and head. Having the appearance of smoldering embers, a pair of eyes took shape.

The surface of the huge phantasm kept churning and shifting. Gazing upon her, the entity ceased its advance.

"You would deny me what is mine?"

The voice of the towering apparition had an eerie quality to it, like that of a throng of snakes hissing in unison.

"We grow ever stronger," the thing continued. "You cannot stop us."

"I have stopped you," Rayden said, realizing the purpose of the posts with their shackles. "You will get nothing this night.

The ones taken to be slaves have been freed, and all the Teverens lay dead."

The dark specter drifted forward, a little further, exposing the central area encompassed by the posts. Moonlight revealed the bodies of five humans who had been concealed within the darkness.

Reduced to husks, the corpses looked skeletal, each covered in a thin layer of dessicated skin. The bodies carried evidence of their identities, from the attire still on them.

Three were garbed in the distinctive armor and helms of Teveren soldiers. Two were clad in long robes, similar to those of priests; and of the man who had taken the small group of children from the Borreni settlement.

Rayden knew the two robed men were more than mere priests, for them to have summoned an entity of the kind now confronting her. Both had been sorcerers of a higher level of skill, capable of working powerful, dark magic.

"You denied me nothing," the apparition said with a boastful air. "I consumed other slaves to feed my hunger."

The gruesome sight explained the absence of any others around the area. The entity had devoured the essence of both sorcerers and their guards in the place of the intended sacrifices; a blood offering of innocents, the children taken from the settlement.

The full realization sickened Rayden, and she felt no pity for the men who had met such a hideous doom.

"I will return to the great abyss soon, but not before I have had my fill with the spirit of one more human," the entity declared.

"I do not serve your Master, and I am no slave," Rayden said. She backed up another couple of steps, drawing the entity forward, until it came to an abrupt halt.

She backed up another couple of steps, but the entity stayed in place, as if restrained by some unseen force.

Rayden looked past the apparition and saw that the darkness trailing it had reached the edge of the space enclosed by the posts. In some way, the entity remained tethered to that interior area, and appeared unable to advance any farther.

"It would seem your reach is limited," Rayden said.

"You know nothing of the power rising in this world," the entity responded. "Barriers are falling."

The entity's shape devolved, transforming into a stream of darkness that funneled into the body of one of the dead sorcerers. When the last wisp of its substance entered the corpse, an icy chill filled the air. Rayden's every breath became visible, like those on a deep winter's night.

The corpse sat up, animated with the power that had entered it. Its dark eye sockets now exhibited the same ember-like quality of the apparition.

The unnatural thing got to its feet. As it looked toward Rayden, a raspy, multi-layered hiss emerged from its throat. With a bestial snarl, the revenant glared, its face contorting into a ghastly visage.

Springing forward and breaking into a run, the thing closed the distance between them in moments, moving much faster than she anticipated. Striking out with her weapons, her sword grazed its upper right arm, and her axe bit deep into its side, but the blows did nothing to slow the entity or alter its course.

Colliding into her with tremendous speed and strength, the corpse took Rayden down hard, smashing her to the ground. Pain erupted throughout her back upon the impact.

Unable to use either of her weapons, she let them drop. Resorting to hand-to-hand combat, she took hold of the creature. Grappling with the thing, it took all of Rayden's strength to keep its jaws from snapping down on her neck or shoulder.

Out of the corner of her eyes, Rayden saw a large, dark shape coming in fast from the side; a moment before it slammed into the corpse, knocking it off of her. A great roar filled the night.

The lion that she had freed in the Teveren camp now straddled the corpse. Biting down, the lion clamped its jaws upon the neck of the thing.

Rayden flinched in surprise when the lion was hurled through the air an instant later, tossed away as if it were a small cat.

The corpse scrambled for Rayden at once. She threw a forward kick as it neared. Fast and powerful, the blow landed in its midsection and knocked it back, before it could set its hands upon her.

Another roar sounded as the lion leaped onto the corpse from behind, knocking it back toward Rayden. On instinct and with quick reflex, she sent a hard left uppercut crashing into the lower jaw of her undead assailant.

Shifting aside, Rayden let the lion continue its assault. Swiping its claws in rapid succession, the lion ripped the corpse's back wide open. The corpse thrashed and whipped about, throwing the lion off once more.

Radyen scurried over to where her sword lay, and snatched it up. She lunged and thrust the sword blade forward, right as the corpse came at her again.

The tip of the blade drove into its mouth. Shattering teeth and bursting from the back of its head, the blade skewered the corpse.

Rayden let go of the hilt. Crying out, she slammed her right knee hard into the thing's midsection, while bringing her left fist about in a powerful hook that hammered into the jaw of the corpse.

Springing to her left, Rayden made for her axe, the corpse staggering for a moment. Gurgling through the sword protruding from its mouth, it turned toward her.

Once more, the night erupted with a tremendous roar. The

lion reared up behind the corpse, unleashing a savage mauling with both sets of claws.

Rayden did not stop to watch what transpired. Locating her axe, she bounded over and picked it up. When she looked back to the corpse and lion, she distrusted her eyes for a moment.

Shredded all over from the lion's attack, the back of the corpse faced her. The lion lay upon the ground inert, whether dead or unconscious.

The corpse pulled the sword in its mouth free. Raising the weapon above its head, the corpse readied to strike the defenseless lion.

Rayden hurled her axe as hard as she could and broke into a run. Spinning through the air, the weapon sent bits of skin and bone flying, lodging in the back of the corpse's skull.

Disrupted, the corpse loosed a dreadful cry and whirled about to face in her direction. Propelling off one leg, Rayden kicked high with the other, snapping the head of the corpse back and sending it rearward.

Tripping over the body of the lion, the corpse fell backward and dropped the sword. Rayden jumped over the lion and retrieved her blade.

She chopped downward as the corpse reached for her, severing its right arm at the wrist. Bereft of an arm, it flailed about, before moving to brace itself with its remaining hand to get back to its feet.

Two hard blows from Rayden's blade separated its skull from its body. Taking no chances, she used her sword to hack the corpse apart until its limbs lay in pieces, scattered about its torso.

Chest heaving, she looked back toward the lion. Relief flooded her, seeing the side of the lion rising and lowering with unmistakable breaths.

Taking up her axe, she carefully gathered the pieces of the corpse together, and set them to flame using one of the torches before the pavilion. Not wanting to risk any more corpses reanimating, she proceeded to burn the four remaining bodies within the perimeter of the posts.

A rustling on the ground telling her the lion was awakening, she took her eyes from the fire and looked over to the beast. Getting back to its broad paws, the lion turned and gazed toward her.

Eyes gleaming in the firelight, the creature remained in place, showing no inkling of aggression or agitation. Though wary, Rayden had no fear of the lion. She made no move to take up her weapons.

One of the most unlikely allies she had ever had, the beast had intervened and repeatedly hurled itself at her supernatural attacker, despite suffering heavy blows.

"Thank you, great king," Rayden said in a low voice, nodding her head to the lion. "I would have been dead without you."

The lion took a step forward, and then another. Gazing into the fire, the beast paused.

A low growl rose from its throat, ebbing a few moments later. The lion looked back to Rayden, its golden eyes shining bright in the firelight.

Rayden had witnessed numerous predators on the hunt, including lions. The movements of the lion with her did not carry the look of a creature about to attack.

Padding forward and keeping a wide berth from the fire, the lion fixed its gaze upon Rayden and emitted a few low puffing sounds. At last, the lion drew to a halt before her.

Taking one more stride, it nuzzled its large head against Rayden's body, nearly pushing her backward. A steady humming sound accompanied the lion's exhales, a sound she found somewhat akin to a smaller cat's purrs.

Rayden spread her arms and ran her hands deep through the lion's great mane. Burying her face into its mass of hair, she hugged the beast to her in a gentle fashion.

"Thank you again, great warrior and king of beasts," she said, keeping her voice low, listening to the comforting hums continuing from the lion on its outward breaths.

Whether a few moments or a long time had passed, Rayden could not say when the lion pulled back. Giving her one more nuzzling from its massive head, it turned away, and headed back into the night.

A state of serenity filling her heart, Rayden watched the regal creature go.

Thinking about what had just transpired, a smile rose on her face. For a few moments, in the aftermath of facing a gruesome adversary, time had stopped. Hints of a better state of being had taken over.

Savoring the peaceful feeling, she took a few more moments to reflect upon the profound experience.

Leaving the hilltop behind a short time later, Rayden set out for the lands of the Tega.

CHAPTER 11

Alcedan, Rayden, and the warriors who had come with them pressed with all haste back to the Gessa lands. When they had returned, the new chieftain wasted no time in issuing a summons for a full tribal council, dispatching messengers to all the tribes.

Many days passed before the response to the messengers became known. As with Eigon's summons, some tribes rejected the Gessa messengers outright. But this time, a few more accepted the request than had done so with the situation involving the Arguntier.

Rayden suspected a few of the ones who had not responded to Eigon's summons had more interest in weighing the new chieftain of the Gessa than in the importance of the council itself. Nevertheless, the presence of additional tribes increased the potential of the council's outcome.

Several delegations from the tribes within closer range arrived over the course of a couple days. Others continued trickling in over the ensuing days, coming in from lands much farther away.

While awaiting the council, the various delegations exchanged tidings and rumors. Those who had not fought against the Arguntier listened with great interest to the descriptions of the creatures and the battle itself. Most professed astonishment at the intervention by the Varganir and the wolves.

The tale of Rayden's prior journey to seek out the enigmatic, lupine beings spread fast, as did the account of her latest one involving the Teveren camp at the border of Borreni territory.

Though a few boasts and insults were hurled about, with a smattering of minor brawls, a general spirit of truce held between the various rivals among the tribes.

When the chieftain of the Pannimbri arrived in the company of his household warriors, having traveled from the farthest corner of tribal territory to the north and east, the rest of the chieftains deemed it time to hold the council.

Though holding little enthusiasm for addressing a throng of chieftains, Rayden agreed to Alcedan's request that she speak to the council at length. Having faced the Teverens in open battle, and fighting in the recent attack on the encampment, she held a perspective that Alcedan judged valuable to the argument for unity.

Further, her name held a strong level of respect within many of the gathered tribes. Regardless of their eventual decisions, the tribal chieftains would listen to the renowned warrior who had gained the help of the Varganir.

***

Rayden could make no more arguments. Taking in the faces of the surrounding warriors, she endeavored not to glower. Frustration boiled inside her.

Councils had never been to her liking, and one that should have been resolved in swift fashion served only to grate further upon her, with every moment that passed. Unsurprised, she found the same kind of short-sighted, stubborn resistance that marked most such gatherings.

She had gone to great lengths to explain why the tribes

needed to unite and march upon the Teverens, and take the fight to the heart of the wicked Empire. Rayden described everything she had witnessed, emphasizing the worst of it, such as the horrific crucifixions running for leagues along the Boreus Way.

She related everything she had witnessed in the Teveren's sack of the Borreni settlement, describing the slaughter of the elderly and the placing of women and children in chains. Rayden spoke of her encounter at the hilltop site where the Teverens had intended to sacrifice Borreni children to feed their dark sorcery.

The expected arguments had been raised.

Chieftains spoke at length regarding the risks of leaving their lands exposed and vulnerable, citing matters of trust and honor in other tribes. Though naming no specific transgressors of those qualities, their comments did little else but provoke an overall tension.

Others questioned whether the Teveren threat truly stood as severe as Rayden and others claimed. Their words tread dangerously close to being insulting to those who had fought against the Teverens, and been eyewitnesses to their cruelties. Rayden could see the ire brimming on the faces of Alcedan, the Gessa warriors who had taken part in the recent excursion, and the Borreni delegation.

A few chieftains gave voice to perhaps the greatest concern of many warriors; the possible cowardice that departing from ages-old homelands represented.

Rayden knew her insistence that the tribes would not be abandoning their homelands, but rather protecting them, fell upon many ears of stone. Working to keep the rising irritation inside out of her voice, she knew that mistrust and isolation would prove the undoing of all the tribes; in the inevitable time when the Teverens pushed north in strength.

Having concluded her long, trying effort, Rayden took a seat on one of the benches in Alcedan's long hall. Her face in a scowl, she stared ahead, and avoided meeting the eyes of any of the other chieftains.

Then, before any others called for a chance to speak, Alcedan stepped forward. An iron look to his eyes, Alcedan's gaze swept across the faces of the chieftains.

"Most of you do not know me," he began. "I am Alcedan, chieftain of the Gessa since the fall of Eigon, in the battle we fought against the monstrosities plaguing our lands. I do not have the years of many of the chieftains gathered here, but I know what I have seen. Rayden opened my eyes, and her words to you are those of wisdom and warning.

"The Arnan, the Cirni, the Rugara, the Marren, the Lanassa, and the Runi know well the nightmare we faced, and how it took all of us to stand together to survive.

"Like Rayden, I too watched the Teveren soldiers set fire to Borreni huts, place women and childen in shackles, and open the throats of the old. This is an enemy that will never rest until all of us are under the shackles of their rule. The Rugara under shackles ... the Pannimbri under shackles ... the Arnan under shackles ... the Gessa ... the Lanassa ... all of us. We must unite and stand as one body to gain the strength needed to defeat an evil that threatens us all. When it is over, we can return to our lands and our ways, each tribe the master of its own destiny."

Alcedan fell to silence. After looking around the hall once more, eyeing each of the other chieftains, he returned to sit at Rayden's side.

One after another, the chieftains of the tribes mentioned by Alcedan stepped forward and spoke in support of his words. The last of them, the burly, thick-bearded chieftain of the Borreni, Otta, finished the orations with a powerful statement.

"My people have already bled and suffered Teveren cruelty, and I would see us take the fight to those bastards," Otta declared in a booming voice. "It is a fool's path to let them build their strength and march upon us. It is true they would take the lands of the Borreni, and the Tega first ... but they will not stop there. They will flood across all our lands. Rayden and Alcedan speak with wisdom.

"Let us all agree to stand together, against the Teverens ... and let us also agree to stand together against any tribe not here, that seeks to take advantage against a tribe that joins this fight."

Like seeds planted in fertile soil, Otta's words took root and sprouted among the other chieftains. A murmur rippled through the gathered leaders, but Rayden could sense the momentum shifting toward cooperation on the part of the tribes.

Many nods accompanied their conversations, and no trace of contentiousness could be found in their expressions.

"The Gessa will stand with the Borreni," Alcedan stated, rising to his feet after a little time had passed. "What say the rest of you?"

Eigon's wish that the tribes could one day stand together in common cause materialized further before Rayden's eyes, as one chieftain after another gave their consent to Alcedan's call to unite. When all was done, not a single chieftain among those gathered dissented from giving their voice to the chorus of agreement.

Rayden looked around the crowded hall, an array of powerful emotions churning inside, pondering what Eigon's reaction to the momentous event would have been like. An army tens of thousands strong represented in the chieftains around her, Rayden found the sight to carry a little bitterness, in that Eigon could not be there in person to witness the profound development.

She knew Eigon's pride in Alcedan would have been immense. The young chieftain had risen to the challenge and exhibited leadership and wisdom that had given life to unprecedented cooperation among the tribes.

If Rayden had needed any sort of vindication for having

lent her voice in acclaim for Alcedan, then the triumph before her would have provided it in abundance. Yet she needed no vindication, or justification. Alcedan had simply taken another great step along the path she had foreseen; that of a Gessa chieftain worthy of being the successor to a man such as Eigon.

Catching his eyes, Rayden shared a glance with Alcedan. He smiled at her, a look of pride resting in his gaze.

A broad smile came to her face, and she gave a nod of acknowledgement toward the young Gessa chieftain; an expression and gesture made on behalf of both herself and Eigon.

CHAPTER 12

Amassive horde of men, women, and children traveling in
their wake, Rayden, Alcedan, many chieftains and a great
number of honored warriors led the people of the northern lands
in the only direction offering a chance to defend a future.

The Gessa, Runi, Cirna, Rugara, Borreni, Pannimbri,
Lanassa, Marren, Arnan, and several other tribes marched
southward, a few tribes joining them along the marching route.
Every leader understood that no respite could be had while the
Teveren Imperator reigned, growing ever in strength and power.

A poisonous serpent gorging itself and enlarging by the
day, the Teveren Empire's lengthening coils would wrap about
increasing numbers of lands and people. Only the severing of its
malignant head could stem the monstrosity's insatiable hunger.

Ranks swelling by the day, the growing sea of barbarians
surged into a tidal wave rolling toward the Teveren Empire.
When they reached the edge of the tribal lands and added the
Tega and the large population of former slaves to their number, a
vast wave stood poised to crash upon the heart of Teveren lands.

While setting up camp for the night, the arrival of the mass
of former slaves brought with it a cause for Rayden to celebrate.
Standing at the edge of the sprawling ocean of cookfires, carts,
and shelters, she watched the multitude striding toward them

from the east, her anticipation growing with every moment of their approach.

Sparks of joy ignited within Rayden's eyes. She broke into a run, a smile blossoming upon her face.

A young dark-haired boy racing out of the mass of people to meet her had a look no less ebullient. His legs churned as fast as they could, his smile beaming.

She swept Hamilcar up into her arms, lifting the boy off the ground with ease. Whipping him around in a powerful embrace, Rayden's heart brimmed with affection.

"I have missed you greatly, Hamilcar," she told the boy, when she had set him back down.

"As I have missed you," the boy replied. "They said you passed through our settlement recently. I was on a hunt with Crassor."

"We had to scout the Teverens," Rayden said. "They attacked Borreni settlements."

"That's what Annocrates said," Hamilcar said. "I wish I was there when you saw him and Doros."

"Was your hunt a good one?" Rayden asked.

"I almost brought down a deer, with a javelin," Hamilcar said. "Crassor said I am getting better."

"He is not one to be generous with compliments, so I am sure you are becoming more skillful," Rayden said.

"I am," Hamilcar said. His voice lowered. "I would have done anything to go north with you."

"My path was not one you are ready to take," Rayden said, her tone carrying a trace of apology, even if she knew she had done the right thing.

The boy nodded, though a glimmer of sadness crossed the surface of his eyes. "I understand, Rayden. Annocrates spoke to me of how you had to face a great darkness for your people, and how you did not want to take me into danger. But I still wished I could have gone with you."

"I wish the situation was different, so you could have gone with me," Rayden said. "It gladdens me that Annocrates explained why I had to go."

"Annocrates has been very good to me," the boy said. "I am thankful for him."

"As I was confident he would be good to you, a guardian and a guide," Rayden said. "He is among the best men I have known. I would place you in the hands of no less."

"He makes me practice with the sword every day," the boy said, a smile coming back to his face. "I am getting better. I would like to show you. I think you will be pleased."

"I will have to see your improved skill for myself," Rayden said, ruffling the boy's thick, wavy locks of hair. "We will have some time before we move onward, and there will be other times along this long march south."

"It is said we are marching on the Teveren Empire itself, to strike at the Imperial City," the boy said, with an air of amazement. "Is this true?"

Rayden nodded, her expression becoming grim. "It is the only choice left to us. Either that, or wait for the Teveren Legions to march on our lands."

"It is said the Imperial City is even larger than Kartajen," Hamilcar said. "Can that be possible?"

Rayden nodded. "I have not seen the Imperial City for myself, but all tales speak of it being the greatest city that any have set eyes upon."

The boy had a look of amazement. His next words echoed Rayden's own concerns. "Will this army of warriors be enough to overcome them."

"We will know the answer soon enough," Rayden said. "Let us not dwell upon that."

"Will I get to help in the attack, since everyone is going on this march?" he asked, a flare of eagerness in his face.

"Everyone is going on this march so the warriors can make sure all are defended, and no one is left behind in a vulnerable state," Rayden explained.

"I want to fight the Teverens!" the boy stated, excitement dancing in his eyes. "I want to fight at your side."

"We will see what happens," Rayden said, wishing the boy could be taken to a safe refuge far away. She knew how the eagerness of the young toward war, thinking of glory and renowned heroes, turned all too swiftly into a litany of haunting memories and a bleeding spirit. "I can promise nothing. We are all caught in this storm."

The forefront of the incoming mass of people began to flow around them. Many individuals called out greetings to Rayden.

Looking around, Rayden said to Hamilcar. "It looks like your numbers have grown."

"Many have come since you went into the north," Hamilcar said.

"That is good news," Rayden said. "More found their way to freedom, and your settlements have grown stronger."

"Rayden!" exclaimed a familiar, female voice.

Rayden looked to her right and saw Doros making her way through the incoming throng.

"Another journey looms," Rayden said, when Doros drew near. The two gave each other a quick embrace.

"I see Hamilcar finally found you," Doros said, grinning at the boy.

"I am glad he did," Rayden said.

"I'm going to show Rayden I can handle a sword better," Hamilcar declared to Doros. "You've seen me."

Doros smiled. "Indeed you have improved your skill. Very much so."

The boy stood a little straighter at her praise.

Rayden looked to Doros. "I trust the journey here was not too difficult."

"Smooth as it could be," Doros said.

"And the mood among the new settlements?" Rayden asked.

"Many are hungry to fight the Teverens," Doros said. "No part of this vast army, save for a few of the Borreni, will understand the threat of the Teverens better than the men and women walking by us now."

"It will be good to have all of them along to remind the others," Rayden said. "Many trials in the days to come."

"Many trials we will overcome," Doros said, resolute.

"And we will overcome them together," Hamilcar stated.

"That we will," Rayden agreed.

Doros looked to Rayden. "I saw something very interesting when we neared this encampment. A recent friend of yours, I think. Not many of his kind in this region. Will he accompany us south too?"

Doros glanced to her right, in the direction of a hillside overlooking the low expanse of ground where the camp had been situated. Near the summit, on a broad rock, a lion reclined on its side, watching over the sea of humans.

Only one lion would be roving the hills in the northern reaches of the Teveren Empire. Gladdened and surprised at the sight, Rayden stared toward the lion.

"You know that lion?" Hamilcar asked.

"We met once in the Divine City, in the Mystic Kingdom," Rayden said. "Our paths crossed again too, in the Teveren camp we attacked, and this time I was able to do something about it."

"He's your lion?" the boy asked excitedly. "He's going with us?"

"He belongs to himself, as it should be, and whether he chooses to go with us, I cannot say," Rayden answered. "But he is a long way from his homeland, and I am the only friend he knows. If he wants to go with us, then he shall."

"Everyone needs to know he is with you, then," Doros said. "Word must be passed not to harm that lion."

"We will see to that," Rayden said. "I want no harm to come to him. He has already made sure that harm did not come to me."

For a moment, she thought of the macabre, living shadow, its possession of the desiccated corpse, and the intervention by the lion. A cold shiver passed through her.

"This sounds like quite a tale," Doros said.

"One I will share with you this night," Rayden said, looking back to her friend.

***

Several days of marching passed, covering many leagues through rolling hills. Though well into Teveren lands, no force had confronted the tribal masses.

Scouts reported no signs of Tevern legions. The estates and small villages they came across had been abandoned, the inhabitants likely fleeing when word of the advancing tribal horde reached them.

Often in the company of Doros, Rayden spent her days at the forefront of the march, lending her skills to scouting, hunting, and foraging efforts. The consistent activity kept her muscles limber, and her mind from the monotony of the long days.

Streams running through the hills held an abundance of fish, and all manner of game dwelled in the forests. Vacant estates and villages produced a little in the way of foodstuffs, tools, and other provisions, though most things of value had been taken away by their former inhabitants.

Nights and early mornings gave her some time to visit with those she knew; from among the Gessa, the settlement of former slaves, and a few individuals in other tribes.

Hamilcar proved to be advancing well in his sword skills.

She instructed him further, in addition to giving some training in the use of a sword to a few other youths he had befriended in the population of former slaves. Rayden cherished the time spent with Hamilcar, looking forward to their visits each day.

Yet Rayden still sought and needed a little time to herself; a precious commodity when she found herself surrounded most of the day by people, from the break of dawn to the last shred of dusk.

Over a week into the march, with the camp in good order and evening approaching, Rayden set out by herself and made her way up the slope of a hill.

Reaching the top and looking back, she sat upon the ground and took in a resplendent sunset. Soft caresses of evening breezes attending her vigil, Rayden let a long, slow breath out.

A little tension seeped from her with the breath and pleasant vision, but not all. A number of concerns weighed upon her mind.

Campfires reaching beyond the edges of her vision, Rayden gazed across the masses of northern warriors with an uneasy heart. Numbers guaranteed nothing against an enemy that could field its own massive force; comprised of powerful legions forged, honed, and wielded upon the battlefield with masterful skill and command.

During the march south, Rayden had listened carefully to every account of the rise of the Teverens. Time and again, over the years, their veteran legions had destroyed opponents holding a great advantage in numbers. Even the experienced and well-equipped Kartajenians had been crushed several times on both sea and land, losing vast swathes of their territory to the Teverens.

Rayden had her own experiences to draw upon, having witnessed the Teveren's sacking of the port city of Iellia, and then standing later against them in open battle with the army of rebellious slaves. She knew that the intervention of the general

Mago had been the only thing tilting the rebel army's fate from destruction.

Waging war with cohesion and discipline unrivaled, the Teverens had little standing in their path toward full dominion. In the Western lands, only the northern tribes and the sorely-pressed Kartajenians could field any kind of force capable of challenging the Teverens on a field of battle.

Yet despite all of their martial strength, the combined legions of the Teveren Empire did not cause the unease churning deep within Rayden. Something far older and vastly more powerful than the Teveren Empire loomed from the shadows of its actions and aims; a threat voracious, cunning, and patient.

The face of that greater menace had presented itself to Rayden an abundance of times, in a number of forms. The leering visage of the crazed man scuttling among the rotting, crucified slaves along the Boreus Way. The bestial abominations of nature plaguing and bleeding the northern tribes. The madman imbued with supernatural strength and powers roving the forest. The living shadow that had poured into a corpse and resurrected it, outside the hilltop pavilion.

All hearkened from the preeminent adversary facing them; an enemy that held no hunger for jewels or gold, bore no lust for flesh, or desired any worldly crown. It could not be negotiated with. Apprehension enveloping her at the thought, Rayden knew full well such an enemy could not be overcome by axe and sword.

Answers would have to be found before its power grew insurmountable. Until then, war had to be waged against the Teveren Empire.

***

The next day saw Rayden, Doros, and a few other warriors in one of the groups warding the eastern flank of the march. Trekking through the hills on a mild day, beneath a bright sun, they looked out for any signs of Teverens.

About midday, they came to a halt and had a little bread and cheese, while giving their legs a rest. Rayden walked over to join Doros, who stood with her back to the others, staring into the distance.

"He is now fighting on our behalf. Or so it would seem from all indications," Doros observed, gazing toward the lion standing upon the crest of a nearby hill. "A scouting group came upon more dead Teverens."

The lion looked down upon a broad river of humans, thousands upon thousands, coursing southward. Alone and far from his home, the noble beast stood tall and proud, its mane flowing in the wind.

A survivor and fighter, the lion continued to endure in a callous and dangerous world. Watching the lion, Rayden knew in her heart that the creature would not lie down and surrender. The creature yet stood strong, despite having been imprisoned and taken across an ocean from the lands he had known.

The lion turned his gaze from the flowing sea of people and looked in Rayden's direction. She met the creature's eyes, the two regarding each other in silence.

She remembered the feel of the lion's mane in her hands, when the creature nuzzled her following the encounter with the corpse-raising dark entity. The lion had flung his body again and again at her attacker, suffering many blows, and never once had threatened her.

The creature showed no sign of fear or hostility while holding her gaze. In the deep, golden eyes of the lion, Rayden sensed a kind of affection. Perhaps looking at Rayden standing atop a hill, with her own locks flying free in the wind, the lion even saw her as a kindred spirit; a fellow warrior who met every rising of the sun with the will to persevere.

Rayden recognized that kind of nature in the lion. It made

no difference what kind of being each of them were, human or lion. Both stood as warriors and survivors in a world unforgiving, and so often cruel.

The lion turned and strode away, disappearing from sight after a few paces, on the opposite side of the high summit.

"Not even one of ours has been killed? Only Teverens?" Rayden asked Doros, still a little incredulous at the reports that had been mounting.

Doros shook her head. "Not a single one has been harmed, or even threatened. But no less than five Teveren scouts have been found slain the past couple of days, and the wounds all point toward their slayer being that lion. All were mauled and ripped open. What is even more surprising to me is that there was no sign of them being fed upon. From all appearances, the lion just slew them, and left their flesh behind for scavengers."

"I am not surprised that lion has no fondness for Teveren flesh, after being caged up by them for so long," Rayden commented. "He has had more than enough of their scent to distinguish them, and for that I can be no less than grateful."

"The lion is behaving like some sort of protector, or guardian," Doros said with a trace of fascination in her voice. She glanced over to Rayden. "It is like he has adopted us, through you, in a way."

"In the southern lands, a male lion will protect his clan or tribe," Rayden said. "Maybe he has come to see us as his clan, in some manner."

"Then maybe he will go ahead to the Imperial City, slay the Imperator for us, and bring all of this to an end," Doros replied, grinning.

"While that would be wonderful, I'm afraid it will not be that easy," Rayden said, smiling at the idea. "I wish it could be so, and see the head cut off the Teveren snake before the ground drinks the blood of many."

Rayden looked over the mass of tribal people marching onward and fell into silence. A number of thoughts pressed upon her mind.

Many days of hard marching lay ahead. War bands had been sent out in all directions, primarily to salvage whatever food could be taken from Teveren villages and the estates of nobles.

In the more heavily forested northern provinces of the Teveren Empire, farms harbored a fair number of pigs in addition to the commonly-found sheep and goats. Chickens, ducks, geese, guinea hens and other more exotic kinds of fowl were raised on some farms.

Cattle, though much fewer in number on an average farming estate than sheep or goats, could be found on most sites. Every last bit of livestock that could be taken was swept up by the tribal horde on their southward journey.

Oxen, mules and donkeys found upon the farms were pressed into immediate service, to help carry the grains, fruit, vegetables and stocks of olive oil seized on the farms. Before long, a sizeable number of carts laden with foodstuffs and other goods rumbled south with the tribal forces.

Most farms had been abandoned in haste before the warrior tide reached them, but a few still remained occupied. Whether foolish, arrogant, insipid, or a blend of all three, nobles, or those entrusted to run the farming estates by absentee nobles, had remained on their estates with their families, guards, and slaves.

These individuals witnessed the estates sacked, plundered, and put to the torch, and any slaves on the land set free. With larger Teveren farming estates having several hundred slaves, more than half of whom were kept in shackles, a spirit of liberation accompanied the taking of each estate.

Even more humiliating, the nobles or overseers in those instances found themselves put into chains and taken captive, along with their surviving guards and family members. With their influence, many coming from powerful Teveren families, all of them held value for negotiations; whether for gaining supplies or securing the release of tribal people who might yet fall into the hands of the Teverens.

Rayden held no pity for any noble who fell into warrior hands and had been taken prisoner. Teveren nobles thrived upon the enslavement of others. Seeing them in chains and stripped of their freedom looked to be a rare kind of justice.

Even then, the justice meted out through the chains and shackles placed upon the nobles fell short of the greater crime. Unlike the slaves who had suffered and labored for them, the nobles' lack of freedom carried no permanent intent on the part of their captors.

The nobles would not endure the lash of a whip, be used to satiate carnal appetites, or find their skin branded with searing iron. They would not be forced to see their children sold off, or be kept shackled in the depths of dusky cellars.

Freed slaves had to be held back from exacting retribution on their former masters in more than one instance. At the insistence of Rayden and leaders such as Annocrates, grievances from those newly-freed would be given voice, with the fate of transgressors to be weighed and judged. No mercy would be given to those guilty of extreme cruelty or the violation of bodies; no matter what value the offending noble or overseer might have in future exchanges with the Teverens.

While a few of the liberated men and women chose to take their paths elsewhere, on their own, most desired to continue onward with the tribal masses surging toward the Imperial City. All who wished to take that road joined their number to those who had taken refuge with the Tega.

Already, several hundred men and women capable of carrying a weapon had bolstered the ranks of the former slave army. The influx swelled the ex-slave force to a level much greater in number than the one Rayden had taken the field with against the Teverens.

No Teveren force had manifested to stop the great advance, but Rayden knew the enemy was far too shrewd to cast away a legion or two in hasty responses. Teveren legions would concentrate, and then, in a state of full preparation, meet the invading force.

Even then, should Tevern Legions be overcome, the matter of the Imperial City loomed with its towering walls of stone and massive gates. Rayden had never set her eyes upon the great city, but the accounts of it all agreed that it appeared so strong as to be considered impregnable.

The walls were not her only concern, once they reached the city. From all the dark encounters she had endured in relation to the Teverens, Rayden suspected even more threats lay in wait; involving things not of human origin.

"Nothing is easy, but it is a great feat that so many tribes joined together in this struggle," Doros said. "Did not many of them war among each other, before all of this happen?"

Rayden nodded. "They did, and some more than others. But the unity I see down there, in that march, is a comfort for a future time. Should we prevail, I hope that this unity leads to a new day in the northern lands."

"Prevailing is the only path to a future," Doros replied. "There is no retreat from this war."

Rayden could not disagree. A great die had been cast, and the fate of the tribes depended on the outcome. At the very least, a sliver of a chance existed in taking the fight to the Teverens. Doing nothing would have invited certain doom, when the Imperator hurled an unstoppable storm across the north.

The sound of footsteps approaching from behind took Rayden's attention from the spectacular view before her.

Head beaded in sweat, Crassor drew to a halt a few paces

away. His chest heaved, and he appeared to be winded from a long run.

Already muscular when she had first met him, the huge man had added even more girth to his shoulders, chest, and limbs in his time spent on Tega lands. With better sources of food and rest, both more available to him as a free man, and the ability to engage in dedicated training with weapons, Crassor had grown into an even more impressive physical presence.

"I bring you good news," he announced, continuing to breath heavily as he caught his wind. "Messengers have reached the Kartajenians."

"Those are welcome tidings," Rayden replied. "Is there a response from them yet?"

"We expect one soon," Crassor said. "But I would not think the Kartajenians foolish enough to avoid the chance to bring the Teverens to their knees."

"They can wait for the Teverens to become invincible and find themselves destroyed, or they can join with us and attack now," Doros commented with a somber air, echoing the thoughts crossing Rayden's mind only moments before.

"Their war fleets would be of great use in the coming fight," Rayden said.

The seafaring Kartajenians remained one of the last who could contend with the Teverens upon the water. Beyond them, only the largest pirate fleets could challenge Teveren warships, and even then in limited scenarios.

"When will these Teveren dogs take a stand?" Crassor asked, an edge of frustration to his voice. "Will they keep falling back? We have not encountered even one legion!"

"Their people take refuge in their walled cities, and you will not see their legions until they are confident of destroying us," Rayden said. "Make no mistake, when they present themselves for battle, they will believe themselves in position to destroy us."

Scowling, and jaw growing taut, Crassor spit at the ground. He loosed several heated curses, before continuing, "Then let us pause, and take one of their walled cities. Great stores of food could be found within the gates of those cities."

"We will strike at the head of this great serpent ... and the rest will follow," Rayden said, knowing her words would do little to assuage the impetuous, fiery man. "The Imperial City means everything to them. It is the head and heart of their empire. We must threaten it as soon as we can. We may even force them to commit to battle before they deem themselves entirely ready."

"I'm ready for them now," Crassor said, his words sounding akin to a growl.

"I've been thinking it would be wise for us to take a closer view of the Imperial City, before our full force reaches it," Rayden said, looking from Crassor to Doros. "Even from inside of it."

"Legions will be easy to assess," Crassor replied in a dismissive tone. "We won't need to go into the city for that."

"Legions are not all they will have to wield against us," Rayden said, casting the big man a hard stare. "I mean to find out what else this Imperator is capable of."

"What could be more of a concern than their legions?" Crassor asked, looking confused. "If we break their legions apart, they are no more."

"The power behind those legions and everything else, including the abominations we faced in open battle in the lands of the Gessa," Rayden said.

"Unnatural beings," Crassor muttered. "I have heard many tales of those beasts while we marched. But they were destroyed, yes?"

"They were destroyed, but we must know more of what the Teverens are preparing," Rayden said, holding Crassor's gaze. "A power capable of raising an army created from wild beasts changed in form, and guided by wicked spirits, is nothing to underestimate."

Crassor took in her words for a few moments. He said in a lower, conciliatory voice. "I have no argument with that."

"We face a dangerous and unprecedented enemy," Rayden proceeded. "It would be best to find out whatever we can in the Imperial City ... and we can have a look at their walls and gates from the inside."

"That would be of great value to the tribes," Doros said, nodding. "I would accompany such a mission."

"I would join both of you in such a task, but I carry the mark of a slave," Crassor said. "I would not get past their gates."

"I do not carry such a mark, and nor do others," Rayden said, an idea forming in her head. "We can deceive them, if you are willing to assume the part of a slave to go into the city."

Crassor nodded.

"But you must hold your anger," Rayden said. "The time will come to spill Teveren blood ... that I can promise you."

"It is a thirst that I fear can never be quenched," Crassor replied. "But I will do anything I can to see to their defeat."

Rayden looked from Doros to Crassor. "Then I think we should all explore the city we intend to sack."

CHAPTER 13

Setting out in the damp chill preceding the break of dawn, Rayden and several others departed from the tribal forces and set out on a new course. With her traveled Doros, Crassor, and three who would be invaluable for their purposes; Polybius, Lucius, and Gaius.

All three of the men stood Teveren citizens, though ones holding irreconcilable grievances with the Imperator. Each had joined the slave rebellion of their own accord, finding their lives untenable beneath Teveren rule.

Polybius had seen his livelihood taken through the maneuvering of a landed noble desiring to convert his estate from renting tenants to a slave-run farm. The small farmers had no genuine recourse when their agreements had been severed, without warning.

Without any other viable options in their province, all of the tenant farmers had been condemned to a life of destitution. For Polybius, the slave rebellion could not have erupted at a better time.

Lucius had seen his only son taken away for legion service; for a war of conquest whose only purpose was to bring status and glory to the wealthy noble leading it. His resentment increased to an irreconcilable level when word of his son's death arrived a year later. He had not hesitated a moment when the flames of rebellion swept across the province he lived in.

Gaius found his world gutted when a merchant of great influence with the senate had usurped all trading rights for wine from his home province to markets in the Imperial City. Unable to bring what he produced from his small vineyard to the most crucial market, Gaius found himself with no path to pay off the debts he had accrued.

He had no leverage, and soon had to sell his holding at a fraction of what he paid for it, to a representative of the merchant. On the verge of selling himself into slavery to cover the debts, Gaius had sought out the rebels and the hope of a life outside Teveren rule.

Though not warriors like Rayden, Doros, and Crassor, the trio brought many needed qualities to the group journeying toward the Imperial City. They knew Teveren customs and traditions, including those that applied to the treatment of slaves.

Teveren coins and finer clothing taken from the sacked farming estates would serve to fortify the masking of the group.

Polybius, Lucius, and Gaius wore finer styles of Teveren cloaks and tunics, and each carried a pouch full of coin. While they would not appear to be from the highest circles of Teveren society, they did carry a look consistent with men of solid means.

Doros and Rayden did not change their garb, other than donning Teveren-style cloaks, but also took along pouches filled with coin. Rayden and Doros would take the role of foreign guests of the Teveren men.

Crassor, in posing as a dutiful slave and guard, carried some coin, albeit in a smaller quantity than the others. He carried a Tevern-style short sword. The weapon would not appear unusual to any Teveren they might encounter, as many slaves of the empire served their masters as guards.

The previous evening, Rayden met in private with Alcedan

and Annocrates, informing them of her intent. She told them of her aims in scouting the Imperial City. Neither tried to dissuade her, both appearing to understand the importance of the quest.

Careful in keeping their purpose to themselves, the fewer knowing of their aims the better, the others had passed the night without saying a word about their departure to anyone. Slipping out of the camp before sunrise, at Rayden's lead, had gone smoothly enough.

Heading southwest, the group started their journey toward the Imperial City. Maintaining a steady gait, they covered several leagues before dusk beckoned. Guided by Rayden, Doros, and Crassor, the three Teverens helped fashion a little shelter for the night.

The first night passed without incident. Setting out at the break of dawn, they traveled another full day, stopping a couple of times to eat some bread and cheese, and rest their legs.

The respites lasted a little longer than they would otherwise have, as the Teverens were not in the same physical conditions as their stalwart companions. For their part, Polybius, Lucius, and Gaius made no complaints, or asked for any favor, but Rayden could see the strain in their faces.

With the sun descending on the western horizon, the group began looking for a suitable place to settle down for the night. The weather remained clear, and a bright moon allowed them enough visibility to continue a little into dark, to find an optimal setting.

Shortly after nightfall they came across a lake nestled among a cluster of low hills. Starlight sparkled all over the surface, the rising moon appearing like an embedded pearl, in gleaming onyx. Gentle breezes brushed the water, leaving a rippling shimmer in their wake.

"I could look upon this vision all night long," Doros remarked, looking out over the waters.

"As could I, but we need to get some rest," Rayden said. "We pressed longer than yesterday, and tomorrow will come all too soon."

"My legs feel like they are made of stone," Polybius said, leaning over and rubbing his thighs around the knees. He looked to Rayden and gave a weary smile. "But by morning they will be flesh and muscle again, I am sure."

"We traveled a fair distance today," Rayden said, in the way of encouragement. "Far enough to tire any pair of legs. I intend to get some good rest, myself."

"Here is as good a place as any to make our camp," Crassor said, looking around.

"Once we finish having a look around," Rayden said. She turned to the three Teverens. "Wait here. We will scout this area out a little more."

Rayden, Crassor and Doros searched out the immediate area, covering the perimeter of the lake, and finding no signs of habitation. Nor did they come across any hints of larger predators, a concern near any larger source of water. Once satisfied that the immediate surroundings stood clear, they returned to their companions.

With no hint of rain and the hour later, the group decided to forgo making any shelter. Dividing up watches, they took to sleeping on the open ground, using their cloaks to ward the night's chill.

Having taken the first watch of the night, Rayden and Doros sat against the wide trunk of an old, majestic tree. Neither spoke at first, both of them listening for any kind of disturbance, no matter how slight.

The chattering of insects, the occasional splash of a larger fish, and the breezes coursing through the trees from time to time were the only sounds to reach Rayden's ears. The night advanced smooth and peaceful.

The moon's position above told Rayden that sleep would soon be forthcoming, when she and Doros turned the group's watch over to Crassor and Polybius. She welcomed the thought, relishing a little rest before beginning another long journey at sun's arrival.

A night spent in the wilderness, especially one with the necessity of maintaining watches, never proved fully restful. For Rayden, having trained herself to rouse in an instant, should any trouble manifest, any sleep would be light in nature. Nevertheless, what little could be attained would serve to recover some strength back to her limbs.

The insects then ceased their incessant prattling. No more splashes of fish came from the lake. Even the breezes died down.

Rayden sat up at the abrupt shift in atmosphere, the cessation of sounds drawing her attention every bit as much as a loud noise would have.

Eyeing the lake, she took note of the deep silence now permeating the still air. Something about the quiet troubled her, prodding her every instinct.

She looked over to Doros, who had a look of concern on her face.

"I do not like the feel of this place," Rayden said in a low voice, rising to her feet. "Something is here."

"We have scouted the area all over, and we found nothing," Doros remarked, getting up.

Rayden looked around, the unease building inside. With soundless steps, she moved out from the tree and drew closer to the water.

Eyes narrowing, her scrutiny fixed upon the lake. She gripped the hilt of her sword and haft of her axe firm.

"Out there," Rayden said, the hackles on her neck standing up. "We did not search the lake itself."

A rippling along the surface of the lake a short distance

from the shore prompted Rayden to take several steps back from the edge of the water. The motion in the water drifted toward the land, heading straight toward the spot where Rayden and Doros stood.

Rayden readied her weapons and took up a fighting stance while Doros raised her bow, notching an arrow in place.

"Crassor!" Rayden said over her shoulder, in a low voice.

"What is it?" he replied, from where he lay several paces away, coming awake swiftly.

"Rouse the others," she said, keeping her eyes honed upon the disturbance in the water. "We may have some trouble."

Skin glistening in the moonlight, water dripping from their long hair and skin, a pair of young women emerged from the dark lake. Naked and voluptuous in form, they drew to a halt, a few strides from the water.

Looking toward Rayden and Doros with calm expressions, they showed no concern at their defensive postures. Rayden heard the shuffling steps of the others from her group, coming up from behind.

"There is no need for weapons," the one to the right announced, in a silken voice. "We welcome all of you as our guests."

"I would like to know who you are first," Rayden said in an even voice, not about to let down her guard, even if the women appeared naked and unarmed. "I did not see you swim across that lake. You came from within it."

Rayden had trod the world's surface long enough to know that an appearance of vulnerability could veil a lethal threat. Further, she had seen more than enough of diabolical things that could take on human guises.

"Do we look like enemies to you?" the other woman said, with an air of disappointment. "We come as friends, and you keep weapons poised to attack?"

"You are not human," Rayden declared, staring the woman directly in the eyes.

The two women regarded Rayden for a moment. She did not soften her stance or waver in her gaze.

"No, we are not," the female on the right finally said, though she still sounded at ease. "Our concern is the water, the trees, and this land. You have nothing to fear from us."

"Are they nymphs?" whispered Polybius, from behind Rayden.

"I have experience with nymphs," Rayden said. "None I have encountered would approach humans like this. They are shy creatures, and like to remain hidden."

"You do not know the ways of all things in nature," the female on the left said, her lips beginning to spread into a smile.

"There is nothing wrong with a proper welcome," the second woman stated, also exhibiting the onset of a smile.

Rayden caught the slight shift in focus within the eyes of the women. Both had cast glances beyond Rayden and her companions. The smiles on the lips of both women stopped short of revealing their teeth.

Everything came together at once.

"You are talking with us to keep us occupied, so that others may come from behind," Rayden concluded. "Crassor! Behind you! Now!"

Rayden cast a glance over her shoulder, as Crassor turned. As she suspected, several other naked female forms stood behind their group, blocking all routes of escape.

The faces of the female figures, both in front and behind, began to distort. The two who had emerged from the water hissed like serpents.

"Nymphs were here, and they are dead," the one to the right said, eyes now solid black, and lips drawing back to reveal a huge set of fangs. "Their flesh was sweet and succulent. Their blood, nectar. Another feast from our Master."

Long of fang and talon, and face of the woman shifted, narrowing such that her visage echoed the form of a muzzle. The entity took a step toward Rayden with deep hunger in its eyes. Saliva dripped from its jaws.

With eerie cries sounding like a blend of a howl and shriek, the entities lunged toward the humans from both sides.

Doros let an arrow fly, and Rayden swung both sword and axe. The arrow drove into the throat of the entity coming at Doros, while both of Rayden's blows connected with the one attacking her, opening up broad gashes in the creature's torso.

Rayden threw a hard kick to the front, sending the bleeding entity tumbling back into the lake. Turning fast, she swung her axe hard at the entity attacking Doros. The blade drove deep into its side, eliciting a shriek before her sword lopped its head off.

Doros took her blade from its sheath, and stood at Rayden's side.

Standing upright, the entity that Rayden had sent back into the water had regrouped. Screeching, the creature hurled itself toward Rayden, opening its jaws wide.

Rayden ducked the vicious swipe of talons that the creature aimed toward her head. Swinging her axe, she caught the entity solid at the knee. Thrusting her sword upward, she drove the blade deep through the underside of the creature's jaws.

The entity twisted and jerked about, crippled and with its jaws pinned shut. Doros loosed a vigorous cry and hacked into its neck, coming close to severing the head with two blows.

The entity flopped over and hit the ground at an awkward angle, appearing dead.

Turning back to the ongoing melee, Rayden saw that Crassor had downed one of the creatures. She did not have time to warn him of the danger now falling upon him.

Another entity springing onto Crassor from behind, the

creature sank its fangs deep into the flesh of his right shoulder.

Crying out, Crassor shoved the creature off from his back. Blood streaming down from his wounds, he turned to face his attacker. A second entity then slammed into Crassor from the side.

Rayden could not go to his aid, prevented when another of the creatures leaped toward her with a shrill cry. She dodged a swipe, and slammed the pommel of her sword squarely into the entity's teeth, shattering several of them.

The creature staggered back, clearing enough room for Rayden to swing her blade. Slashing the thing across the eyes, Rayden kept free of the creature's wild flailing. Howling in pain, the thing turned to make for the water.

Rayden jumped after it and drove her sword deep into its back, while bringing her axe down atop the creature's skull. It fell into the water, face first, and lay still.

Turning, Rayden's eyes widened. Clutching onto his legs, one of the creatues had begun dragging Crassor toward the water's edge.

He thrashed about, trying to free himself. The creature proved too strong, the water drawing closer and closer, with every passing moment.

Rayden darted across the ground, knocking another of the things aside with her shoulder and racing toward Crassor. Leaping across him, she brought her sword overhead and down in a vicious chopping strike, cleaving the entity's head into two halves.

The thing's body remained upright a moment longer. Crassor shook free of the grip still affixed to his legs and scrambled backwards, the creature toppling over and hitting the ground to his left.

Polybius and Doros stood at an impasse, a few strides away. Shoulder to shoulder, they held weapons up, facing another one of the vile creatures.

Rayden spared a quick look around to assess what remained.

Lucius and Gaius had been slain, and the bodies of two more entities lay upon the ground. The fighting had narrowed down to one last creature.

Crassor moved aside and snatched up his sword, while Rayden stepped toward the last creature from behind. He hurried over to stand on her side, and a few moments later they had the final creature surrounded.

The creature looked back and forth, from Doros and Polybius, to Rayden and Crassor. Gnashing its teeth, a raging hatred filled its eyes.

"You are going nowhere," Rayden told the thing, her ire building with the thought of their dead companions lying nearby.

The thing loosed a hideous screech, and then said in a breathy voice. "I will go to the Master, but not before I drag you with me, into the endless dark!"

The creature hurled itself at Rayden, slashing with its talons. With outward swipes of her blades, Rayden batted its attacks aside, twisting her head as the thing's jaws snapped shut where her face had been a moment before.

Rayden brought her right knee up hard between the thing's legs, jolting it, while crashing the hilt and haft ends of her weapons into the sides of the thing's neck. The creature gurgled and choked, releasing a pungent breath into Rayden's face, causing her to gag.

The creature then released a grating cry, jerking about several times. Life abandoning its dark eyes, a final, scratchy hiss left its throat, as it slumped downward.

Crassor and Doros stood behind it, both of their blades freshly bloodied. Lifting his leg up, Crassor stamped down on the back of the creature's skull, pulping flesh and bone with a loud crunch.

"It won't be taking you anywhere, Rayden," Crassor announced, glaring at the dead thing.

The area fell into silence once more. Looking about, Rayden searched for any more of the things that might be lurking in the shadows.

She examined the bodies of Lucius and Gaius, holding onto a faint possibility that one of them yet clung to a sliver of life. Both had been shredded in savage fashion, with throats and guts torn open. Closing their eyes, Rayden wished both of them a smooth and rapid journey to a better afterlife.

Polybius remained the last Teveren in their group. He had suffered a few light wounds in the attack, but nothing that would prevent him from continuing onward.

Kneeing at his side, Rayden assisted Crassor in cleaning and binding his shoulder wound. He winced as she applied the makeshift bandaging.

"That fanged pile of dung got me pretty good there," Crassor said, grimacing.

"It will heal up," Rayden said, though she did not give voice to her concern about what the bites of some creatures could do. She knew she would have to keep a close watch upon Crassor, and watch for any signs of changes.

"All that talk of a Master," Polybius said, coming over to join them. "What was that all about?"

"Even these things are tied to the same power behind the Imperator," Rayden said, getting back to her feet. "That's what it meant."

"A Master? What Master?" Polybius asked.

"Best not to dwell on what it is," Rayden said. "It is the will that drives all of this darkness."

"Like some sort of dark god," Polybius said.

"In a way," Rayden said. "And maybe something more than that."

"I don't like the sound of that at all," Polybius said, looking anxious.

"It's why there is urgency in striking at the Teverens," Rayden said. "The roots of something dark are set in place, and we don't want to give it the time to grow to harvest."

Polybius looked around. "All these bodies. What are we going to do with them?"

"First, we burn every last bit of those foul things," Rayden said to Polybius and the others. "I want no chance of them returning to threaten anyone else."

"And Lucius and Gaius?" Doros asked.

"We will honor them, and not sully their remains with the filth of those creatures," Rayden said.

Gathering up wood, the survivors of the attack set about burning the remains of the creatures. After collecting up the coin pouches and weapons of the fallen pair of Teverens, they arranged a second fire for their bodies.

Flames licked with insatiable hunger at flesh, and a terrible stench wafted from the fires engulfing the corpses of the creatures. Crassor heaved and vomited, before having to walk a good distance away.

Though nausea plied at her with increasing strength, Rayden stayed in place until she deemed the fires had completed their course in devouring the remains of the entities. Nothing could be left to chance when it came to creatures of the ilk they had faced.

A short vigil at the makeshift pyre would serve to pacify any concerns.

Fire sealed the doom of most such entities. Ash scattered in the winds stood no chance of regenerating.

Looking at the smoke twirling up in slow coils, ascending toward the sky, Rayden said at last. "It is time we are back on our way."

CHAPTER 14

Traversing hills and valleys over the course of the following few days, Rayden and her three companions made steady progress. Keeping to the wilderness, they avoided encounters with other Teverens easily enough.

Vineyards, orchards, and fields, both fallow and filled with crops, marked the locations of farms and settlements. All remained tended to.

It was all Rayden could do to continue onward after observing a group of slaves, shackled and chained together, laboring beneath the lash of a gruff overseer.

Despite a burning desire to intervene, Rayden restrained herself. No risk could be taken while so close to the Imperial City.

If Rayden and her companions set the slaves free, even one eyewitness who could recognize the members of her group could jeopardize any chance of learning more about their enemy; knowledge that might well mean the difference between victory and defeat for all the tribes now marching south.

With victory, all the slaves would be freed, from the ones laboring before her eyes to those in bondage on all the estates, farms, and in the cities of the Teveren Empire. With defeat, everything would get much worse; for slaves and common folk alike.

Rayden had to continue the journey; even if every part of her desired to pummel the dreg wielding the lash, until his face could not be recognized.

Using her bow, Doros secured a little game from time to time along their way, downing a pheasant, a couple of rabbits, and even a small deer. The meat, along with the small quantity of bread and cheese they carried with them, ensured that the group ate well enough on the journey; keeping their strength up, despite the long, arduous hikes each day.

For the most part, the skies remained clear, save for a light rain that fell while they were making their way through a series of larger hills. The Teveren cloaks proved capable enough for dealing with rain, and Rayden passed an afternoon listening to the gentle patter of drops on the woolen material.

Polybius proved to be a pleasant companion, acclimating as best he could to the rigors of a long journey by foot. He shared many things about his life before joining the slave uprising, and answered all the questions that he could from the other three.

With the loss of Lucius and Gaius, the burden of watches at night grew with fewer in the group to take them. But they encountered no further surprises, of natural or supernatural kinds, and were able to attain a pattern that provided for a little sleep.

After a few days, Rayden slept so well that she found herself in the midst of a vivid dream.

***

Rayden stood in the midst of an exuberant crowd. The edifices of a great city rose all around her. Statuary, colonnades, temples, palaces, and other magnificent structures stood in view, no matter what direction she turned her head.

A roadway made of smooth stones ran through the teeming

masses. To her left, a towering archway loomed, an inscription carved across the facing of the transverse segment crowning the portal.

A statue of a proud-looking man rose from the center of the archway's lofty summit. Clad in a solid cuirass sculpted with the contours of a muscular chest and abdomen, the figure wore an ornate helm, fitted with wings on each side. Arms upraised, one hand gripped the hilt of a sword, while the other held a flaming torch.

Rank after rank of Teveren soldiers, in exquisite order, tromped down the roadway in square formations. Weapons and armor shining, their steps pounded in a rhythmic cadence.

Soldiers wearing animal skin cloaks in each formation carried large, curving horns and spear-like standards adorned with golden torques, silver discs and tassles. At the forefront strode men in more ornate armor, wearing greaves on their legs, and with helms exhibiting high horizontal crests of feather or horsehair.

After several formations of soldiers had passed, a mass of people in shackle and chain came into view. Rayden's gut clenched, recognizing men of the northern tribes by their garb and styles of hair. Gessa, Rugara, Runi, Pannimbri, and several others were represented in the dense multitude.

Herded along the route, most looked forlorn and defeated, though a few held looks of defiance.

A few large carts pulled by oxen trundled forward in the midst of the captives. Serving as rolling platforms to display individuals chained to high posts, the carts sparked a great uproar from the gathered crowds.

Rayden stared in dismay, seeing Alcedan being paraded in one of the ox-drawn carts. A somber look on his face, Alcedan looked ahead, showing no reaction to the barrage of mockery and insults coming from both sides.

Other carts carried chieftains she recognized from other tribes of the north, such as Grogner of the Tega. A deep scowl on his face, he hurled curses at the shouting throngs lining the roadway.

The final cart carried a figure that left Rayden stunned, her breath catching in her throat.

Staring at the figure of herself being paraded before the howling mobs, an icy chill crept through Rayden. Looking around, she tensed, noticing solid black eyes in the faces of every single man and woman around her.

Though the sounds of laughter and shouts came from their lips, no true sense of merriment reflected in their dark eyes. With no changes in their expressions all began weeping tears, the drops streaking down their faces consisting of blood.

Despite the blood rivulets streaming from their eyes, the crowd yelled and cheered louder, becoming more frenzied by the moment. The maniacal adulation took on a surreal atmosphere, with each one of the thousands upon thousands of participants appearing to be in the clutches of a greater power.

Rayden's gaze fixed upon a child near to her, of no more than eight or nine years of age, whose face alone of all others displayed no attempt at gaiety or excitement. Rather, her state reflected a much more genuine expression of the macabre scene unfolding.

The little girl's heaving cries and wails brimmed with a forlorn sadness; innocence bereft of hope and condemned to a horrific fate. A single tear of blood trickled from the girl's right eye, a sight that distressed Rayden far more than the adults surrounding her with streams of blood coming from their eyes.

Thunder rumbled across the skies, and an icy wind picked up, coursing through the crowd and whipping all with its icy tendrils. Her long locks tossed all about in the grips of the chilly blasts, Rayden shivered as the cold sank bone-deep.

The ambience dimmed fast, pulling Rayden's attention toward the skies. Rolling, dark clouds swept across the heights, blanketing the sun itself behind a thick wall of vapor that no ray could penetrate.

Dread filled Rayden, seeing much more than clouds in the air over the city. Like a storm of ash, dark forms filled the heights. Shadowy wraiths darted and drifted through the sky; a rain of menace descending from the roiling cloud masses toward the city below.

The atmosphere continued to darken, and the chill inside Rayden progressed. Around her, the crowd persisted in its feverish cheer, though the voices now carried a shrill, desperate edge to them.

"Awaken now, and speak with me, away from the others," a voice whispered into her ear, one she recognized as that of Dreaghen.

The voice snapped her out of the horrid nightmare. Waking with a start, sweat beading across her brow, Rayden took a moment to gather herself from the traumatic dream.

Crassor and Polybius were sitting together quietly, attending to their watch. Doros lay deep in slumber close by.

Sitting up, Rayden looked toward the two men and said, "I'll be back soon."

"Still awhile till next watch," Crassor replied. "Get some more rest in."

Rayden nodded to him, getting to her feet and heading away from the others. She hoped Dreaghen would not take long to manifest, as she did want a little more rest, if it could be found.

The images from the nightmare continued to prod her mind. She wondered at the meaning of the various things that had occurred; from the people with the bleeding eyes, to the gathering storm, to the host of wraiths.

Once more, her mind's eye filled with the vision of the

crying child with the single blood-tear crawling down her little cheek. Everything within Rayden wished she could go back into the dark dream and snatch the child out of it.

Nothing could be done, but Rayden held the consolation that the things of the dream had not come to pass. Nor did she intend them to. For her part, she would die fighting before being taken captive and paraded through the streets by the Imperator's legions.

Breaths steady, and footsteps silent, Rayden continued through the shadows of the forest.

***

Walking toward her, Dreaghen's form had a silvery luster. His steps carried no sound, and left no print in the ground.

Looking around, a wistful expression crossed his face. He raised his eyes up, gazing toward the gleaming orb enthroned in the night sky. A trace of a smile came to his face.

"The air of a forest night, under a magnificent moon ... the taste of it, the scent ... the feel of it on your skin," Dreaghen said. He brought his eyes down to meet those of Rayden. "You know what I speak of."

"I do, as does anyone who dwells in the north," Rayden said. "I wish circumstances were in a place where I could savor a night like this more."

"One day, and may it be soon," Dreaghen said.

"I know you didn't summon me from a dream to speak of forest nights," Rayden said. She paused, before adding, "A dream that was less than pleasant."

"Even were the Teverens to cheer the victory of their legions, they would be applauding their own doom," Dreaghen said, his mien growing austere. "When none are left who can oppose the Imperator, the trap will be sprung upon every last man, woman ... and child."

His emphasis on the final word invoked the image of the terrified little girl from her dream, once more.

"I've seen more than enough to know the nightmare that awaits, should the Imperator prevail," Rayden said. "I needed no lesson in that."

"The rabble in the streets are all fools, easily cowed, placated, or subdued," Dreaghen said. "Just tools in the hands of those who seek greater power."

"As it is in most kingdoms and empires," Rayden said. "I cannot count on more than one hand the number of rulers whose reigns I would be swift to defend."

"I would think it would take a broad search, across all the lands of this world, to come up with enough to require the use of a second hand to count them," Dreaghen said.

"It would take such a search," Rayden said. "Most are despots of a much different mind than those they rule ... and now we find ourselves pitted against one of the worst of their lot, one who wields tremendous power."

"Power far beyond mortal soldiers, and force of arms," Dreaghen replied.

"Power that raises an army of beasts that have been transformed into beast-men. Power that resurrects a corpse, and gives it strength beyond any man or woman. A power that gives one of its thralls the power to strangle me with invisible hands, and summon a pack of wild boars to devour my body. A power that brings monstrosities veiled in beauty from the depths of a lake." Rayden paused, and then added with a curt edge. "Yes, Dreaghen, I am well-aware of the deeper levels of power our adversary enjoys."

"Remember, all these things are roots of the same tree," Dreaghen said, in a tone of caution.

"Not something I ever forget," Rayden said. "It is the reason we are going into the Imperial City. To learn what other roots may lie in wait. You are aware of all of this, so why have you summoned me tonight?"

"The roots and branches of a tree are all connected," Dreaghen said. "Everything in thrall to the power behind this has that kind of connection. You have made many enemies in the abyss, in a short time."

"I try not to think about that too much," Rayden said. "I'd rather my adversaries to be of flesh and blood, where my sword and axe can resist them."

"Word of you has traveled among their incorporeal kind," Dreaghen said. "Do not forget that you have contended with them long before you came back to the north.

"While your name spread on the tongues of humans, your name also spread within other realms. Every time you stood against an evil, or thwarted a wicked aim, a root of that greater tree became aware of you.

"Those kinds of spirits will recognize you on the streets of the Imperial City ... surrounded by thousands upon thousands of Teverens ... and many leagues from the warriors coming from the north. I assure you, there are many dark spirits within the walls of the Imperial City; including several that are very powerful among their kind. They will do all in their power to make certain you do not return to the tribal army."

Rayden understood the sorcerer's meaning at once.

"Then should I turn back? And leave the other three to a task I decided upon?" Rayden asked, disliking the taste of the words on her tongue. Her eyes narrowed, casting the sorcerer a hard stare. "Is that what you are asking of me? If you are, then you will be gravely disappointed with my response."

Dreaghen shook his head. "I did not come here to dissuade you from your path. In a world where courage like yours is scarce, you are needed in this struggle ... especially against an enemy such as the one we are both facing."

"Then why did you come here to speak with me?" Rayden asked, her irritation rising along with a growing impatience. "To tell me what I am already aware of? You speak of facing an enemy ... Need I remind you that it was my life in the balance against all those things I spoke of, like the beast men and the resurrected corpse? I was the one alone in the forest, being choked high off the ground ... the grip on my throat impossible to break."

"I came here to give you what help I can, in the final stage of this struggle," Dreaghen said, his voice lowering. The lilt in his tone told Rayden that her words had struck a powerful note in the sorcerer. "I know what you have faced, Rayden."

"Why don't you come down here in your own flesh and join with us?" Rayden asked, a humorless grin spreading on her face. "Or do you fear coming within my reach, after all the times you have confounded me with your words and appearances? You speak of courage ... do you have enough courage to stand before me?"

The sorcerer stared at her for a moment. "Must I always remind you that I have always helped you? Without me, you would not have returned to the north, until it was far too late."

"It would have been too late for everyone, everywhere, not just the northern tribes," Rayden stated. She fixed her gaze on the sorcerer. "Too late for you as well."

"It would have been too late for all of us, if you had not responded to me, and undertaken the journey," Dreaghen admitted. "But few could survive what you survive. Few could stand against what you have confronted, and then continue forward. Because of you, there is still a chance to stop this great darkness. You have seen its face, and you know what price all will pay should it prevail."

"Then what help are you offering now?" Rayden said with an air of vexation. "The night grows late."

"What I do for you now will reduce my strength greatly, to

where I don't know if I can even manifest to give you counsel," Dreaghen said. "But you will not survive the Imperial City with things as they are now. The minions of the abyss are watching for you, everywhere. Within an animal, or a high priest of the Imperator's cult ... or a man deemed consumed with madness on the streets, or even in the kind of disembodied form you've already witnessed on that hilltop. Make no mistake, Rayden, the things of the darkness are keeping a watch for you, from a great many vantages."

The sorcerer's tidings were of little surprise to Rayden. More than once, she had been recognized by the things of the abyss, in places far removed from each other, where word of her could not have spread through normal human means.

It stood to reason that their ilk within the Imperial City could do the same. She intended to keep a low profile in the streets of the Imperator's great city, but the risk would be constant.

She did not wish to imperil her companions, but neither could she begin to think of abandoning them.

"Then what do you intend to do, sorcerer?" Rayden asked, the harshness in her tone ebbing.

"I intend to shield you, and to veil you, to whatever extent I can," Dreaghen said. A look came over the sorcerer that she had not seen before; one holding elements of sadness, affection, and even a little fatalism. "I will give to you all I can muster, Rayden, and I hope it will be enough to see you through your foray into the Imperial City."

Seeing his change in demeanor, Rayden wondered what the sorcerer intended. The sense of finality in his face unmistakable, the sight troubled her.

As frustrating and enigmatic as the sorcerer could be at given moments, he had never led her astray. In a physical sense, he had not been with her during the perilous moments she had spoken of. But then again, she did not know everything about

Dreaghen's own path. Rayden surmised there were many things about him yet to be learned.

Dreaghen then spread his arms wide, palms open, and began chanting in an unfamiliar tongue. A few moments later, a tingling sensation arose all across Rayden's body.

She remained in place, stifling a few defensive urges at the presence of magical arts, trusting to the sorcerer and her core instincts.

As the sorcerer continued with his chanting, Rayden watched in amazement as her skin began taking on a silver glow. With the manifesting luminescence, a sense of weightlessness filled her body, to a level where she expected to begin floating off the ground.

A sweet scent filled the air. Not unlike the burning incense found within some temples or at a ceremony, the aroma had a pleasant, soothing effect upon her. Rayden closed her eyes, basking in the immersive sensation, before looking back to the sorcerer again.

Dreaghen stepped forward, now holding an upturned shell and long feather in his hands. Giving off a light smoke, a short bundle burned within the shell. Without any pause in his chanting, he waved the feather over the shell, fanning the smoke toward Rayden, starting at her head and lowering to her feet.

He walked around her, repeating the sequence again and again.

A calm feeling flowed through Rayden, easing her mind into an even more tranquil state. Her breathing coming slow and easy, she savored every instant.

Dreaghen stepped away from Rayden, and his chanting drew to an end. The glow emanating from Rayden's body ebbed, and her sense of weight returned.

His movements slow and ponderous, the sorcerer turned to face her.

Weariness filled his eyes and face, though a smile rested on his lips. His voice also reflected a great level of fatigue. "It is done. Go onward to your task ... and know that their eyes will be confounded for a time. Learn what you can of our adversary. I do not know when we will speak again. I have bestowed you with all that I can. I have held nothing back."

Eyeing his drooping posture, Rayden knew the sorcerer had exerted himself to a tremendous degree.

"Thank you," Rayden said, giving him a slight bow. "I will do all I can to honor what you have done here."

"I know you will, Rayden Valkyrie," Dreaghen responded, his face now showing a high degree of pain in addition to the weariness. He mustered another smile. The look of pain increased further, and his voice sounded strained when he continued. "I only hope that I have honored what you have done, and will continue to do."

With a final look that reflected sheer anguish, Dreaghen's form dimmed, and then vanished, leaving Rayden alone among the shadows of the trees. The last expression on his face distressed her, but she knew he had accepted whatever burden had transpired.

In her heart, she knew a change had taken place within her, due to the sorcerer's actions. In addition to whatever mysterious veiling the sorcerer had invoked on her behalf, he had girded her, and even cleansed her, in preparation for what would come. She felt renewed and invigorated, not just in body but also in mind.

Wherever Dreaghen dwelled, Rayden wished a quick healing and recovery for the sorcerer, yet she doubted that would happen. No matter how much she wanted it otherwise, she knew he had incurred a great trial to do what he had done.

She did not understand the things of his world, but could only imagine the kinds of prices a sorcerer paid to wield their power to the highest levels.

From pushing the limits of endurance, to calling upon every last reservoir of strength, warriors taxed their physical bodies in carrying out an onerous task or prevailing in battle. A warrior also paid a terrible price in mind and spirit; from experiencing the horrors born of war and battle.

Dreaghen might have paid a heavy physical price, but Rayden suspected that other, greater, costs, of a non-physical nature and unique to the arts of sorcery, had been suffered. Knowing how even the best of warriors could be worn down in body, mind, and spirit, to a point where they were mere shadows of their former selves, she feared for the sorcerer.

Rayden knew she could do nothing at the moment for him. She did not even have an idea of where he could be found, in a physical manner.

The uncertainty of Dreaghen's fate would have to be accepted for the time being. Rayden could honor him in giving her full focus to the Imperial City, and discovering the things it might be harboring. Every insight about their enemy that could be gained could well prove to be the difference between victory and defeat for the tribal army; in addition to numerous other lands and people falling under a Teveren shadow.

Failing to stop the Imperator held far more in the balance than the usual war over territory between kingdoms, or a change in rulers. Defeat meant the unfolding of a horrific age; one that would enslave numerous lands and populations, with nothing capable of stopping it.

With a broad range of feelings, Rayden started back for the area where she and her companions had camped for the night. There still remained a little time for rest before the next watch, but she doubted sleep would come easy.

***

Stretching her limbs in the first rays of morning light, Rayden drank in the crisp, cool air. She looked over to where Doros worked at the clasp on her cloak, readying for the day's journey.

"Rest well?" she asked her friend.

"As well as one can, while traveling through the wilderness in unfamiliar territory," Doros said. "I think I would give over half of the coins in my pouch if I could get a night in an inn."

Rayden thought upon Doros' words for a moment. "Didn't Polybius say we would come across a Teveren city before we reach the Imperial City?"

Doros nodded. She looked over to where Polybius sat quietly, munching on a little cheese.

"What city will we see, before we reach the walls of the Imperial City?" she called over to him.

"Verrannus, a trading town of good size," Polybius called back, after swallowing a bite of the cheese. He dusted a few crumbs off his tunic. "Probably reach it by midday, in fact."

Rayden looked from Polybius to Doros. "You could get a night in an inn, and we could see what we can learn about the state of things in the empire, before we reach the Imperial City."

"Going into Verrannus?" Doros asked. "Is that what you mean?"

"For one night," Rayden answered.

She left one reason unspoken. Dreaghen had invoked power to shield her from dark spirits, and it stood to reason that such creatures roved the streets of Verrannus as much as they did the Imperial City. The sorcerer had mentioned several different forms that the dark spirits could be found in; and one in particular tugged at Rayden's thoughts.

All Teveren cities held temples.

Testing her new, unseen shield a little before they walked the streets of the Imperial City would be as reasonable as putting a newly-crafted weapon to some trial before carrying it into battle.

Rayden knew she needed to come across someone appearing

to be gripped in the throes of madness; or search out a high priest.

Then, she would know the strength of Dreaghen's gift that night.

CHAPTER 15

Coming down from the hills, Rayden looked upon the walled city nestled in a bend of the great Golden River, whose waters did indeed have a light golden hue. Though far from being the biggest city she had visited, Verrannus' walls and main gate looked stout enough to hold off a large force for a good while.

Verrannus itself did not concern her as much as the construct visible just outside the northern end of the city did. Arranged in the shape of a rectangle, a great fort had been erected; one far larger and containing more elements than the encampment they had sacked on the edge of Borenni lands.

Bordered with a deep ditch and high earthen embankment, the latter crowned by a wooden palisade, with open-roofed, platform-like towers set at regular intervals, the fort contained a number of elongated structures inside. Several of the timber edifices sat in orderly rows, and a few had been arranged in square configurations, at the center of the fort.

As with most times she set her eyes upon Teveren edifices, Rayden could not help but appreciate the discipline that the arrangement reflected. Sharpness of purpose and dedication emanated from every aspect of the fort's visual appearance.

Unlike the tribal army confronting them, the Teverens

harbored no differences that could undermine their efforts. They shared a solid foundation, one that girded every province within their empire.

Rayden harbored a little envy at the thought, wishing the northern tribes could embrace a similar, strong sense of common purpose. If they had been like the Teverens in that regard, the tribal force marching toward the Imperial City would have been twice as strong, if not even greater in number.

Rayden eyed a few buildings, into which horses were being taken. A calvary force quartered within the fortress indicated the presence of a legion with strong capabilities.

With Polybius at the front, Rayden and Doros flanking, and Crassor bringing up their rear, they walked along the road, joining the light foot traffic and a few carts heading toward the city.

After Polybius answered a few questions from guards warding the city gate, the group proceeded inside the walls. A maze of narrow, winding streets spread before them.

Walking through a corridor of shade created from the multi-story structures looming on each side, Rayden and the others pressed through the congested path. Listening to the incessant noise from people and animals alike, Rayden wondered how anyone could enjoy living within such an environment.

The warm touch of the sun fell upon her face, breaking through the wall of adjacent tenements, where one of their number had collapsed and now stood in ruins. Seeing wooden posts buttressing the walls of some of the other high structures, Rayden doubted the fallen edifice to be an isolated incident.

The streets became even more difficult to navigate where ground level shop owners plied their wares and artisans labored in front of their spaces and workshops. The sounds of spirited haggling, and clack and clang of tools, melded into the noisy environs.

Rayden found herself relieved that it did not take long to find a tavern and inn. A few low tables and benches outside the front entrance identified its nature readily enough. With no desire to observe the dense flow of people through the street, Rayden led the others past the tables and into the tavern.

The dusky interior held the usual array of patrons. A few quiet loners, others in low conversations, and some more boisterous, showing the effects of the strong wine they had imbibed, occupied a few of the tables and other spaces within the establishment.

Rayden and Doros drew more than a few looks their way, including gazes that lingered with reflections of lustful desires. The ones casting the prurient expressions took quick note of the weapons Rayden and Doros carried, as well as Crassor's presence with them.

Rayden doubted any would be foolish enough to try and act upon the thoughts they harbored. But the ability of strong drink to lead some to stupid, reckless decisions could never be underestimated.

A couple of serving women flitted among the crowd, working alongside a stocky, grizzled-looking man who acted with the kind of confidence that identified him as the tavern master.

Rayden's group found an open table near to where he stood, and took seats on the benches set around it. Walking over to them, the tavern master eyed Polybius, Rayden and the others, and a smile grew on his face.

"Welcome," he greeted, in a scratchy, deep voice. "From the looks of you, I'd say you've been traveling a fair distance."

"Making our way to the Imperial City ... too much uncertainty in the north," Polybius replied, with a formal air, sliding with ease into the role he had undertaken. "At least my companions and I can conduct some business there, while we wait for the legions to take care of the disturbances."

"Looks like your companions can handle themselves well enough, and your slave would give any bandit pause," the tavern master replied, appraising the group with the kind of eye honed from years interacting with an extensive variety of people. His gaze settled upon Rayden. "You must be one of our latest group of friends. Can't tell from which of the two tribes, just by looking at you, since the women of both have similar appearances. I only can tell the tribes apart from the way the men of the tribes wear their hair. But whichever you are from, we're glad to have your help at this time."

Rayden took the surprising news in stride, showing no outward reaction that would indicate the unease sparked by his words. She knew the northern tribes well enough to hazard a guess; at least with one of the more disagreeable of the tribes, whose men wore their hair in a distinctive knot atop their heads.

"Alettani," she ventured, all but certain she had named one of the two that the tavern master had in mind. The word tasted bitter on her tongue, as the Alettani had rejected the messenger sent from the Gessa to gather the tribes to face their common threat.

"Good bunch of horsemen they are, we'll raise a drink to your tribe," interjected a younger, clean-shaven man seated with three others like him at a table nearby.

"I am honored," Rayden said, nodding to the quartet and playing along with the development. They all had the air of soldiers, in good physical condition and dressed simply in tunics and capes.

"Prefer your lot much more than the Sarrimena," one of the other men at the table added. "We already got into a heavy brawl with a bunch of those ruffians. But they learned quick enough that legion men are not to be messed with."

The soldier's companions cheered his words. Clanging their vessels together, they took a drink.

The mention of the Sarrimena carried a sting. Like the Alettani, they had also rejected the Gessa messenger sent to them by Alcedan. Evidently, both had already made another choice, regarding the path they would take.

"You'll find us much better skilled than they at our mounts," Rayden said, though in her heart she knew both tribes to be exceptional warriors on horseback.

"All the better to aid us in clearing up the rabble from the north," the first solider said. "I know most of them bear little love for us. But they are wise enough to know who will prevail."

"I am sure a little coin and guarantees of land had some influence on them too," the second soldier commented, with a laugh.

"What legion are you men from?" Polybius asked the soldiers, in a polite and curious manner.

"6th Antiochus," the man replied with an air of pride. "We will be moving out soon, in a matter of days, to join the others near the Imperial City gathering to deal with the upstarts."

"Your words come as a relief, there's been far too much disruption these past months," Polybius said.

"For all of us," the first soldier said. "My back and knees still ache from constructing our fortress. Nothing like building a road. Entrenchment tools are the last things I want to see right now. We were hard pressed to build it as fast as possible, with the barbarians moving so quickly into the heart of Teveren lands."

"We're taking no chances ourselves," Polybius said. "We will continue on to the Imperial City come morning."

"Don't worry yourself too much," the first solider said. "These barbarians have avoided all walled cities on their march. They seem to aim for the Imperial City itself. But I wouldn't stay anywhere outside of a city. Lots of pillaging and destruction going on in the villages, farms and villas."

"I have friends whose holdings have been overrun by these

barbarians," Polybius said. "They are taking everything, and setting flame."

"This scourge will not last long ... the legions will bring this to an end, soon enough," the first soldier said. He paused, and then, after a glance toward Rayden, added, "Along with our allies, of course."

"I am sure our presence will come as a great surprise to the invaders," Rayden said, casting an amiable grin at the man.

"It will ... I hear they are holding the Alettani and Sarrimena back, until the barbarians squat before the Imperial City's walls," the first soldier said.

"Walls they'd break themselves upon anyway," a third soldier in the group said.

"Several legions, two tribes filled with good horsemen, and the walls of the Imperial City ... order will be restored across Teveren lands in a rapid manner," the first soldier said.

"And the Imperator may have other surprises in store for the barbarians," the second soldier said, chuckling.

Rayden's expression did not change, but she doubted the soldier had any idea of what the Imperator truly stood capable of. Like Teveren citizens, he served a use for the moment, but had no inkling of the malignant world the Imperator intended to bring into being.

Rayden knew the Teverens would use the two tribes they had recruited in a concentrated and unique way. Teveren legions fought in a specific way; with components of a legion assigned dedicated roles during the course of a battle.

Tribal cavalry would not be used in a way that would disrupt that cohesion. Rather, they would be wielded in a manner that would tilt the course of the battle. Striking at a flank, or charging in from behind the tribal army, the Teverens' new allies would enter the fight at a critical juncture.

The first significant fruits of their journey, the information regarding the alliance of the Alettani and Sarrimena would be of immense value to the tribal army.

The northern tribes would have to be careful to veil their awareness, while preparing for the attack of the two renegade tribes. If the Teverens thought they still held the advantage of surprise, their scheme could be thwarted all the easier.

Rayden could only imagine the face of Alcedan when learning word of the betrayal. She knew that he and the other tribal chieftains would desire to inflict a terrible punishment on tribes who had willfully chosen Teveren masters.

"The Alettani will look forward to celebrating with the Teverens, in days soon to come," Rayden said, raising her cup toward the men in a salutatory manner.

"We will be marching together in a great Triumph together, through the streets of the Imperial City," the first soldier replied. A wistful look in his eye, he continued, "All my life I've imagined what it would be like to march in a Triumph."

At the soldiers's words, Rayden thought of her recent dream, and kept her face still. The image of her shackled to a post, and paraded on a cart through throngs of jeering Teverens, traipsed across her mind's eye.

"May it not be much longer before you take part in one," she replied to the first soldier, forcing a smile upon her face.

"I am no fool, though," the soldier replied. "I know days of hard marches, labor, and fighting lay ahead."

"Tonight is not a night to dwell upon such concerns," Polybius said. He looked to the tavern master. "These men of the legion have already labored hard for the defense of the Teveren citizens. Let me pay for a round of your finest wine, for each of these noble soldiers. It is the least I can do to show my gratitude."

The four men at the table gave a hearty cheer toward their new patron at the declaration.

"Who may we say shows us such generosity?" the first

soldier asked.

"Polybius, of Tarna," he answered.

"Tarna ... the vines there make for some of the best wine I've had," the second solider said, appreciatively.

"It is what we are known for," Polybius replied.

"And we happen to have a couple amphorae of such, full and ready to be enjoyed," the tavern master said.

"Then delay no longer, and fill the cups of these men with the exquisite nectar of Tarna," Polybius replied.

The tavern master fulfilled the request, and then proceeded to fill the soldiers' cups a couple of times more at Polybius' direction. The soldiers, comrades given a night away from the cares of the world, accepted the outpouring of generosity with raucous salutations.

The tavern master personally attended Rayden's group and the legion men, letting the pair of serving girls see to the needs of the other patrons. By then the tavern rooms had filled to capacity, the air brimming with spirited conversation, jests, boasts, laughter and the clatter of dice.

Rayden knew the tavern master's persistent personal attention reflected the respect he had for the legion men, as much as it did the largesse of Polybius.

She nursed her own cup of Tarnan wine, savoring the taste, but not about to put her wits at risk. Watching the soldiers, she slipped a question in, when the legion men displayed advancing effects of the wine.

"Does the Imperator have a temple close to here?" she asked. "One dedicated to him?"

"Getting a bit late for worshipping, don't you think?" the first legion man said, his words beginning to slur. "It's almost night! Stay with us ... let us drink, my new Alettani friend! The temple will still be there in the morning. So will your journey. Enjoy the moment at hand!"

"If we had more time," Rayden said, smiling. A part of her did wish she could indulge in several cups of wine, but she had just one night in the city. "We continue our journey tomorrow, at dawn's light, and I wanted to visit a temple tonight."

"Both a new ally and a new worshipper," the first soldier said, a little wine dribbling from a corner of his mouth. "Getting ready to become a Teveren citizen!"

"I would like to pay my respects to the divinity of the Imperator," Rayden said.

"The divinity of the Imperator," the second soldier muttered, repeating her words with a trace of derision in his voice.

"A temple is built to a god, yes?" Rayden asked.

"A temple to a man! A man ... who proclaims himself a god, and builds temples to himself," the second soldier stated in a lighthearted air, shaking his head. His words drawing silence and hard glances from his companions at once, the soldier did not appear to notice their abrupt shift in mood. Laughing, he continued, spreading his arms wide, as if making a grand gesture. "Maybe I can do the same after a few more cups! Make myself a god. Then the legion can build a temple to me! You all can be my high priests!"

"Do not let drink get your tongue wagging foolish," the tavern master interjected, a sharp edge to his voice. Glancing around toward the other patrons sitting at tables nearby, he continued admonishing the soldier. "Not a word more. Let that be the end of it!"

"Oh, we are just having some fun here," drawled the soldier, taking no notice of the irritated expressions on his companions' faces.

"I said not a word more, or you will not be welcome in this tavern," the tavern master replied, continuing to look around in a nervous manner. He turned his attention to the other three soldiers at the table. "Get the lad under control."

Rayden suspected the tavern master harbored serious concerns regarding the patrons within earshot. She wondered what could provoke the kind of fear she could see reflected in his eyes.

"Best keep your mouth shut," the third soldier told his companion.

"What do you mean?" the second soldier slurred. "I'm just joking around here. Me? A god? I—."

"That's enough, or I'll shut you up myself," the first solider said, cutting his companion off. "Before you find yourself hanging from a cross, or becoming fodder for beasts in front of blood-lusting crowds."

"No joking about that, and not here," the tavern master added in a firm tone, glaring at the soldier. "I don't think you need any more wine tonight."

Rayden caught a trace of panic within the hard stare he cast the soldier. The open mention of the Imperator in such a manner had crossed a line that all the Teverens within hearing distance recoiled from.

Looking around and seeing the angered expressions on his comrades' faces, the soldier's smile and joviality faded. With a frown, he nodded to all of them, looking well chastised.

"Fine ... I didn't mean anything by it," he muttered, becoming contrite in demeanor. His mood darkening, he stared down at the cup in his hand, and fell into a brooding silence.

The tavern master looked back to Rayden. His tone lightened. "There is a temple here in Verrannus ... turn right, outside the tavern entrance, and go down the street. You'll come to a baker's shop. Turn right on the street that crosses there ... follow it, and you'll see a temple on the hill to your left. Big temple, broad columns. That will be the one you are looking for."

"Thank you," Rayden said.

"You are certain you will be going there tonight?" the tavern master asked.

"I have little choice, as we are leaving for the Imperial City when the dawn arrives," Rayden said.

"Be on your guard if you go, then," the tavern master said. "The streets turn dangerous when night falls. From the looks of you all, I sense you are capable enough, but I must caution you anyway."

"I do appreciate the counsel," Rayden said.

"I try to look out for my patrons when I can," he replied. "Few ever listen, but I try."

She smiled, understanding his words. "Few ever heed counsel born of experience or wisdom. It is why the world is as it is today."

"And why I see the same mistakes repeated over and over again," the tavern master replied, with a grin. "If you would excuse me for a moment, it is getting busy in here now."

The tavern master walked off, and Rayden finished her cup. Taking a deep breath, she knew the time for seeking a test had come.

***

Turning right outside the tavern entrance, Rayden headed down the street, just after sunset. The clatter of wheels and noise of animals now filled the air, with a number of carts rumbling over the stones of the street surface.

Having insisted on accompanying her, though not knowing her purpose, Crassor strode along beside her, eyeing the shadows and side streets with a pensive, wary eye. "Once this all slows down, we will have to keep our eyes out for trouble."

"If it is trouble someone wants, trouble they shall get," Rayden said in a low voice, casting a sideways glance toward her companion.

"Would feel good, after all this endless walking," Crassor

replied. He then added, in a voice low enough for her ears only. "I would welcome a chance to break a few Teveren skulls."

"Over here, follow me quick," Rayden told Crassor, looking up, and shifting toward the opposite side of the street.

Crassor followed her over, just before a pile of refuse plopped onto the street where they had been about to step. He looked up the height of the tenement, glaring.

"If I could get my hands on whoever pitched that out," Crassor said.

"The joys of living in a city," Rayden commented, as they continued onward.

"I remember enough of this from my days in bondage," Crassor remarked. "I did what I am doing now for my former master, more than once. Only a fool would walk streets at night without guard."

Rayden had taken note of more than one city dweller appraising them from the shadows, with more than a passing interest. She knew their kind well enough.

Most would seek out easier victims. Only the boldest or most foolhardy of rogues would seek to harass a pair such as Crassor and herself. Better pickings stumbled out of taverns and wandered about in other areas.

Recognizing the sign of a baker's shop perched on the corner of intersecting streets, she turned to the right as instructed by the tavern master. Looking up and to the left, she eyed a large temple stucture, rising from the top of a hill.

Rayden followed the winding street to where the first of a long array of marble steps climbed the hill, up toward the temple.

Turning to Crassor, she said, "I do not intend to be here long. There is something I must learn, and my best chance will be here."

"Do what you must," Crassor said. "I trust it is something of importance. I will stand with you as long as it takes."

Rayden gave him a nod, and began surmounting the steps, making her way to the top of the hill.

Large charcoal braziers cast a reddish glow onto the front of the temple, illuminating the row of stout columns supporting the portion of the roof sheltering the entrance.

A number of scenes had been carved into the facade high above. Many depicted various images of war, set on either side of a prominent, central scene; exhibiting a man pulled in a grand-looking chariot, riding through the midst of a triumphal procession.

Rayden stared at the figure, taking in the sight of his sculpted cuirass that followed the contours of his torso. The statue atop the great arch in her dream rose up within her thoughts; the man displayed a match for the one in the facade above.

Continuing forward, she climbed the wide steps leading to the temple entrance, and proceeded inside.

A series of braziers and oil lamps cast a number of great, dynamic shadows throughout the spacious interior. An altar of stone stood at the far end, atop a dais. Behind the dais and altar arose a towering sculpture.

Imbued with solid muscle tone, the figure presented an image of strength and vitality. The face of a clean-shaven man with angular features and short-cropped hair looked out over the temple floor, from a height equivalent to many of the tenements Rayden had seen in the streets below.

Crowned with a laurel, his head had been wreathed in rays of light, or perhaps tongues of fire, that left no doubt of the figure's divine nature.

The sculpted cuirass he wore matched that of the image in the facade and the statue in her dream.

Rayden knew she gazed upon an image of the Imperator; a man who declared himself to be a god. He was not the first such man she had come across in her journeys, but nowhere had she witnessed the kind of scale like that displayed before her eyes.

The sounds of footsteps drew her attention back from the massive statue. A narrow-faced man attired in a long dark tunic and sandals walked toward Rayden and Crassor.

His steps carried no sense of urgency, but his eyes were filled with scrutiny as he eyed the two of them. A thin, silvery chain around his neck disappeared underneath his tunic, hiding whatever pendant might be hanging from the bottom of the loop of finely-crafted links.

"It is a late hour," he said, looking between the two of them. "We do not have many come at this time. What business do you have with us?"

"We are on our way to the Imperial City, and just staying one night in Verrannus," Rayden answered. "I wanted to visit the temple while I am in the city."

"You are welcome to render adoration to his divinity," the priest said.

"May I speak with the high priest?" Rayden asked. "I would also like to make an offering to this temple, while I'm here."

The priest raised his eyebrows at her mention of an offering. He nodded to her. "We welcome all offerings. I shall leave you here, and see if he is available to speak with you."

The priest left Rayden and Crassor where they stood. She doubted he would return by himself, when the mention of an offering had been made.

In her experience, priests and kings alike tended to react favorably to any prospects of gaining more treasure.

The priest soon returned with a taller man clad in similar attire. He also bore a thin chain around his neck, with some manner of pendant or amulet hidden beneath his lengthy tunic.

Behind the two were a pair of younger men, clean-shaven on both face and head, and garbed in tunics of a lighter hue. She guessed them to be priests or acolytes, of an even lower rank than the first.

"The High Priest of the Temple of the Imperator," the first priest announced.

An air of threat surrounded the high priest, whose physical appearance seemed benign enough. Looking to be many years older than the first priest, there was nothing remarkable about the lean, narrow-faced man that could justify the deep sense of unease he gave Rayden.

The high priest regarded them in silence at first, his gaze harboring a cold edge. His scrutiny lingered on Rayden, and the disquiet within her rose. Something about the man provoked her instincts to a greater degree than a wild beast, or even a hostile, armored warrior.

Rayden had little doubt she stood in the presence of a dark spirit, dwelling within the man before her.

"A barbarian woman, in the company of a slave," the high priest commented, in an even tone. "Unusual visitors at this late hour."

"Alettani, friends of the Teveren Empire, and in the service of the Imperator," Rayden replied, giving the high priest a respectful nod. She glanced toward Crassor. "He is the slave of Polybius of Tarna, who I am traveling with to the Imperial City. We leave Verrannus tomorrow. I just wanted to make a visit to a temple dedicated to the Imperator, and make an offering."

"It is wise to embrace his divinity," the high priest said, with no change to his timbre. "It was very wise the Alettani chose friendship rather than a path of war. A great and terrible price will be paid by the enemies of the Imperator."

Rayden drew out the pouch at her waist. Loosening the string closing it, she took out several gold coins, a substantial sum for a random visitor to a temple.

She handed the coins over to the high priest.

"Accept this gift to the temple, to honor the Imperator,"

Rayden said.

"A highly generous gift," the high priest acknowledged, accepting the coins. "The first we have received from one of the Alettani."

His stare held glints of suspicion and mistrust, but his demeanor remained unruffled. He turned the coins over to the priest at his right.

"A sacrifice will be made on your behalf this night at the altar," the high priest stated, looking back to her. "What is your name?"

"Vallassia of the Alettani," Rayden said, using a female name common in the north.

The eyes of the high priest narrowed slightly. She could sense the man's concentration, even if it barely showed on his face.

The air inside the temple grew colder, taking a sharp plunge to where she could see the ghostly wisps of her breath. Showing no reaction to the abrupt shift in temperature, she endured the biting chill; and increasing scrutiny from the high priest.

"You have a mystery about you, Vallassia of the Alettani," the high priest declared. A hint of frustration echoed in his voice.

The light from the oil lamps and braziers dimmed. Swarming shadows pressing in their glow, the lamps and braziers looked like fragile islands of luminescence within a sea of darkness.

In her peripheral vision, Rayden could see movements higher above, within the broader darkness. Though tempted to look upward, she kept her attention fixed upon the high priest.

"A mystery?" she asked.

"You keep much about you hidden," the high priest said. "A very guarded woman."

His words seeming like those of a seer or common fortune-teller, Rayden could tell the truth in his icy gaze. Stymied by Dreaghen's sorcery, the high priest, or whatever dwelled within him, could not recognize her identity.

"Life has not been an easy path for me," Rayden said. "If I appear guarded, it is the caution I must take to survive each day."

"Caution is something we all must heed," the high priest replied, a gleam in his eyes and the wisp of a grin on his lips. "But your generosity must be rewarded. I will allow you to witness the sacrifice to be made in your name."

"Thank you," Rayden said, keeping her manner respectful, though sensing the priest had made some sort of determination.

"We allow no weapons near the altar, and your slave must await you outside," the high priest told her.

Rayden's instincts prodded her further, warning her of something amiss. Behind the high priest's invitation lurked a menace, but she could tell that her identity had still not been fathomed.

Suspecting an ultimate test of the strength of Dreaghen's sorcery, she chose to continue with her act. Drawing out her sword and axe, she turned to Crassor.

"Take these into your keeping, and await me outside," Rayden said.

Crassor looked uncomfortable, a horde of questions teeming in his eyes. Rayden held his gaze firm for a moment, hoping he did not break his discipline.

His jaws grew taut, but Crassor did not lose his composure. Reaching out, he gave a curt nod and took the weapons from her. The two younger acolytes moved forward to stand on either side of him.

"Come with us," one of them said to Crassor, taking a step ahead of him. He nodded back to the acolyte, after giving Rayden one last look; a glance filled with concern and worry.

Turning, he left Rayden behind, in the company of the priests. The two acolytes escorting him close, Crassor headed for the temple entrance.

When he had gone outside, Rayden watched as two massive wooden doors creaked shut. The sound of a bar being set in place followed. The two acolytes returned and came to a stop a few paces from Rayden.

Rayden observed the closure with a sense of finality, knowing a perilous confrontation loomed.

"Come with me," the high priest instructed her. He looked to the priest at his right hand. "Retrieve the sacrifice."

The priest gave a bow and walked away, leaving Rayden alone with the high priest. He regarded her intently for a few moments, and she could feel a tingling sensation all over her skin.

Sensing the presence of sorcery, and on the verge of striking the high priest, Rayden stayed her hand when the man told her, "Follow me."

With the acolytes behind them, the quartet proceeded down the center of the great temple, striding toward the altar, dais, and statue at the far end. When they arrived at the base of the low dais supporting the altar, the high priest gestured for Rayden to stand in place.

The pair of acolytes then took positions, one at each side of her.

The high priest continued up the short flight of marble steps to the platform, and then walked around to the far side of the stone altar. The priest he had dispatched returned at that moment, carrying a small cage with him. The contents inside the cage remained hidden from Rayden's sight as he climbed the steps toward the high priest.

Whether a trick of the eye, or a change in luminance, the two great braziers at the corners of the dais appeared to brighten. The stronger light afforded Rayden a clear look at what stood confined within the cage.

Her chest tightened, seeing the diminutive winged figure trapped within the cage. Narrow of face, the humanoid being had a lean structure, with long, thin limbs. Standing on the ground, the creature would rise to no more than halfway up Rayden's shin.

It had been quite some time since she had set her eyes upon one of the fairy-folk. Secretive and cautious, the creatures were adept at evading the eyes of all who they did not wish to make their presence known to.

Though small in stature, the creatures were not to be trifled with. With stealth, magical arts, and lethal skill, the fairy-folk had seen to the end of many would-be hunters and adversaries.

Seeing the pitiful-looking creature in the cage came as a tremendous shock to Rayden. The fairy appeared bowed and broken, resigned to whatever fate the high priest intended.

It did not even look once in Rayden's direction.

"A worthy sacrifice to be made in your name, to honor a most generous and unexpected gift," the high priest declared, setting the cage down at the center of the altar.

The high priest opened the cage and reached in. The fairy did not resist when the high priest grabbed it around its midsection, and withdrew the creature from the cage.

Rayden could now see that the fairy had been bound at the wrists and ankles. Set down in the middle of the altar, the creature lay prostrate, and made no movements.

The lower-ranking priest drew a dagger forth, from a sheath at his waist. With his palms up, supporting the dagger at the hilt and blade, he presented the weapon to the high priest.

The fairy-folk were no different than humans in that some chose darker paths and others more benevolent ones, with every variation in between. Rayden had no inkling of the nature of the creature on the table. But knowing who intended to sacrifice it, she doubted the creature to be a being of the darkness.

"A king of its kind, to be offered in your name ... to a greater Master," the high priest announced, with emphasis on the final word.

His gaze lingered upon Rayden for a few moments before he began chanting. In a slow, deliberate fashion, he began to raise the dagger upward, holding it in both hands.

Revulsion filled Rayden at the sight. One of the fairy folk, a king no less, had been utterly subdued, and reduced to await the plunge of a dagger wielded in dedication to the power behind everything she contended against.

She had stopped a sacrifice to a dark god before, and now she was called to do so again; no matter what the cost. The time had come to draw the blood of wicked priests.

The high priest continued with his chant. In a ceremonial manner, he raised the dagger higher, still holding it using both of his hands with palms up.

Rayden snapped her left arm out to the side, hand flat in a chop, catching one acolyte square in the throat. Stepping slightly to her right, she launched an elbow into the face of the other acolyte.

Both men crumpled the ground under the blows, giving her an opening. Springing forward, she raced for the steps. Surmounting them in a couple of bounds, she ran around the left side of the altar.

The high priest gripped the dagger in his right hand and slashed at her, a look of pure hatred filling his eyes. Avoiding the blade with ease, she trapped his hand against his body and drove her fist hard into his jaw.

The dagger clattered to the dais and the high priest fell backward, toppling down the steps.

The two acolytes, now back on their feet, began rushing toward the steps, angling for the area where the high priest had fallen.

Rayden continued her attack without hesitation. Stepping through the space where the high priest had been standing, she delivered a powerful, forward kick into the midsection of the other attending priest. Grunting, the air knocked from his body, he doubled over; right into the hard uppercut that Rayden already had in motion, launching him down the side steps of the dais.

Spinning about, she stooped and picked up the sacrificial dagger, and went after the high priest. Struggling to gather himself midway down the steps, the acolytes now attending to him, he shouted in desperate warning at her approach.

The two acolytes stood in front of the high priest. Blade flashing in glints of firelight, she felled both in swift fashion.

The high priest tried to run, but a severe limp impeded him from getting more than a few steps away. Rayden bore down upon him with no intent of mercy.

He rotated and brought his arms up in a futile attempt to fend her off. His eyes snapped wide as she drove the dagger deep into the soft flesh of his throat.

Yanking the dagger free, she leaped away from the gurgling, dying figure, and rushed toward the remaining priest. Disoriented from the uppercut and subsequent fall down the steps, he flopped about, trying in vain to get to his feet. Knees buckling, he sprawled onto his stomach.

Rayden fell upon him, thrusting the dagger into his back and delivering a killing blow.

Straightening up, Rayden turned back for the altar, where the fairy still lay bound atop it. Movements in the darkness drew her eyes upward.

Something flitted in the heights above. Rayden kept moving, heading toward the large braziers anchoring the corners of the dais, working to gain as much visibility as she could if another danger lurked.

The area around the altar being the most lighted part of the temple, she caught several flickers of dark forms at the edges of the light. Something flew within the shadows, keeping hidden.

Taking a step at a time, and looking all about, she climbed

toward the altar. She reached the top of the dais and set her eyes upon the fairy.

Its gaze fixed on something beyond her, and its eyes widened with alarm, giving her just enough warning to turn around and face the attack.

Sharp, spiky teeth bared in a rat-like visage, the winged creature barreled toward her out of the shadows. The size of a small dog, and structured similar to a bat, save for the longer tail streaming from behind it, the creature was something Rayden had never before encountered.

She ducked it at the last moment, but gasped when a hot sting pierced her left shoulder, where the creature had whipped the barbed tip of its tail. Catching further movement out of the corner of her eye, she lunged to the right, when another of the flying creatures darted toward her from the darkness.

One of the things then alighted on the altar. The fairy-being, still tied, saw the creature, and began crying out in a high pitch.

With its tail held high, the barbed end swaying in a slow, threatening fashion, the rat-faced entity stalked forward. Bracing upon its folded wings in the manner of a bat, the creature fixed its serpentine eyes upon the helpless fairy.

Unlike a bat, it could now be seen that the creature had no fur of any kind. Instead, tiny black scales covered the surface of the creature's extended body, save for its leathery wings.

A few drips of saliva spilled from the thing's extended jaws. It crept closer, drawing within a step of the fairy. Its lips drew back farther, exposing an array of spiky teeth culminating in a set of long, curving fangs.

Rayden hurled the only weapon she had at hand. The tip of the dagger's blade drove into the creature's left wing, continuing into its torso and knocking it from the altar.

The thing emitted a high-pitched keening, twisting and jerking about where it lay two steps down from the dais' surface.

Another one of the creatures glided toward Rayden out of the shadows. Having an angle to strike at it, she chose evasion, as hitting the creature would leave her exposed to its lashing tail.

The creature passed over her, giving her an open path to the wounded one lying on the altar's steps. Impaled by the dagger, it writhed and squirmed, incapacitated.

The creature could do little more than gnash its teeth at Rayden before she stomped her right heel onto its head, crushing its skull against the marble. After retrieving the dagger, she dragged the sole of her leather boot along the surface, wiping off most of the gore.

She looked around for the next attack, while moving back toward the altar. Another risk loomed; a danger beyond the flying assailants.

Rayden did not want to leave the fairy bound. Yet she could not discount the encounters in her past with creatures of its ilk possessed of a malevolent nature. She had killed such fairy folk before, but others more benevolent had given her aid and refuge.

If truly a king, the fairy on the altar would have considerable powers, no matter how beaten it might appear to be at the moment.

Another winged entity rushed her from the darkness. Sidestepping the thing, she slashed at its tail, severing the appendage at about mid-length.

Having just begun to poise its tail for a strike at her, the creature screeched. The bottom half of the tail pitched forward, falling harmlessly to the ground. It did not try to continue with its attack, flying off into the refuge of the darkness.

Rayden moved to the front of the altar. The fairy looked up at her with weary, glassy eyes of a solid emerald hue. She sensed no hostility or wickedness within the depths of its gaze.

Scars riddled its little body, including some fresher ones, made from burns and blades. The marks told a gruesome story of the treatment it had received at the hands of the priests in the temple.

The tortured fairy's wings had been sliced and gouged in many places, and Rayden knew it could no longer fly. She could not imagine the suffering that the creature had been subjected to.

Looking upon the fairy and its wounds, a growing rage filled Rayden.

"I will not leave you to their mercy," she declared, sparing not a moment longer in setting the dagger blade to the bindings on its wrists and ankles.

Before she could aid the fairy any further, she reacted to another attack coming in from the shadows. Rushing from behind and low, flying up from the ground level, it maneuvered its body at the last instant and avoided her dagger trust.

Slamming into her body, the creature's momentum carried Rayden back into the altar. She hit the stone edge hard, while also absorbing a full strike from the creature's tail, the barb penetrating her left side.

The creature shifted and clawed furiously at her right hand, causing her to lose hold of the dagger. Grabbing the creature by its wings, she held it as tight as she could, and pushed it away from her body.

Straining to bite her, and immensely strong for its size, the creature clashed its teeth within a hand's span of her face. With a loud cry she pulled down hard with her right hand while pushing upward with her left, using similar force.

Her ears filled with the piercing shriek of her assailant as she tore its left wing off. Still holding onto the creature's remaining wing, she yanked her left hand downward, smashing the thing against the dais surface.

Keeping her grip on the wing, she slammed it down a few more times, before flinging its battered remains far from the altar.

Numerous shrieks erupted from the darkness above,

coming from all over the temple. Rayden braced, knowing a great number of the creatures, enraged at the blood of their kind spilled in such a way, had become emboldened and would attack at any moment.

Looking around, Rayden's attention shifted from the upper reaches of the temple to the surface of the altar. An unexpected sight met her.

The fairy had gotten to its feet, but swayed in a precarious manner. Face a mask of pain, the being could not take to the air with the shredded condition of its wings. Even if the wings had been intact, Rayden doubted it could muster the strength to fly.

Through the raw expression of anguish, a look of determination and focus broke through upon the little being's face. Jaw clenched tight, it held its arms out, and began uttering words in a voice too low for Rayden to hear.

The light of the braziers and lamps surged, rapidly growing in brilliance and driving back the darkness. A number of angry shrieks met the advance of the light, as the creatures flying in the upper reaches of the temple reacted to the swift-changing ambience.

The light exposed the danger Rayden had been about to face. A horde of the flying creatures, a dark flock well over two dozen in number, roved the air far above the temple floor.

Rayden gripped her weapon firm and took a deep breath. Seeing far too many of the creatures to overcome if they attacked en masse, she intended to take as many as possible down with her.

Though agitated from the swelling light, the creatures began to gather, orienting their eyes upon the altar and the two figures atop the dais.

Behind Rayden, the fairy continued chanting. The light had taken the advantage of surprise from the beasts. At the very least, she would see all attacks coming well in advance.

Rayden turned about in place, eyeing the hovering mass of creatures and awaiting their first movements of attack. The tone of the fairy's chant then changed in timbre, its voice now sounding strained.

A phenomenon then occurred, all throughout the temple. Rayden gave a start, both uneasy and fascinated at the sudden development.

The fires within all the braziers in the temple snaked upward in coiling tendrils. Like so many blazing serpents, the extending flames slithered among the columns and began angling toward the flying beasts.

Emitting loud screeches, the flying creatures scattered about, causing the fiery lengths to accelerate in speed and shift directions. The fires hunted the creatures in a relentless pursuit, chasing wherever the things tried to flee.

When drawing near to one of the creatures, the flames struck with tremendous speed, engulfing the vile things in fire that pulsed white-hot. The winged entities shrieked and flapped their wings in desperation, a few crashing into columns or walls. The fires consumed their scaly bodies in rapid fashion, reducing them to ash in a few moments.

The ash began drifting down, slow in descent, alighting all over the interior of the temple. Rayden watched the dark ash falling for a few moments, astonished at the power she had witnessed.

In the wake of the rain of black ash, Rayden turned toward her unexpected benefactor.

The fairy-being had collapsed to its knees, its face wracked with signs of pain and exhaustion. Remembering what Dreaghen had told her about his last exertion of power, Rayden could only imagine what it had taken for the fairy to wield the kind of power necessary to fill the temple with light, and stream fire from the braziers, to beset the dark entities.

She moved over to the side of the altar. The fairy looked up to her, the movement slow and appearing arduous to Rayden's eyes.

The little creature winced, and then mustered a smile, before lowering its head toward her. She realized the gesture came not from any pain or weakness, but rather served as a bow to her.

"Thank ... you," the fairy said, in a faint, higher-pitched voice.

Surprised at the reaction of the fairy and its expression of gratitude, Rayden shook her head, sadness welling up fast from within. "No, no, no ... it is you who I must thank. And you that I owe. I am so sorry. You gave your strength to save me."

"We ... all must fight ... the darkness," the fairy said, its every word an exertion. "You ... let me fight. Spared me ... from being a sacrifice."

Its breath grew more labored. The fairy slumped down on its side, and Rayden could sense the creature's life was fading.

"Please, tell me what I can do," Rayden said, finding herself at a loss in aiding the creature, its pain and weakness derived from a non-physical source. She feared its large exercise of power had drained its life force to a level irreversible.

"Stay ... with me," the fairy said, in stilted words. After a couple of pained breaths, it repeated the words again. "Stay with me."

Rayden did not have to clarify anything to understand that the creature's request reflected something desired by most humans. Knowing its life to be ebbing fast, it did not want to die alone.

Gently, she reached out, and let the tip of her finger touch one of the fairy's hands. The gesture brought the trace of a smile to the creature's weary-looking face.

"I am here, and I will stay with you," Rayden answered in a soft tone, letting all other thoughts and concerns move to the side. "It is my honor."

The hint of a smile broadened upon the fairy's face.

"Take ring," the creature said. It glanced down, looking toward its hand.

The hand Rayden touched now displayed a ring that she had not seen there before. She hesitated for a moment, and the fairy lifted its hand into hers, letting it rest within her palm.

"Take ring ... my people ... will know you friend of Roggar ... of the Mist Vale," the creature said.

With great care, she slipped the small silver ring off its tiny finger, and cradled it in her palm, continuing to hold the little being's hand. She remained silent, nodding and giving him a smile in acknowledgment of the gift.

Her heart thundered with ache, knowing the little creature was nearing its last breath. A couple of bright tears slipped from her eyes.

"Do not cry ... I go ... to the undying realm ... free ... not as sacrifice," Roggar said, looking into her eyes. "Thank you. I will ... remember you..."

His attention shifted from Rayden. Turning his head slightly, he focused upward, on an area beyond her.

His eyes reacted to something, but this time no trace of alarm shone within his gaze. Instead, his emerald gaze sparked with liveliness, a warm, peaceful smile spreading on his face.

A brief glance revealed nothing to Rayden in the area where Roggar looked. To her eyes, he stared at empty air within the temple. Yet everything about the little fairy's expression shone with the purest joy, overflowing all the signs of agony and weariness so prevalent just moments before.

Rayden wished she could perceive whatever sight the fairy beheld. Having witnessed more than one such reaction from someone on the cusp of death, she took the response to heart, counting it a consolation and tiding of a far better horizon.

The fairy breathed once more. Wings sagging, its body became still.

Rayden took great care in closing the little fairy's eyes. Another tear fell from her, alighting upon the creature's face; a face now looking serene, and no longer in agony.

She drew her hand away and straightened up, continuing to look upon the fairy. Taking a few slow breaths to steady the sorrow inside, she readied to take the little creature's body with her.

She would not leave it behind in the baleful temple, surrounded by the corpses and ash of wicked beings.

A spectacular transformation then occurred. The fairy's body shimmered, before transforming into a host of tiny silver and gold particles. Sparkling and swirling, like a dancing cascade, the tiny elements rose up from the altar before fading from sight.

Rayden did not understand the things of magic. But the passing she had just witnessed, culminating in the bright display of particles, carried a beauty within it; one that transcended the cruelties the little creature had suffered. Another part of her hungered for justice, hoping the high priest paid a heavy price in whatever dark realm his spirit had sunk into.

The silence in the temple pressed in from all around her. Rayden took a few moments to gather her emotions and focus together. Glancing at the empty altar surface one more time, she walked down the steps from the dais to the temple floor.

Finding the temple doors barred from the inside, she decided to leave them shut. In the near term, anyone coming to the temple would assume nothing more than the site being closed to open worship, due to some purpose of the high priest.

Plenty of time could be purchased before anything else was suspected. By the time the deaths of the high priest and others had been discovered, Rayden and her companions would be within the walls of the Imperial City.

Further, it remained possible that no eyewitness could connect them to what had just transpired within the temple.

Having been in several temples before, in many lands, Rayden knew the front doors would not be the only entrance to the structure. Those who administered the temple would have another means of entering and leaving, a portal inaccessible to the common worshipper.

A brief search at the rear of the temple uncovered a small door, well-concealed from the outside. A steep escarpment lined the back side of the temple, with a narrow ledge allowing her a path for walking around to one side of the edifice.

Rayden made her way to the front of the temple. She found Crassor standing at the edge of the long staircase leading down to the street level. Gazing out over the city, he turned at her approaching footsteps.

"I am finished here," she said.

"That took you awhile," Crassor said in a gruff demeanor, a scowl on his face. "Long sacrifice. So can we get out of here now?"

"We will need to," Rayden said. "And no sacrifice took place."

Crassor cast her a quizzical look. "Need to? And no sacrifice? What happened in there?"

"Did you not hear a thing?" Rayden asked, knowing that even by the staircase edge he should have heard the shrieks and shrill cries of the flying entities.

He shook his head, looking perplexed. "I heard nothing."

"I'll explain as we go," Rayden answered, not surprised that Crassor had heard no sounds of the ferocious struggle inside the temple.

It stood to reason that sorcerous arts would have been used to cloak many things transpiring in the temple from being noticed by those on the outside. The true nature of the place had to be veiled from the people of Verrannus.

He stared closer at her, his brow furrowing. "You've got blood on you. A lot of it."

"This blood brings us another problem," Rayden said, taking notice of the extent of the blood on her clothing. "We don't want to be identified with the death of a high priest and three others."

"You killed Teverens without me," he said with a terse edge. "How? I didn't hear anything out here."

"Sorcery kept the air silent out here. Even if you did hear anything, the temple doors were barred inside. I'll tell you more as we go," Rayden said, with an air of urgency. "We should not leave by the same way. Not with this much blood on me."

"Spilling Teveren blood is a good thing," Crassor said.

"Most is not even Teveren blood," Rayden said.

"What? Then ... whose blood is it?" Crassor asked her.

"I have no idea what they are called, but the priests kept some winged pets in there," Rayden said, her side aching from the sting she had taken. "Nothing I've ever seen before."

"Seems to be a lot of things in recent times that none of us have seen before," Crassor remarked.

"And more will be coming, until we overcome our enemy," Rayden said.

Crassor gave Rayden back her weapons. He removed his tunic, revealing a chiseled muscularity marked in a few places with scars.

"Get rid of yours, and wear this for now," Crassor said. "Slaves are known to go about with bare chest. I will not arouse suspicion."

She took his tunic, and before she could say a word he turned around to allow her privacy to change. Removing her own, she slipped the other one on. Fitting her loose, and hanging down farther than she liked, it would have to suffice.

"I'm ready," Rayden said.

Crassor turned around and smirked. "It looks a bit baggy on you."

"I wonder why," Rayden said, with a grin. "Let's get back to the inn. I've had more than enough of this city for tonight."

Rayden took Crassor around to the back of the temple, where the escarpment led down into another area of Verrannus. She studied the rocks and eyed a route of descent. Then, she discarded the tunic over the edge far to her left, letting it catch on the rocks, well out of the way of their intended path.

With plenty of hand and footholds, they descended easily enough. Still, she took her time with each step and grasp. Fatigue lent itself to mistakes, and she did not wish to tumble down a cascade of jagged rocks.

Sizeable gardens filled with trees spread outward from the base of the escarpment. The plentiful foliage afforded Rayden and Crassor an abundance of cover as they worked their way back to the streets of Verrannus.

With the night advancing, the traffic in the city had dwindled and now stood sparse. Beyond encountering a larger group under heavy guard, presumably a citizen of high rank returning from a late hour social engagement, only a few individuals braved the later hours. Rayden suspected most of the latter to be less than savory in nature.

Rayden and Crassor drew a few looks from the shadows, but none dared to test the pair.

***

Striding back to the inn and within close reach of it, Rayden heard the distinctive sounds of a scuffle coming from around the bend of a narrow side street. She drew to a halt, Crassor coming to a stop as well.

"Please, I beg you ... take what you will ... but spare me my teeth," a sobbing voice brimming with fear pleaded from the shadows.

More than one voice laughed in response, telling Rayden all she needed to know about the situation. Few sounds stoked the flames within her more than hearing raw delight in the suffering of others.

"The joys of living in a city," Rayden muttered, with an incensed look on her face. She turned toward Crassor. "You wanted a chance to crack some Teveren skulls? I believe this will be the chance you wanted."

He nodded and grinned, looking almost eager, following Rayden as she started down the side street.

Two men had another down on his knees. Their victim clutched his side, and Rayden had no doubt that he had already suffered a terrible beating.

Rayden came up behind one of the standing pair. A large man, a little taller and broader of shoulder than Rayden, he turned at her approach.

"This is our street! What are you—." he managed to get out in an angry tone, before Rayden's left fist cut him off, a short, tight hook crashing into his jaw. With a hard knee to the groin, and a thunderous uppercut that lifted the man off his feet, Rayden sent the man sprawling onto the ground.

Hearing several heavy thumps and a sharp crack, she turned in time to see the other rogue slumping down unconscious. Crassor had slammed his head into a timber post supporting one of the buildings lining the street. Neither scoundrel would be getting up anytime soon.

She looked over to the man who had been spared from further injury. Still holding his side and on his knees, he looked to them with terror glistening in his eyes.

At close proximity she caught a strong whiff of the reason he had been on the streets after dark. The scent of wine carried on his breath, and she knew he had partaken of more than a few cups.

"Will you be okay?" she asked him.

Crassor moved away and went over to the two downed men.

After a moment, the man nodded. "They had just started ... to beat me ... I gave them what I had. They ... weren't going to stop."

"For that kind, the beating is more rewarding than what they take from you," Rayden said. She then admonished, "Don't let love of drink have you falling into the hands of the likes of those creatures."

"Thank you," the man said, a little subdued, and looking ashamed at his predicament.

"Can you get to your feet?" Rayden asked him.

He nodded again. Accepting the hand she extended him, the man pulled himself up to his feet. He swayed with a little unsteadiness, before regaining his equilibrium.

"Here, I believe this is yours." Crassor extended a small pouch in one hand toward the man. In his other, he had a couple of additional pouches. "And take these. Those two scum have taken enough from others. This serves as some recompense."

Accepting the first pouch, the man hesitated in taking the latter two. "I shouldn't. They'll just find me later. They won't hesitate to kill me."

"Very stupid to be walking streets like this alone at night," Crassor said, glowering. He glanced over toward the two unconscious rogues. "I'll make certain those scum won't find you later. They won't be killing anyone."

He walked away, moving over to the two would-be thieves. Cracking sounds pierced the night a few moments later. Necks snapped, the pair lay still as stone.

"You have nothing more to worry about with those two dung piles," Crassor announced to the man. "Now go, and stay off the streets at night."

The man nodded, looking fearful, eyeing the inert bodies of the two who had assaulted him. Collecting himself, he headed down the narrow street, and disappeared around the bend.

Rayden and Crassor resumed their walk back to the inn. She had not intended the deaths of the two thieves, but knew that two ruthless predators had been removed from the streets.

"Feeling a little better now?" she asked Crassor, noticing him walking with a more brisk step.

A spark to his eyes, he smiled at her. "I didn't like getting locked out of that temple. I felt worse when I heard of what happened inside it. This made up for it just a little. I do feel much better now. Teveren scum."

"Maybe we can all get a little rest now," Rayden said. "Seems like forever since we drank in the tavern."

"It has been a long night," Crassor said. "I would rather we had stayed in that tavern until dawn."

"As would I," Rayden agreed. "But time is no friend to us."

They did not have a long distance remaining to the inn. To Rayden's relief, no more incidents occurred.

Returning to their room, both soon found themselves asleep.

CHAPTER 16

After a slight morning delay, in which Doros and Polybius secured a new tunic for Rayden, the group set out from Verrannus. A couple full days of traveling on foot at a modest pace remained, before they reached the walls of the Imperial City.

Clear skies, and a warm day accented with cool breezes, made for a comfortable atmosphere to walk in. Winding through the hilly region south of Verrannus, the road had few travelers.

For the most part, Rayden's group traveled in silence for the early part of the day. After the dangerous night she had endured, Rayden welcomed the quiet.

Content to dwell in her thoughts, she ruminated about what had been learned, and what might come to pass.

The stop in Verrannus had been fruitful, gaining them knowledge of the Teveren alliance with the Alettani and Sarrimena. It had also allowed Rayden to test the strength of the veiling enacted by Dreaghen over her.

The high priest, undoubtedly harboring a dark spirit within him, had been unable to recognize her like the others of his kind before. She had observed his growing frustration when thwarted by Dreaghen's veil.

The experience gave her insights that would have to be kept in mind when she was within the walls of the Imperial City. To the high priest, she had been a blank parchment; a void with nothing to read or identify.

While the high priest could not discern her nature, her anonymity had provoked him into action. He had determined her a danger worth getting rid of.

Walking in the streets of the Imperial City, she would have to be cautious about direct encounters with those who might harbor dark spirits. At best, the mystery she represented to them would draw heightened curiosity. More likely, their response would be similar to that of the high priest; they would seek to eliminate her.

Nevertheless, her lack of identification would prevent them from fathoming her greater purpose. Dreaghen had bestowed her with a highly valuable gift, a shield that increased her chances of surviving.

When the sun neared midday, Rayden decided to break the silence in the group.

"Have you ever heard of a place called the Mist Vale?" she asked the others, looking over her shoulder from where she walked at the forefront.

Polybius nodded. "A beautiful place. Said to even have a good presence of fairy folk there. You'll find the Mist Vale just to the north of the Imperial City. You needing a place to relax when all this is done?"

"I had never heard of it, before Verrannus," Rayden answered.

"Is it something to do with the fairy you said they were going to sacrifice?" Doros asked.

Rayden nodded. "It mentioned Mist Vale ... a place I am not familiar with."

"That was some powerful blood sorcery they were preparing to do," Doros commented. "To sacrifice one of the fairy folk. And a king at that, from what you said."

"It is something I didn't expect," Rayden said. "I could sense a mounting threat, but didn't know what they intended fully, even when I attacked the high priest."

"Either going to conjure something really powerful up, or they wanted to overcome you in some way," Doros said, matter-of-factly.

Her words made sense. The high priest, in failing to be able to read Rayden's mind and past, had deemed her a threat without hesitation. In sacrificing something as rare and powerful as a fairy king, he had endeavored to work a high level of blood magic.

His purpose stood clear. He had wanted to pierce whatever power had stymied him in identifying Rayden. He had desired to gain answers, before attempting to kill her.

"They didn't overcome me, thankfully," Rayden said, grinning. "I just hope it will be a few days before their bodies are discovered."

"I think it will be," Doros said. "Most people are afraid of high priests and the things of gods and sorcery. They won't readily break through the doors of that temple."

"Unless other priests arrive," Rayden said.

"Then let's hope none do, and we are able to gain some distance," Doros said.

"Nobody lived who witnessed us when we were up there at the temple," Crassor said. "Even if they do discover the bodies, they will have no idea of who to search for."

"And the two thieves you killed? What of the man you saved from them?" Doros asked. "He saw the both of you."

"He will not want to be tethered to that in any way," Crassor said. "He will fear anyone angered at the death of the two scum coming after him."

"It would seem we are in good steading then," Doros said.

"It would appear to be so, but it is better that we do not relax our guard," Rayden cautioned them. "We do not contend against just flesh and blood."

"You won't find me letting my guard down," Crassor said.

"Nor I," Doros added.

"And I will always heed the advice of veteran warriors such as you three," Polybius said. "I must admit, I've never felt safer walking about a Teveren city as I did when we were in Verrannus."

"Well, if that is true, you should show your appreciation by paying for our cups of wine next time," Crassor said, giving a rare chuckle.

Rayden enjoyed seeing a little levity in the large, brooding man. For all the times they had not seen eye to eye, when Rayden knew Crassor's blood lust for Teverens would lead to poor decisions, the man had proven to be stout-hearted; a warrior she would not hesitate to have at her side during a battle.

"I agree with Crassor ... pay for our wine next time, Polybius," Rayden said, laughing.

"Make that three of us, in agreement," Doros said.

Polybius rolled his eyes. "I already know it would be folly to argue with three warriors of your skill."

"You are wise," Crassor said, smirking.

"Good thing we took an ample amount of coin with us," Polybius stated. "I am aware of how the three of you can take in wine."

"If we need a little more, I'll take care of it," Crassor said. "I've been known to prevail at dice."

"I wish I had that kind of luck," Rayden said. "For me, it is like throwing away coins, which is why I avoid it."

"I'm the same way," Doros said.

"Then it is settled. Polybius buys our wine, and I gain back the coin spent through a few rounds of dice," Crassor said. "We may even emerge from a tavern with an increased amount of coin."

"A solid plan if I ever heard one," Rayden said, smiling.

Her words drew another chuckle from the big warrior. "I am astonished, we are finally in agreement on a course of action. I had expected you to give a big, long speech in opposition. Try to tire me out with an abundance of words. But yet here I am ... agreeing with you."

Rayden laughed. "They say miracles do happen from time to time in this world."

"Or is this some sign that the world is about to end?" Doros asked in a merry tone, bringing laughter from all the others.

"I hope not," Polybius said, grinning. "I have a few ambitions in this world yet. I am not ready to explore the afterlife."

"Do not worry yourself too much, Polybius. I am sure Crassor and I will find something to disagree on soon enough," Rayden said with another laugh.

"I am very sure of it," Crassor said, shaking his head with a deep chortle.

"Like the sun rising, and Rayden and Crassor in disagreement, it is good there are some things in the world that one can always count on," Doros said, causing another round of laughter to erupt.

"What I wouldn't give for a little more of that Tarnan wine from last night," Crassor said.

"Many find it to their taste, and I am sure we will have no difficulty finding it in the Imperial City," Polybius said.

"Makes me want to press a hard march and get there in a day," Crassor replied. "You still guessing two days at this pace?"

"Yes," Polybius answered. "This road will shadow the path of the Golden River and lead us right to the Imperial City. Then it will be a matter of choosing the gate to enter by."

"Choosing the gate?" Doros asked.

"Nine gates through those walls," Polybius said. "This is a city like no other you have seen before. The harbor alone is a sight to behold. Vessels from across the seas, bringing people and goods from far lands. Exotic animals too. Many of those are used in the great arena for blood sport."

Thinking of the lion she had freed, Rayden asked, "The arena?"

"Beast against beast, man against man, man against beast," Polybius said. "Thousands gather in the seats to watch blood flow."

"I have seen such contests in other lands," Rayden said.

"I imagine not like these," Polybius said, his voice growing somber in tone. "Dozens of condemned men and women put in the arena, unarmed, with a horde of ravenous beasts loosed upon them ... shredding them apart, to the cheers of the crowd. Do they have such contests in other lands?"

Revulsion filled Rayden. "What kind of sickness brings so many people to cheer such a vile thing?"

"The greater the promise of blood, the more who squeeze into the seats," Polybius said.

"Teveren scum," Crassor muttered. "No surprise."

"Not just Teverens, but the people from many lands within the city," Polybius said. "It is a sign of high status to put on these kinds of contests. Often they run for days on end, with many thousands in attendance."

"All the more reason to cut the head off this loathsome snake," Rayden said, angered.

"At least it doesn't sound like we will draw much notice in a city that large," Crassor said.

"A very good thing," Doros interjected.

"The less notice, the better," Rayden said. "We are there to observe as much as we can, and then get back to the others. And I want to have a look at as many of those gates as we can, from the inside."

"We just have to be sure to get out of the city before our

friends arrive," Polybius said. "They will shut all of them, and nobody will get in or out until the city is taken or defended."

"We will be sure to get out of there in time," Rayden said. After a pause, she added, "But we will be getting back into it soon enough, with thousands more at our side."

"A return I await with eagerness," Crassor said.

They talked amongst each other a little longer about the city. Polybius spoke of other things less troubling. He described great temples, lavish gardens, and vast bath complexes, where a person could immerse in heated water, engage in exercise, give orations, eat and drink, or swim in cool waters.

The more he spoke of the things they would see, the more Rayden got the sense she was about to experience a city like no other.

Finding it regrettable that such a marvel served as the seat of the Imperator's power, she reminded herself that rivers of blood had been spilled in many lands to empower the city. Wars bringing countless men and women into the bondage of slavery secured more lands to exploit and divide among the powerful in the Teveren Empire.

New provinces received Teveren governors appointed by the Imperator, with everything feeding into his voracious appetite for power. Underneath it all, powerful blood sorcery grew ever stronger, channeling dark power from every source possible; whether a war, a slave put to shackle and lash, a wicked ritual, a captive nailed to a cross, or anything rooted in blood and suffering. Rayden did not even want to think of the true purpose of the arena described by Polybius.

When the group fell into silence once more, Rayden and Doros walked a little ahead of the other two.

"I am glad you are with us," Rayden said. "I know you desire to begin your search for your family."

"If we fail to bring an end to the Imperator, any search will be futile," Doros stated with a rueful edge.

"You'll find no argument from me," Rayden said.

"I do not intend to survive to witness a Teveren shadow spread across all lands," Doros said. "I will fight until we prevail, or until they cut me down."

"And I as well," Rayden said, resolute.

"Do you think we stand a chance?" Doros asked.

"We do, and we are going to increase those chances with what we learn on this journey," Rayden said. "We already know of the two tribes in league with our enemy. We will discover much more."

"I fear for what we will discover of the children taken by the Teverens," Doros said, looking grim. "The ones sold to them and taken to the Imperial City."

"I have braced myself for what may be uncovered," Rayden said. "You must also prepare yourself for the worst."

"What can they possibly gain from mere children?" Doros queried.

"Dark power, and great amounts of it," Rayden answered, dour and firm. "Blood sorcery feasts upon the sacrifice and destruction of innocents. The shedding of even one innocent's blood is a treasure deeply coveted by one steeped in dark arts.

"The sorcerers in league with the Imperator have gained themselves a host of innocents. I have no doubt it is for a dedicated, very particular purpose."

"How can we begin to find where they have been taken in the Imperial City?" Doros said.

"I do not yet know," Rayden said, wondering herself how they could find a trail among the shadows in a city so vast. "We must keep our wits about us, and think carefully."

"Even if we do come across a trail, what if it leads to palaces, or other places under heavy guard?" Doros said.

"I will just have to find a way," Rayden said. "I will ask no one take an undue risk."

"I am not about to let you risk yourself alone," Doros said.

"We must make certain that word of the Alettani and Sarrimena reaches the ears of Alcedan and the other chieftains," Rayden said. "That knowledge could decide the fate of thousands."

"Polybius and Crassor are capable enough," Doros said.

Rayden cast a hard stare at her friend. "Sometimes a single person can prevail, where even two is folly. You will have to trust my judgment."

Doros scowled. "I do trust you, but I am not one to walk away from something. It's why I'm here now."

"I know," Rayden said, her expression softening into a smile. "And we will get through all of this."

"Sometimes, that task looks impossible," Doros said.

"Sometimes the things that appear impossible must be challenged, to show what is truly possible," Rayden said.

"There has to be a way," Doros said, a look of anxiety and concern shadowing her face. "Far too much hangs in the balance."

"If the Imperator prevails, the world will see the rising of a dark sun at dawn," Rayden said. "Bringing a day that will shroud the world in darkness."

"Then we must prevail," Doros said.

"It is our only path," Rayden replied.

Looking ahead, and feeling the warm rays of sunlight upon her face, Rayden continued striding along the winding road. Every step brought her closer toward the Imperial City.

***

Rayden stood awestruck.

Gazing down from the hillside, she could not say a single word. In silence, she took in the tremendous vision spread far and wide before her.

Towering walls protected a massive city, one much greater

than any she had ever witnessed before. Built atop and among several grand hills, the immense city flowed across the landscape in a cascade displaying elegance, strength, beauty, and undeniable power.

Gleaming temples and lavish palaces crowned the most prominent rises within the city. The multi-level facades of some palaces took the form of beautiful, curving arcades, while a few of the temples held a circular form, graced with magnificent domes.

Winding streets lined with prominent edifices of all kinds filled vast tracts of ground within the walls, interspersed with sprawling gardens, forums, amphitheaters, and open marketplaces. Colonnades, sparkling fountains, and statuary adorned the city all throughout; jewels in the fabric of Teveren pride and affluence.

Massive structures of a distinctive nature drew Rayden's eye, wherever she espied them soaring up from among the city's dense host of constructs.

Her gaze lingered upon one such edifice, an immense, circular construct, rising several stories high with an interior left open to the sky. Extensive rigging fashioned of ropes, timber masts, and supported on corbels held a series of what looked like giant sails in place all around the top of the structure.

Another open structure, located near a colossal palace, had the shape of a great, elongated oval. Ringed with rising tiers of stone, the oval featured a long line of statuary down its center.

Unique constructs existed outside the city walls as well.

Disappearing into hills, and covering long segments of ground toward the city, were several intriguing stone structures. Ranging from one to three arcaded levels in height, sparkling channels of water ran along the tops of the segments. Rayden realized the segments were pieces of extensive constructions, like human-made streams; a gigantic continuum bringing water toward the city from afar.

Constructs of such tremendous scale, inside and outside the walls, testified to an empire steeped in wealth, power, and luxury.

Cradled in the bend of the broad Golden River, the Imperial City looked out over a waterfront teeming with activity. Vessels of all kinds plied the glittering waters, from barges, to large cargo vessels, to tiny boats of the kind manned by one or two people.

In one area of the harbor, an unmistakable line of warships rested in good order along an extensive stretch of the banks. Rayden took account of the multitude of galley sheds in view, with many attendant buildings supporting repairs and quartering.

She knew without doubt that the Teverens could muster a substantial naval force in a short amount of time to confront any threat by sea.

Within the river channel, a number of small islands could be seen. Connected to the shorelines via bridges, a couple of the more sizeable ones among them contained a number of edifices.

A few extensive bridges spanned the river itself. They connected the bank nearest the main part of the city to a smaller, walled sector filled with an assortment of various buildings on the opposite side.

Rayden eyed the bustle of activity filling the streets and open spaces all over the city. A steady stream of traffic could be seen entering and exiting at many portals along the walls. As Polybius had indicated, nine primary gates could be counted along the course of the city's stout perimeter.

Rayden had been inclined to believe the tales of the Imperial City as exaggerations spread by a boastful empire, but her eyes told the full truth of it. No city that she had ever seen or explored came close to being the rival of the opulent vision before her.

Looking upon the magnificent city bathing in the golden light of a midday sun, Rayden found it hard to believe that a ravenous darkness lay just underneath. Somewhere within the walls, whether in a palace, temple, or a chamber deep underground, the Imperator and a host of sorcerers advanced ever closer to the realization of wicked aims; on a scale unsettling to ponder.

Even more distressing, a great obstacle lay in place before any army could reach the city walls.

Visible from the hillside and deployed not far from the city, occupying great swathes of land girded with trenches, embankments and palisades, multiple legion encampments could be seen. No less than three legions had already been set in place outside the city's boundaries.

The tally did not include any force quartered within the city walls, or others still coming; such as the one about to break camp in Verrannus.

The Teverens had conceded the southward march of the tribal army, choosing to gather in force and await their arrival in a position of strength. While not afraid, Rayden could not avoid the sinking feeling taking place inside her. She could see the Teveren acumen for war on bold display in the presence of the encampments, and the harsh reality it represented.

The tribal army would have to overcome Teveren legions of a strength more than capable of contesting the tribes in an open field of battle, before even reaching the walls of the city. With the addition of the Alettani and Sarrimena, and it remaining uncertain of how many additional Teveren legions were still coming to the city's defense, a daunting situation loomed for the tribes of the north.

She could not deny the conclusions from her observations. The tribal army alone would not be enough to see to the end of the Imperator. Rayden could only hope that the Kartajenians understood how dire things stood; and even then she wondered if they could bring enough strength to overcome what she had assessed along the banks of the Golden River.

Taking a deep breath, Rayden steadied her focus. She had

come for a purpose; to learn what she could of the Imperator's power and hidden threats.

No matter how dispiriting the greater situation might appear, she could not allow herself to be distracted by things she could not change.

She simply had to carry out her chosen task, and enter the Imperial City.

Rayden looked to Crassor, Doros, and Polybius, where they had gathered around her. Doros looked spellbound, while Crassor appeared unsettled. Only Polybius retained an expression of composure.

Doros shifted her gaze to Rayden. Beneath the astonishment in her eyes lurked a trace of fear.

"It is hard to believe a city could be so large," Doros said. "Have you ever witnessed the like?"

"No, nothing of its kind," Rayden answered.

"What can be done against a power such as this?" Doros asked, her tone rife with doubt.

"I heard the tales for years, but did not deem anything like this possible," Crassor said, with a somber air.

Rayden caught the distress in the large man's voice, a sound she had never heard from his lips. She turned to face him.

"We must not waver. Not now," she said, holding his gaze.

Crassor's eyes, like Doros', carried an unmistakable hint of fear. "Not even an army three times the size of the one we have gathered could take this city. Even if they get past the legions."

"We will just have to find a way to break them and take the city," Polybius declared. "The four of us are here to help in finding that way, and that is what we will do. We will each play our part in this task, and glean what we can. I agree with Rayden. We must not waver, not now."

The determination reflected in his voice and face came as a surprise to Rayden. Where the two seasoned, battle-hardened warriors had expressed doubt and fear, a merchant displayed confidence and encouragement.

She knew Polybius harbored fears and doubts, no different than the others. The nature of courage involved the suppression of fear; and the will to act, in spite of it.

Polybius had proven to Rayden once again that courage could be summoned from within any heart.

"Polybius speaks truly, we all have a part to play in this," Rayden told the others. "No use standing here and waiting any longer. It's time for us to go find some answers in that city. Gird yourself, for appearances in this city labor to veil a great wickedness. We must keep our wits and be on our guard."

The others nodded to her, all of them looking more confident.

Rayden looked out over the city and beyond. "Let's get going. I want to be inside the walls before the rain begins to fall."

With a resolute heart, Rayden stepped forward and started down the road toward the great city. A dark mass of storm clouds lining the far horizon, a ripple of thunder echoed in the distance.

To be continued in Book Three of the Dark Sun Dawn Trilogy

About the Author

Stephen Zimmer is an award-winning author and filmmaker based out of Lexington Kentucky.   His works include the Rayden Valkyrie novels (Sword and Sorcery), the Rising Dawn Saga (Cross Genre), the Fires in Eden Series (Epic Fantasy), the Hellscapes short story collections (Horror), the Chronicles of Ave short story collections (Fantasy), and the Harvey and Solomon Tales (Steampunk).

Stephen's visual work includes the feature film Shadows Light, shorts films such as The Sirens and Swordbearer, and the forthcoming Rayden Valkyrie: Saga of a Lionheart TV Pilot.

Stephen is a proud Kentucky Colonel who also enjoys the realms of music, martial arts, good bourbons, and spending time with family.

Find Stephen online at:
Website: www.stephenzimmer.com
Facebook: www.facebook.com/stephenzimmer7
Twitter: www.twitter.com/sgzimmer
Instagram: www.instagram.com/stephenzimmer7

Transcend reality with Seventh Star Press!

On the following pages we would like to introduce you to some of our titles featuring Sword and Sorcery, Post-Apocalyptic Fantasy, Epic Fantasy, YA Fantasy, and more!

To get more information on Seventh Star Press and our titles, please visit:

www.seventhstarpress.com

or connect with us at:
www.twitter.com/7thstarpress
www.facebook.com/seventhstarpress

Single author author collections of short stories
from Seventh Star Press!

Now Available!

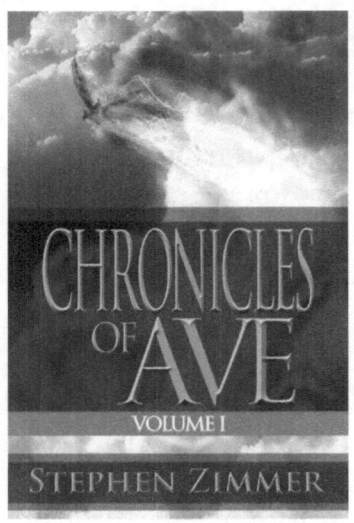

Have many action-driven fantasy adventures in
the world of Ave in Stephen Zimmer's
Chronicles of Ave, Volume 1.

Softcover: 978-1-937929-30-5
eBook: 978-1-937929-31-2

Grand Epic Fantasy from Stephen Zimmer!
Explore the world of Ave in the Fires in Eden Series from
Stephen Zimmer! Epic Fantasy for those who enjoy authors
like George R.R. Martin and Steven Erikson!

Softcover ISBN: 9780982565612

eBook ISBN: 9780982565698

Softcover ISBN: 9780983108627   Softcover ISBN 9781937929855

eBook ISBN: 9780983108610   eBook ISBN 9781937929862

Now available from Seventh Star Press! The Rising Dawn Saga, a series that explores the dystopian and the apocalyptic from author

Stephen Zimmer

Book One: The Exodus Gate
Softcover ISBN: 9780615267470
eBook ISBN: 9780982565674

Book Two: The Storm Guardians
Softcover ISBN: 9780982565636
eBook ISBN: 9780982565681

Book Three: The Seventh Throne
Softcover ISBN: 9780983740247
eBook ISBN: 9780983740223

The Rising Dawn Saga titles feature
cover art and illustrations from the
award-winning Matthew Perry

From Bram Stoker-Award-winning Michael Knost

Softcover ISBN: 978-1-941706-27-5
eBook ISBN: 978-1-941706-29-9

Author's Guide to Marketing with Teeth is a collection of essays and interviews on marketing and advertising for authors and books. Michael Knost has spent more than a quarter of a century in marketing, working in the radio, television, and newspaper industries, as well as serving as marketing director and chief marketing officer for several large companies, including those in the automotive industry.

Mr. Knost has taken the lessons he's learned from his extensive experience and captured the best tips and advice for authors (or anyone in the publishing industry) who hopes to increase sales and/or name brand recognition. Each chapter covers a different subject with tips on theory and execution.

And let's not forget the interviews. Michael is also including several with successful authors to learn about their personal marketing strategies—from when they began their careers to now. You'll hear from superstars such as Charlaine Harris, Diana Gabaldon, Jonathan Maberry, Kevin J. Anderson, Lucy A. Snyder, and Dan Poynter.

From Bram Stoker Award-winning Editor Michael Knost!

Softcover ISBN:
978-1-937929-61-9
eBook ISBN:
978-1-937929-62-6

Writers Workshop of Science Fiction and Fantasy is a collection of essays and interviews by and with many of the movers-and-shakers in the industry. Each contributor covers the specific element of craft he or she excels in. Expect to find varying perspectives and viewpoints, which is why you many find differing opinions on any particular subject.

This is, after all, a collection of advice from professional storytellers. And no two writers have made it to the stage via the same journey-each has made his or her own path to success. And that's one of the strengths of this book. The reader is afforded the luxury of discovering various approaches and then is allowed to choose what works best for him or her.

Featuring essays and interviews with:
Neil Gaiman, Orson Scott Card, Ursula K. Le Guin, Alan Dean Foster, James Gunn, Tim Powers, Harry Turtledove, Larry Niven, Joe Haldeman, Kevin J. Anderson, Elizabeth Bear, Jay Lake, Nancy Kress, George Zebrowski, Pamela Sargent, Mike Resnick, Ellen Datlow, James Patrick Kelly, Jo Fletcher, Stanley Schmidt, Gordon Van Gelder, Lou Anders, Peter Crowther, Ann VanderMeer, Joh Joseph Adams, Nick Mamatas, Lucy A. Snyder, Alethea Kontis, Nisi Shawl, Jude-Marie Green, Nayad A. Monroe, G. Cameron Fuller, Jackie Gamber, Amanda DeBord, Max Miller, Jason Sizemore.

Enter the world of the Fey, Faeries, and all things magical in two exciting anthology volumes from
editor Scott Sandridge!

Tales of the Seelie Court
Softcover
ISBN: 978-1-937929-47-3
eBook
ISBN: 978-1-937929-48-0

Tales of the Unseelie Court
Softcover
ISBN: 978-1-937929-49-7
eBook
ISBN: 978-1-937929-50-3

www.ingramcontent.com/pod-product-compliance
Lightning Source LLC
Chambersburg PA
CBHW030958260626
47169CB00002B/597